Toxic People

TOXIC PEOPLE

S. D. MONAGHAN

LUME BOOKS

LUME BOOKS

Published in 2023 by Lume Books

ISBN 978-1-83901-516-8

Typeset using Atomik ePublisher from Easypress Technologies

www.lumebooks.co.uk

To Anne – the arc of my story

1

Friday Night

It was after 11.00 pm when everything started to unravel.

The warm summer night ensured that the pavements of Clareville were still bustling. It was like that for a few months, when the area filled with blow-ins turned on by being near true wealth. Then it would go quiet again for the rest of the year, when there was little noise except for the hush of luxury and money.

Although Shane liked the summer evenings, his neighbours considered the descending crowds to be like children dragging muck in along the carpet. He found the Clareville residents to be generally untrusting, anxious, pompous and wary of strangers. It wasn't their fault, really. It just seemed to be something that happened when people made a fortune every year.

Walking by Pellicci's, the local Italian eatery, Shane looked through the glass. He almost expected to see the diners staring out, their retinas in sudden, dazzling whiteout, examining him, curious as to what had gone wrong in his life. Instead, he saw the truth of himself within his translucent reflection: the settled, attentive husband, the researcher, the writer, the oarsman, the Xbox gamer. Being forty-four suited him. Shane had a swimmer's body, dark mussed-up hair – dusted at the sides – and full lips. He was one of those men who could still wear black jeans and trainers and not look ridiculous.

But in the glass of Pellicci's, he also saw the man who was no longer an easy sleeper. He saw the loving, interested father that he'd never become. 'Not just yet,' Jenny used to say – as if, should she ever change her mind, they'd be able to order one, like a table from a catalogue. He'd always known that she had never wanted a child. He'd just hoped that one day she would change her mind.

Up ahead was their house: a sturdy, three-storey Victorian end of row terrace. Among their neighbours were a businessman, a famous actor and a widower judge who still referred to England as 'the mainland'; all splitting their time between town and country estates. Assessing the strip of lit-up front rooms, Shane saw that most were spending the evening in their studies, decaying away with their private art collections. None of the people living in this wedge of homes socialised together. This made Shane's neighbours feel even more important, even more special, as if they had all that space to themselves.

Living in a nice neighbourhood, near the city centre, did have the odd limitation. Shane and Jenny had no garden, just a decked-out yard. There was no driveway, only a garage around the back leading to a dark, grey laneway. However, pros and cons did not matter anymore because, just a few months previously, they'd received a year's notice to vacate. The notice had come from his mother-in-law.

Shane had always told himself that it didn't matter where they lived, that a house was just a geographical location, that as long as

Jenny and he were together, they'd be happy. However, Shane was also aware of how much he was going to miss the area. *Money...* Shane pictured his boat. He pictured a better one. *I'm not above it.*

He wondered if it wasn't just because of Jenny's mother; if somehow, *he* was the real cause of Jenny losing the house. Could Shane have done more? Perhaps, unconsciously, he was dispensing retribution on Jenny for her refusal to give him children?

Taking out his phone, he texted his wife:

Home early.

Scanning the screen of emoticons, he chose a straightforward red heart.

They had been barely talking before they'd gone out – he to meet a student researcher and she to give a talk on interior design. His wife wanted to stake all their savings on a daydream, the fantasy being that a particularly clever and opportune investment would turn their four-hundred-thousand savings into over one million euros in a year. Then, with that incredible return, Jenny would anonymously buy their Clareville house from her mother, using the funds for both the mighty deposit and leverage for the mortgage. To Jenny, it all made perfect sense. Which it did, as long as the investment performed; or, in other words, as long as her horse won.

It infuriated him how Jenny persisted with her belief that, unlike her, he did not really understand money. It was as if she actually believed that unless you came from a particular class, then you couldn't possibly know what to do with substantial sums of cash. It was an innate snobbery that supposed that only people from a certain rank were trained to be wealthy. But Shane knew that money was *not* confusing – being poor was.

Despite the frustration, the disillusionment, the disappointment, part of him still wished that he could make the investment. How surprised Jenny would be. But Shane knew that he was 100% correct in turning it down. Cars, houses, Breitling watches – they were all just more accumulated trash that people hauled with themselves towards the grave. Shane also understood why Jenny had found it impossible to let the house go. For her eighteenth birthday she'd been given a silver Mercedes – Shane had received one hundred old Irish pounds for his, and he'd spent it on books. That had pleased his father and that in turn had made his father's incredibly generous gift even more special.

But Jenny came from a family that had everything, had once promised her everything – and had then unfairly snatched it all away. Now, Jenny wanted it back. She wanted it back before she was too old to enjoy it. She didn't even want her fair share. Her sister could get the majority of it. But she did want something. If her mother wasn't going to give it to her, then she'd try and take the only thing she could – Clareville.

Most people started off with a sports-car vision of their future. Then they hit thirty and realised that wasn't going to happen. But even though Jenny was forty-three, everything she wanted was still in the future. That was why she had to try and force him to gamble everything away for the chance of quick money – for the opportunity to claim this precious, precious house; to show her mother that she had underestimated her youngest and that she was so much better than the golden child, Joan. Her mother would finally see just why Jenny had been her father's most prized favourite.

Shane was about to run up the steps to the front door but found the best he could do was walk fast. Time slowed. It was like he was trying to build a tower to the moon; the more progress he made, the more he realised just how far away it truly was. He hated lying to his wife and that was what he was about to do, when she got back from her own meeting. Jenny would ask, 'Have you been drinking?' He had. Four pints. But he would reply, 'Just the one.'

He thought of the last time they'd made love. It had been over a month ago. When had they last gone to the movies? A month ago. To a restaurant? For a walk? A month ago. The thought flashed through his brain like a bullet: *All of this wouldn't matter if we'd had kids.* People can lose trust in each other but stay in love – when they have kids. People can fall out of sex but stay in love – when they have kids.

The moment Shane stepped through the front door he knew something was wrong. The hall led past the study and the drawing room, proceeding into the kitchen, where the back door was open. He looked about at the island, the range, the closet-sized fridge, the coffee machine which fed his habit, and shouted, 'Jenny?' – making it sound like a question because he wasn't expecting her back yet.

There was a thud upstairs. Suddenly, Shane was very aware that he was an unarmed forty-four-year-old man who weighed under twelve stone, with no real fighting skills. He considered going back outside. Or should he just call the police?

A wave of territorial aggression surged over him. Most of the furniture had once been Jenny's father's – from the big brass bed to the cutlery. *Don't let that little prick ruin your day, week, year*. Because that's what Shane pictured the intruder as – a young, skinny, teenage creep, who had no idea of the value of the things he was stealing, of the emotional vacuum he was about to create in Jenny's life.

Shane shouted, 'Hey!' and ran up the stairs.

He rounded the landing on the first floor and went straight to the master bedroom. Everything was as he'd left it three hours ago.

Entering the en suite, Shane turned on the light and scanned from the claw-footed tub to the frosted door of the step-in shower.

The sound of boots again. *Thump. Thump. Thump.* Running down the stairs.

Shane exited the bedroom, gripped the top banister pole, swung around onto the staircase and began a rapid descent. He knew there were rules as to how you were supposed to play this game – run, call the police, even hide until it was safe to check what had been lost. Yet, it was a conveniently ignored reality that those who always followed the rules were always punished. Eventually.

That was not going to happen to him.

Sprinting through to the kitchen where the back door remained ajar, he hit it with an outstretched palm. Then, Shane was running across the decking towards the garage door, which was closing after being swung open seconds before. Instinctively, he entered the storage area in a non-sensible half-crouch, as if there was a sniper waiting to pick him off.

'You fucking dick,' Shane shouted and could only picture which of his late father-in-law's personal items the thief was carrying, rather than whether he was armed or how big and violent he might be.

The garage entrance was a rolling metal sectional door, like a shutter, which had already been raised two feet, to let the burglar escape into the laneway. With a furious heave, Shane raised the clunking metal all the way into the roof.

The night air was stagnant, out on the laneway. Nearby, in one of the back gardens, someone beat a rug. From somewhere nearby, an engine revved in the darkness. It was not over yet.

A car accelerated and Shane knew that the thief was driving in the wrong direction. He was going east, where the laneway ended in a T-junction – both options abrupt dead-ends.

The idiot has trapped himself. I can block him.

Without Shane even noticing that he had extracted them, his car keys were clutched in his fist. A moment later, he was sitting in his chunky, ten-year-old, second-hand Land Rover, his body on autopilot, starting up the engine like he was about to pop down to Lidl. Beside him, one of Jenny's jackets was carelessly scrunched up into a ball, and with the car being a dump bin between home and wherever she was working, the back seats were covered in interior design magazines, material samples and colour charts.

Reversing out into the laneway, he nosed the Land Rover in a direction it had never driven before – east. Shane went to turn the lights on and instead the wipers sprang to life, dragging caked grit across the dry glass in a half-moon of stained strata.

Jenny, you should've seen me. You should've been there. He needed to make himself confident. He needed to turn this into an adventure.

The burglar was a few hundred feet away, at the end of the lane, caught in a snare. Shane watched him as though his prey was a dumb nocturnal animal lacking the cunning to undo the clamp. Trying to turn the brightly lit red Ford Focus about the T-junction, the burglar awkwardly reversed and then moved impatiently forwards until, finally, his car faced Shane's.

Its lights went off.

The laneway was in darkness. The engine of the Focus revved histrionically as it sped in the wrong gear. Out of the shadows, it accelerated straight at him. Expecting to hear the squeal of brakes, Shane grimaced – but it didn't come.

Shane's body was about to break. Glass and metal would tear his face apart. This end would please so many people. Jenny's mother. Jenny's sister. The blur of red metal spread across his line of vision.

His heart clenching, he closed his eyes and waited and… his life *didn't* flash before his eyes.

That was just a lie, just more bullshit he had believed in. Instead, he remembered the two rabbits he'd had as a boy. One died in the jaws of a cat. A week later, two magpies killed the other one. His rabbits had taught him that you can never anticipate the end, until it arrives in any of its surprising ways.

2

As Jenny walked home, the moonlight pressed down hard upon her, making her feel like she was in a painting. After giving a talk on contemporary lighting at the Shelbourne Ladies' Club, she was worn out – but in a good way. There was pleasure in being too busy to think.

While strolling along, Jenny's bleached-blonde head bent to check her emails. There were nervous queries from a few clients having second thoughts about a dining room colour scheme, doubting the stone she'd chosen for a kitchen island, worrying about the height of an imported Japanese hand basin. Her job frequently revealed how the wealthier a person became and the better the stuff they procured, the more anxious they became about everything.

She checked her Instagram, Facebook and Twitter notifications. Her accounts were pre-set with updates she'd written that morning, to be revealed periodically throughout the day, as if she was writing them on the go. The last one would soon be automatically posted. It was effortless for her to keep track of, because she found social media compulsive. Shane was always amazed at how she kept up with the inexorable hot lava flow of online discussion. 'Infobesity' he called it.

Much of Jenny's interior design business came from her online presence. She was so expert at marketing herself that *Home Designs Magazine* had recently referred to her as an 'influencer'. Upon noticing that she had fifteen new followers, the warmth from the online numbers radiated out from her phone to the surroundings of the Clareville neighbourhood. Thumbing her phone off, Jenny had almost no awareness of getting from the Shelbourne Ladies' Club to her own road. No smells. No sights. No sounds. She had been *in* her phone.

Now that she was almost home, she inhaled deeply, as if her neighbourhood had a fine aroma. There was a moneyed hush in the air – like she'd entered the innermost sanctuary of a private members' club. She loved Clareville, even though outsiders considered it pretentious, arrogant, up itself. But once you were in, you were in. Clareville was a safe, quiet neighbourhood and home to a great many interesting people, who would acknowledge each other with a courteous nod or wave, as a familiar frisson of satisfaction sizzled between them all. These were the executives of multinationals, airlines, communication networks and the bankers who advised them. Jenny knew their type – her father had dined with enough of them. But these people were not like her dad, who had never forgotten where he'd come from. These people were the kind that went out of their way *not* to socialise with normal people. Civilians with real jobs bored them.

She passed Pellicci's. That was where Jenny had often said hallo to someone she recognised – only to realise that she did not, in fact, know them. They were just famous. Inside, the Clareville locals loved to gather informally in that searing atmosphere that pervades a room full of couples who have inherited their families' boom-time businesses – those riches-to-ultra-riches magnates. There, they would all get excited over the same thing: property. They could also moan about the trying issue they all faced – being property millionaires. Just a week ago, a house in nearby St Catherine's Hill went for over three million and now everyone was wondering what their taxes would be the next time one sold in Clareville. The most salacious news was when someone had to downsize. 'Downsize' – the most wounding expletive in the neighbourhood's vocabulary. It meant divorce, financial ruin, legal woes; probably all three.

She checked her texts and saw Shane's message. She replied:

Cool. Home in 2 mins.

Scanning the screen of emoticon items, she chose an exploding champagne bottle – the sexual connotations obvious. Jenny didn't mean it, but she was trying. Shane and she were at the tail end of their biggest fight in years. She wanted to invest in a sure thing. He didn't. And just like that, their marriage had hairline fractured down the centre.

Her husband's naivety about money was excruciating. It was like he didn't realise how the bank notes in his wallet were worth so much more than the loaded weight of the coins in his jeans. Instead, he seemed to believe that the heaviness in his trouser pocket was what made a person powerful and free. Shane also insisted that she'd always known that he had never been driven by money, had never been very interested in it… *Yet any time we've had some, he's always found new and fun ways to get rid of it.* Anyway, it didn't matter that he'd never misrepresented himself. People do evolve. People are supposed to change. They grow together.

Jenny had watched over the last few years as the Dublin shopkeepers, barmen, taxi drivers had once more come to believe that they were players; maxing themselves out to get the new car, the new kitchen, the second home in Turkey. Dublin was, yet again, a site under construction, the city stain spreading, giving its people huge suburban houses with nominal finishes and bargain basement accoutrements. Jenny wanted to stick the knife in for her share of that sticky, gloopy, sugary pie and get rich quick before the inevitable crash.

It wasn't greed that drove her. It was her family. Finally, she had a chance to break free of them.

Approaching their end-of-terrace Victorian home, she gazed up at the oak tree growing in the pavement outside the front gate and admired its lush leafy fingers splaying across the violet sky. She pictured her bed, the warm lampshades, the excellent hardback she was close to finishing. Jenny loved being in the centre of it all, living in that spacious building, feeling that her claim on the Clareville property was akin to acquiring another limb.

Until recently it had been easy to forget that Jenny's mother, Vera, owned the house and that they were only tenants who paid Vera rent. Just a few months ago, they'd received a letter from the family's solicitors giving them twelve months' notice. Her mother could have told Jenny to her face, but that would've been normal behaviour and therefore lack the drama and subterfuge that made Vera's life so self-absorbing. The twelve months' notice was ruining Clareville for Jenny. Everywhere she looked, there was someone living the life that had once been reserved for her.

SMASH. It came blasting through the night, so loud, the air seemed to move. The noise came from above the roof of their house. It came from the laneway behind the backyard. Jenny went to insert her key, but the front door swung inwards from the slightest pressure. She stared down the hallway to the kitchen, where the back door swayed in the breeze.

Something had happened to Shane. Something awful. Something that wouldn't have happened if she hadn't been late home. The thought entered her mind and was staying there – like woodworm in a chair, like cancer cells, like vermin under the boards. Nothing would eradicate it. She longed to protect him from the knowledge that, this time, the sky had actually fallen.

But it was too late; *she* was too late.

Jenny pictured Shane in tangled metal, wanting to live but being denied his last and fullest wish. *Please let there be no pain. Let it have been so violent that he just evaporates. Vaporises.*

Jenny, too, wanted to be atomised. She looked up at the tight cluster of stars that were surprisingly visible above the city, like a ragged tear in the galaxy. There was a whisper in the air, and it took her a moment to realise that it was her own. 'Let him be OK… Let him be OK…' She envied those, like her mother and sister, who had the crutch of God. It still seemed incomprehensible that God should exist and yet, for the first time, it somehow also felt incomprehensible that He should not.

Jenny was on the decking in the backyard. It was as if she'd magically materialised there. She hadn't been aware of running through the hall and kitchen. It wasn't fair. They'd only had fifteen years together and she'd never told him her biggest secret. There it was, taking over her brain like an exploding firework lighting up the sky.

Her secret should've been dead, gone, lost in the past, down the back of life's sofa along with those memories of wetting herself at school, being humiliated by the cool girls, being disgraced by losing when she should've won. And finally, a flaunting image above all those memories. Mother.

3

The air shifted and the breeze hit Shane's face like a shout. Glass beads were scattered over his knees and the front of his shirt. Shane had felt like this so many times in the past – car-crashed, stuck, buried alive. He'd gone through so much to get the life he now had with Jenny. He had a career. She had a future. They had their savings, enough to finally walk away from Jenny's family.

Yet here I am. Stranded. Maybe dying in a grubby laneway.

Moving his toes, Shane felt the shoe leather cling, taut against his feet. His digits thrummed the steering wheel from thumb to little finger. Holding his breath, he slowly moved his neck left and then right. *No paralysis.* Releasing the steering wheel, Shane grabbed the rear-view mirror with such force that he nearly ripped it from the ceiling. He saw himself in the yellow glow of the interior light that had come on after the passenger door blew open.

No bleeding. No scarring.

Then, Shane noticed him. Wearing a balaclava. His body lay horizontally on the mashed bonnet of the Land Rover. Behind the man, the front of the Focus had ceased to exist, its engine crumpled inwards to become almost one with its steering column.

Shane tried to ask him if he was OK, but only succeeded in swallowing. The man's eyes stared at him through the twin holes of the mask. Blue. Piercing. Accusing. The man's mouth opened and the startling red lips, surrounded by black fibre, silently mouthed, 'Fuck. You.' It was like a heart monitor bouncing back from a flatline. The young man was furious. Furious survives. Usually. That was good.

Shane's gaze moved down the balaclava to the man's shoulders and upper body. His legs were broken and twisted at a gruesome angle up behind his lower back, his knees concertinaed to his buttocks as if he was an escape artist. Shane noticed his green jumper. It had the look of something second-hand, from a charity shop – as if the aura of other people's sadness radiated from the acrylic.

Someone else is here.

The gloomy vision of a second man was sketched in the laneway shadows. He seemed to have no natural curves, a hasty line-drawing rather than a real person. Shane tried to move, but his feet were jammed beneath the steering wheel. This second man was going to do something to him. He wanted to move his hands to protect his face, but they retained their grip on the leather steering wheel. He opened his mouth to call out, but realised that he was only breathing in sudden gasps. In a whisper, he said, 'Don't…' But he didn't know what else to say. *I can beg him to leave me alone*. He didn't need to play the part of a desperate man. He *was* a desperate man.

Shane heard a voice. It was a low, deep whisper; 'This is just the beginning…'

'What?'

'You have no idea what's coming.' The voice was stronger now, emphasising how the effects of the crash, for him, had been fleeting.

The man stepped away from his colleague's body, and Shane listened to the footsteps fade down the laneway. Just as they were about to disappear completely, they began to increase in volume again. *He's coming back.*

Louder and closer they came, until Shane felt the man's hands on his forehead, running through his hair, then the skin of his cheek against his. The man had Jenny's voice and he was repeating, 'Thank God. Thank God. Thank God.'

Shane wanted to warn Jenny about the other burglar, but the one on the bonnet wouldn't close his eyes, wouldn't stop staring at him.

Jenny said, 'You are the only thing that matters in my life.' She leaned in further, placed her hand over his and repeated, 'The *only* thing that matters', as if saying it twice would make it more true.

Shane said, 'The second one.' It was barely a grunt.

Jenny looked to the guy on the bonnet. 'Yeah. I'll check him out. Don't move anything.'

Neighbours were emerging from their cosy cocoons of abundance and Jenny scanned their faces like an anxious parent at the school gates. She shouted, 'Get the doctor,' as if there was only one in the whole world.

Leaning over the bonnet of the Land Rover, she grimaced at the twisted, broken body lying across it. Placing her hand on the side of the man's neck, she waited, staring into the Land Rover at her husband's face. 'I can't feel a pulse.'

Her fingers dipped under the rim of the balaclava before carefully peeling it up.

The nearest neighbour surveyed the sight revealed before her and exclaimed. 'Oh. My. Word.' Her tone, her expression, her wide eyes – it all filled the air with emergency.

'Fuck me,' Jenny muttered.

'Jesus Christ,' Shane said.

Lying across the bonnet was a young woman, dark hair clipped to the sides. Her pale skin was smooth, eyebrows sculpted. Even in death, she was quite beautiful.

4

Now

12.30 pm: It was Monday, three days after the crash, and Shane was back in Clareville, making a promise to himself that whenever he was to die, it would be at home. After just one night in hospital, his room had begun to feel like an asylum. He'd had visitors; he'd had peace and quiet; he'd had unrelenting queries of concern. By Sunday, he'd wanted to leave – but the doctor had insisted that he stay for at least one more night.

Reluctantly, they let him depart that morning with a three-month prescription – not for painkillers, but for serotonin reuptake inhibitors for post-traumatic stress. Before getting a taxi with Jenny, he'd scrunched up the Zoloft slip and binned it. Shane had no intention of becoming medicated. He would prefer to feel bad things than to feel nothing at all.

The moment he got home, Shane checked out the laneway, from where the emergency services had eradicated every last trace of both vehicles. Looking for evidence that Friday night had actually happened, all he found were diamonds of glass brushed to the sides of the wall.

Now that he was back in Clareville, he felt up to dealing with the administrative issues concerning the crash. For example, the Land Rover was a write-off and, because of its age, they were only due about four thousand for it. Their next second-hand car would have to be something way more pedestrian. He wondered how much that would perforate Jenny's self-esteem. Jenny's first car had been the silver Mercedes that her father surprised her with on her eighteenth. Hard to believe that was twenty-five years ago. Back then they'd drive down to Dublin Bay, where they'd undress each other with the enthusiasm of two people who felt that they'd just invented sex.

Shane returned to the house and went upstairs to the master bedroom. After showering in the en suite, he stood before the mirror to examine the smattering of small wounds across his body, the light discolouration on his legs and bruised forehead. Physically, he'd been lucky in life. Outside of a few adolescent-era punch-ups, the only true corporeal suffering he'd experienced had been when confined to the dentist's chair.

As Shane knelt to get his shoes from under the bed, he noticed a wicker basket containing Jenny's old letters and photos. His wife had kept all their historical mementoes – Polaroids of them arm wrestling, cinema stubs, a poem he'd written for her at college. In hospital, Shane had found himself thinking of things he no longer owned – school yearbooks, diaries, even mix tapes – and he cursed himself for once believing that he was going to be young forever and that memories were there to be replaced by better, newer ones. Now that it was too late, he realised that without mementoes or the stimulus of children to share reminiscences with, the past just withered away and died. How he would've loved to have had kids with Jenny.

Is it too late? Are we now too old? Can science help? The answers didn't matter, because Jenny had never even intimated that she'd change her mind. While in hospital, it had occurred to Shane that aging was a process of gradually relinquishing everything of value until, in the end, you have absolutely nothing.

He turned to face his father-in-law's full-length antique mirror and focused on the lines of his forehead, the darkness beneath his eyes. *I've begun my gradual extinction.* It was as if he was witnessing the moment when the great herds of his cells, dividing and subdividing across the vast plains of his anatomy, paused, and sensed a shift in nature, a darkening of the sun, the first rousing draft of an ice age.

Despite their never having had children, being in love did feel good. It was like winning at roulette every day. But that would mean there would come a time when he was destined to lose. Probability demanded it. Shane thought about his year at college with Jenny – back then, they'd talked about the future with a certainty that it would contain them both. Despite everything that would happen, they had eventually been right. They'd been right until that very month – when they just might be wrong.

Shane sat at the edge of the brass-framed bed as the electric shaver droned on. He remembered waking in hospital on Saturday. It had been as if he'd no idea about the previous night. Zero. It was a movie he'd never seen. It wasn't that he'd lost his memory. It was just that he'd refused to think about it. The police, Jenny and the doctor had all asked him questions. He'd said the same thing to each of them – 'Not yet.' Then, on Saturday evening, he'd finally spoken to the detective who eagerly took down every scrap, until he came to the fact that he'd seen a man. His outline. A sinister charcoal drawing next to the smashed red Ford. The man had been there,

Shane was certain. *And I think he said something. I'm sure he did. But what?* It was a story that kept telling itself to him, but always leaving out the end.

So far, all the police seemed to have done was to arrange for the girl to be brought to the morgue. Writing true-crime explorations had armed him with the knowledge that often the police just go through the motions, simply to reassure the public that their taxes are not being wasted and to make them believe that they're protected from the people who want to rob and kill them – because, when a serious offence was committed, then in most cases the guilty party was either known from the start, or unlikely ever to be apprehended.

Shane pictured the woman on the bonnet of the Land Rover. She'd looked frightened, and young. True, she could've stabbed Shane in the house. She could've poleaxed him in the garage with his own hammer. But she hadn't, because she'd been scared. *She tried to kill me with her car*. No – she tried to escape. She'd done what he would've done in her situation – run. Just like everyone else, she had imagined what it would be like to have more.

Dressed, Shane was ready to face the detective, who was due any moment. He descended the stairs, rubbing his hand along the banisters as if he was extinguishing the last vestiges of the dead girl from the planet. In the hallway, he opened the front door to check for Monday's mail. Lying there on the mat were wrapped white lilies. Scooping them up, he flicked open the small card. Four lines were scribbled in black pen. The first read:

This is just the beginning.

That's it! That's what he said on the laneway. I knew it. I was right. But what does he want? Is it the girl? Does he blame me for her death?

Shane read the remaining lines, as a dark and slimy tide swamped him:

Do you know what I'm going to do to you?

Think of the cruellest things.

By sunset today, I will have destroyed your life.

5

1.15 pm: Jenny sat at the island counter. The kitchen was her favourite room in the old Victorian house. It was where she watched TV, did most of her paperwork and relaxed. The kitchen was like something from a catalogue, perfectly in tune with the current fads – every cabinet handle, each smooth-sliding drawer, even the constitution of the tile grout had been chosen by Jenny to generate serenity.

She still could not accept that she was going to lose Clareville. Not just because of what the bricks and mortar represented about her father – his sworn promise, his legacy to her, his loyalty. But also, Jenny loved her life inside it. Shane had made her Clareville home a pleasant sanctuary; because, to him, that was what a home was supposed to be. Shane's family had been so laid back, sometimes it had been annoying. He'd grown up in a house where no one had to yell or cry or scream because that was the only way in which you could have your feelings heard. His parents were, basically, nice people. When times were good, they celebrated. When times were bad, they were optimistic.

Jenny had grown up in a noisy house. Her mother had struggled with peace and quiet. Vera had her three children addicted to family showdowns and tear-jerkers; since she had never worked, she didn't have the petty back-stabbings of the office to keep her appetite sated.

A year ago, in what had appeared to be an unaccountable act of generosity, Jenny's mother had assigned her a substantial budget to renovate the kitchen. However, now that Jenny knew the house would soon be on the market, she saw that for what it was. Vera had made an investment for Vera, and used the expertise of an interior designer without having to pay for it.

Vera hadn't called since the crash on Friday – which was strange. With all the coverage in the press over the weekend about the break-in, surely Vera would have some concern, if not for Shane, then for her youngest daughter's welfare? After all, their family was no stranger to dynastic tragedy. *Something must've come up. Maybe she's not well. No – Joan would've told me in a text.* It irritated Jenny that even when Joan was away in Florida or London, her sister remained more aware of their mother's whereabouts than she ever was. Jenny sighed, as she usually did whenever she thought about her mother; Vera – the only person who could ruin her day without actually being in it.

Pushing her coffee to the other side of the island top, she scanned the kitchen and hated the fact that it could soon be taken away from her. It seemed impossible to think that in a year, someone else would be sitting here having breakfast; someone else would be loving this kitchen. She knew it was her mother's fault, but it felt as if Shane was equally responsible. He believed their lives were on cruise control. They had no debt. They could drive an hour to the countryside and take his boat out on the lake. They ate in chic restaurants. They took exotic holidays. He could spend an hour every night playing video games. Life was good. Why risk it all for more of what they didn't need?

What Shane refused to understand was that she *needed* this house. Jenny's father had promised it to her – only for the rest of her family to deny his wish. Jenny remembered the first time her financial advisor had run the idea past her, and he'd concluded with, 'Jenny, it's simple. Do the maths.'

She'd done the maths. She'd exclaimed, 'Jesus Christ!' The mere sound of the figure had mesmerised her. It had made her lose her thoughts to contemplation. It was like staring into infinity or tasting pure power. To even mutter the number had been like rolling wealth around in her mouth. With that investment opportunity, she could anonymously buy the house when it hit the market. She could outsmart her mother and yet also give Vera what she wanted: money.

That was important to Jenny – getting the house fairly – because it was not vengeance she sought, but justice.

Outside in the hallway, she heard the office door close. *He's working already?* In hospital, Jenny had sensed Shane's impatience to get back to hammering words onto the page. Now that he had been home for less than an hour, he'd already retreated to the sanctuary of his study.

That weekend had been the first time in fifteen years they'd slept apart, and Jenny had missed him. The great thing about her husband was that he would appear at the right moments – when she needed someone to talk to, when she was turned on, when she wanted to laugh. Other husbands did not seem like that. With them, there appeared to be hours and hours of listening to them talk about things that weren't important and having to nod along as if they were. It seemed exhausting. No wonder so many didn't make it.

She knew that he secretly followed the Instagram account of one of his old girlfriends, and every few days Jenny would spy on whatever was keeping him interested after all these years. His ex had documented the journey of her latest pregnancy on her feed; from shots of the bump to a stylish online gender reveal party, where pink balloons popped out of the box and dozens of people put heart emojis in the comments. Every morning, Shane's ex put up a brand-new sepia-toned portrait of herself and her perfect children – all styled in Tommy Hilfiger.

I should've given him the children he wanted but, how could I? There was always the other thing; and the other thing was the main thing. Everything else was just camouflage.

Jenny blinked twice, as if that would clear the choked memory cache of her brain.

She checked her watch; 1.32 pm. The detective was twenty minutes late, which was like a punch in the gut to a person who checked her watch with a tic-like frequency. It was her experience that, if someone was late for a meeting, they were either an incompetent arsehole or they were trying to make a power statement. She reckoned that with this detective it was the latter option.

Footsteps in the hall. A moment later Shane entered, and the first things she noticed were the lilies he held by his side. 'Who are they from?'

'Just a reader. Nice, huh? I'm appreciated!' He laid them on the far end of the counter. 'I saw the get well cards from the neighbours, in the hall. They must've been afraid I was going to lower Clareville's tone by dying.'

Shane was dressed in black jeans, black shirt and black jacket – but he looked a husk of himself, as if he'd been caught in a spider's web and drained of blood. She wasn't used to seeing her husband like this. He was always in excellent health, always fit; one of those men who improved with age.

Jenny tried to sound breezy. 'Everything OK? You're pale and…

You sure you shouldn't have stayed in for another night? They're always angsty over head trauma. The doc suggested another twenty-four hours of cranial observation for a reason.'

He was thrown, which surprised Jenny. Her husband clearly assumed he'd been doing a reasonable impression of every-day Shane.

'Observation of my wallet, more likely. I'm fine. If it hadn't been in the papers, they wouldn't have bothered asking me to stay in.'

'I'm just worried about you, babe. Next weekend, we'll be down the country, on the boat, cruising the lake… OK, *rowing* the lake. Soon I'll be like you and prefer cows to people.'

'When have you last seen a cow being an arsehole? Or a horse? Or a sheep?'

'A very valid point, Shane.'

For a moment he looked pensive. Then he said, 'Admittedly, goats can be arseholes.'

She laughed and felt some of her tension melt away into the tranquillity of their home.

'Did Mum visit while you were in hospital? Like, you would've told me, yeah?'

'No,' Shane answered quickly. 'I mean, no, I didn't see her.' He swallowed. 'Why? Has she been in touch?'

Jenny shook her head. 'Just wondering.'

They kept each other's gaze.

The doorbell sounded and Jenny, in her new black Zara suit, answered it. It was Detective Murray, twenty-three minutes late, dressed – on a hot day – in brown chinos and a navy jumper beneath a blue jacket. He had a smooth, round face with full, well-fed lips – though there was a weakness about his chin, as if they'd run out of clay when making him.

She looked at her watch. It was deliberate. She knew the time.

Jenny didn't like the detective but tried hard not to show it. She knew that he saw her as a spoilt rich girl who thought that poverty was to be restricted to the 'by the glass' section of a fantastic wine menu. Jenny had no intention of correcting his mistaken impression. That was, after all, the image she needed to project as an in-demand interior designer. It was important for the world to see her living in a beautifully furnished Clareville home and driving a Land Rover. It would not be fine if the world knew that the house was not hers, that the furniture was her father's leftovers after her sister had taken first dibs and that the Land Rover was second-hand and ten years old.

Detective Murray stepped into the hall and said, brightly, 'You're all dressed up?'

'LaLucia is opening its first European department store. They chose Dublin and not London. That's a big deal – and I worked on the interior for the kitchenware department. Usually, I do domestic. So, this is my first corporate.' Her fingers made a pyramid before her almost juvenile-looking face, to demonstrate the sharpness of her queen-sized thoughts. 'Because of that, I gotta be at the opening.'

'Yeah, well, nice suit. Seriously. It's sick, as the kids I arrest say.'

'Um… thanks.' Jenny tried not to sound grateful, but she appreciated the compliment. With Shane arriving home from hospital, she'd only had thirty minutes to get herself ready, when she generally allowed herself a minimum of an hour.

Leading Detective Murray into the kitchen, she gestured for him to sit at the antique hunting table. He turned the chair outwards, so he could stretch his legs. Jenny retook her stool at the island next to Shane, pleased that they were both now higher up than the policeman.

Detective Murray asked, 'How's it going, Shane?'

'Not awesome.' He gestured to the morning newspaper before him, which was open at page eight and included a small story about the break-in. 'Have you found the second burglar?'

'There was no trace of anyone else in the stolen car. Just the young woman.' The detective's tubby round face reddened, and he reminded Jenny of a traffic light.

'I *know* what I saw.'

'Think about it, Shane. How can you be sure you saw what you saw? I mean, you never mentioned anything about someone else being on the laneway when Jenny arrived. Or when the police and ambulance got there. You never mentioned anything until the next day; Saturday at 7.00 pm, in hospital, to be precise. Until then, it had been a straightforward situation.'

Jenny suppressed an audible guffaw. So, it was official – her husband's experience had been downgraded from 'horror' to 'situation'.

Shane said, 'I never mentioned anything about *anything* on the laneway because I was just involved in a head-on collision and there was a dead body lying prostrate two feet from my face. Detective Murray – I *know* what I saw. He *had* been there.'

Jenny watched Shane's face darken. Her husband didn't particularly care for the police. His experience until now had been that they were responsible for giving them speeding tickets and, years ago, making them paranoid any time they'd carried recreational drugs. Then there was the fact that clearly, due to the nature of his research, he didn't rate their work methods.

'Okay, listen to me, Shane,' Jenny said, about to get assertive. 'I arrived what… two minutes after the crash? And there was no one there.'

'Great. Here we go again.' The fact that she had jumped in to support the detective bothered Shane. 'I just love hearing how even my wife doesn't believe me.'

'Of course I believe you. I believe that you believe. Get me? But I know what I *didn't* see. And the police are right about one thing – you're lucky not to have been seriously injured. On top of all that, we weren't even robbed. I mean, *nothing* was taken. Like I've been telling you – just forget about it. You'll drive yourself nuts, otherwise.'

Shane failed to mask his disappointment. Jenny held his gaze. A silence stretched.

Finally, the detective said, 'Don't you believe your wife is being honest with you?'

There followed a traffic jam of silent exchanges. Jenny looked at Murray and couldn't think of anything to say. Shane, too, shifted his attention to the detective, who sat there waiting, genuinely curious.

Jenny's mobile bleated the arrival of a text. She glanced down to the screen. It read: **Still going to the LaLucia launch?**

Picking up the phone, she typed: **Y**.

A moment later, the reply read: **Will meet u there**.

Jenny slid off the stool and planted her feet onto the floor. Again, she typed: **Y**.

The two men were looking at her. Jenny cleared her throat. 'Right, gotta go and be worshipped in the church of my genius.'

Shane asked, 'Going alone?'

'Yep.'

'Not meeting anyone?'

'No.'

'I can still come, you know? It's only ten minutes in a taxi. You need a wingman, then it's not a problem.'

'I'll be fine.' Then, with more confidence, she added, 'I know you hate these things, so I do appreciate it. You're the best. But that outline isn't going to write itself by Friday. Get on it when you're done here.'

Shane nodded; the detective gave a half-wave, and just like that, Jenny slipped away to the privacy of her outside world.

6

1.55 pm: With Jenny just gone, Shane rounded the island, picked up the lilies and passed them to the detective.

'I didn't want to show you in front of Jenny. Read the card.'

Murray did so and said, 'Don't let it spook you. I mean, "I will destroy you" by sunset of today? When's that – nine this evening? Ambitious, huh? It's just a sick joke from your averagely nasty person. Happens all the time. Especially when there's media coverage. Believe me, there's many sickos out there but most of them are not "act-out" dangerous.'

'So therefore, some of them *are* "act-out" dangerous. Anyway, that's not the point. The point *is*, that when I read the note, I suddenly remembered that the first line is what the guy said to me in the laneway.'

Murray almost stood up. But then he relaxed, cleared his voice and spoke softly. 'I understand what you're experiencing, Shane. You've been through a terrible trauma. And I don't use that word lightly. But until now, you've never mentioned anything about him actually *talking* to you. Shane, you've just read a line in a card and decided you've heard it before. You're in shock. Don't worry about scaring your wife. She seems fine to me. In fact, get Jenny to go through your mail for the next few days. There'll probably be more crazy coming your way and it would be better for her to see it first, maybe.'

Shane wasn't surprised that Murray did not believe him. He'd experienced the egos of detectives before, when researching long-dead cases. The fact was, Shane was messing with Murray's standard schtick. Part of that schtick was telling recovering victims that everything bad that could happen had just happened and therefore the chances that more harm would occur, were miniscule. In other words, that a recovering victim was, by default, safe.

Shane said, 'Look man, I appreciate all you've done. But at the same time, I can't help noticing that besides the second burglar, you've no problem with anything else I've told you.'

'But Shane, we *have* taken your belated Saturday recollection into account.' He smiled, as if letting Shane know how much of a favour he'd done him. 'That's why we've already searched the back gardens along the laneway, to check for any trace that someone had been hiding there. But… we found nothing.'

Shane tried to imagine Detective Murray out there, in the field, actually doing his job. 'Check the car for prints?'

'Of course. We've matched hers. But then there's lots of other fingerprints. It was stolen on Friday afternoon from outside a community centre. It was an old man's, who'd owned it for five years. So, there's prints from passengers in the past week, month, year. But we have her phone – a grotty old thing with dirt clogging the sockets and buttons and melted lipstick smeared across the screen. Alas, no calls or texts to anyone who seems like an accomplice. So, what we mean is, there's absolutely zero trace of a second perp in that car on the night of the burglary.' Again, he flashed a condescending smile; a smile Shane liked even less than the first one.

'What about *her*? Did she have a boyfriend? You did investigate her, right?'

'Yes, Shane. I had a quick look at who she was. And by quick look I mean going back through the archives fifty years.' Murray looked away to the window and Shane imagined him rolling his eyes. Then he continued. 'I'm not trying to be smart. I'm just trying to demonstrate that I'm with you in this. We have your back. We want you to feel safe again. She was twenty-two. Deirdre – or Dee, as her few friends knew her. Her people were from rural Cork. Parents – dead. Left home at sixteen to be with her twenty-two-year-old boyfriend, who played in a band. They broke up and she lived for a while in a hippy commune in the west. But you don't have to be long in my job before realising that kids wearing Extinction Rebellion badges or who have Hindu tattoos are some of the most violent, thieving menaces you'll ever meet.'

'How'd she get from hippie commune to my house?'

'Out west she got a record for trespassing and shoplifting a few years ago. But she's been out of the system since then. Finally grew up, seemed to get her life together and studied computer science in Galway. Graduated a year ago and worked for six months designing websites. Then, with the money she'd saved, went backpacking in Asia. She was an outsider. No close friends. No *steady* boyfriend. She got around, for want of a better phrase. I talked to people who knew her in Galway. They were all surprised – not by the burglary, but that she'd rammed your car. She was… "feisty" is how one described her—but not liable to do something off the wall like that. However, people change.'

Shane wasn't satisfied. 'And…?'

Murray held Shane's gaze. 'Well, unless something comes to light, it's case closed.'

Shane could see what was happening. Their burglary had already been chalked up as a win for the police. They'd got the perpetrator. Dead or alive was irrelevant.

Murray said, 'Look, I didn't just knock in to see how you are. Though that's important to me. To us. To the investigation. But I also wanted to let you know the post-mortem results and… well, if I learn anything from the results that I didn't see with my own eyes, then it'll be evidence that I'm not doing my job. And I'm doing my job. God put two eyes in my skull, not a pen in my hand.'

Murray took out his phone, opened an email and began reading it aloud. Murray listed Deirdre's height, weight, age and the general health and condition of her corpse, before describing some of the injuries in detail – each with an ascribed cause. All in all, the post-mortem report was indistinguishable from Shane's crashed vehicle report, which the dealership had emailed that morning; both filled with words such as 'abrasions', 'fracture' and 'rupture'. Shane knew the detective was trying to make him grateful to be alive.

Having finished, Murray began to fasten his jacket but abandoned the attempt, as if surprised to find that he had put on weight recently. From the bottom of the kitchen, he said, 'This is where it is. That girl broke into your house and tried to rob you. You disturbed her and to escape, she knew that she'd have to possibly kill you. She tried this and died. Nothing was stolen and you're relatively unharmed. Shane…' He drew out his name, demanding silence like a patronising but all-powerful headmaster. 'You could've lost everything. And I mean *everything*. You should be grateful.'

'Look, I know what I saw. But yeah… I get what you're saying. And thanks, man.'

'I'll be in touch with any updates. Now, look after yourself and rest up. You've been through the wars, my friend.'

The door closed and Detective Murray let himself out.

Shane remained at the island counter, staring down at the note that came with the lilies. He checked the time – 2.08 pm – and then wondered just how many ways his life could be destroyed by sundown. Something terrible could happen to Jenny. Could his career be ruined in the next seven hours? He could be killed, mutilated, crippled. Could he be framed for something? He could lose all his money.

This is pointless and stupid.

Coffee mug in hand, he entered the front room where the walls contained his ceiling-to-floor library and a sliding ladder. Shane's own oeuvre was in the process of stretching to seven books; all but the first were in-depth explorations of contemporary Irish true crime. He preferred to examine cases where there wasn't a conviction, where there was nothing known except confusion.

Behind his desk were three shelves containing copies of his books, each one in a different language – Chinese, French, German and so on. It was his trophy cabinet. Despite this altar to his success, he often felt dwarfed by the room: the heaviness of the gold curtains, the thickness of the carpet, the flock wallpaper, an antique chess set, the sheer weight and bulk of his late father-in-law's furniture.

On the neat writing desk, the laptop was waiting. Shane sighed into the face of all the work that was waiting for him – a whole day of it – like a wall he was about to smash his head into. Taking his seat at the vintage writing desk, he stretched. He was good at taking his time. His current work in progress was a highbrow examination of a very lowbrow tabloid-baiting murder of a model/influencer that had occurred last year in Cork. It was very 'now', and incorporated all the buzz-themes that his publishers and agent were currently loving – the speed of communications, smartphones, Twitter, Facebook, fame.

He looked at the bay window. It begged him to approach and stare through it. Deadlines belonged in the real world. *Apparently, I'm a writer – so what's the mad rush?* He walked to the window and looked out to the pebble pathway leading to the wooden gate and the low stone wall topped with a decorative white metal railing. Had Deirdre watched their house before trying to rob it? She would have been out there, walking by, looking in through this window, watching him. He may even have seen her and thought, *just another pretty Clareville neighbour walking by.*

Out on the road, a man had stopped at the garden gate. He faced the house full on, staring in, as if their building was somehow historically important. Shane was well aware how people got excited about horrible things when they were *not* happening to them. *Yes, the protagonists of page eight of your morning paper live here.*

'Move on, buddy,' he muttered. 'Move. On.'

The stranger remained at the gate. He had a beard… and was he bald? Shane squinted. No. His head was just shaved, which was at odds with the density of his facial hair. He was wearing a thin black leather jacket and white earbuds which, in summer, made him look punkish in an affected catwalk manner rather than the grungy real thing. The stranger met Shane's gaze and did not turn away.

As if encountering a rival tribe member within his encampment, Shane experienced a primitive hostility towards this person. He wondered if he should knock on the glass but that seemed like such a suburban thing to do. *Maybe I should go out to him. Tell him to get lost. But what if he refused to do so? What would I do then? Hit him?* Holding up the partially pulled blind, Shane focused on what was unsettling him. It was a long time since his one and only truly violent encounter: a confrontation he'd never forget. *Do I really know how to fight? Why is he even making me think these stupid thoughts? Just walk on. Walk. On.*

As if hearing Shane's plea, the man with the shaved head and white earbuds sauntered off behind the neighbour's hedge. *It was nothing. No one's stalking. No one's spying.*

His phone buzzed. Unbuttoning his jacket beneath the window-magnified sun, the vibrating shell of his phone lifted away from his chest. *Is it Jenny?* Taking it out, he read the text and muttered, 'What the…?'

YOU HAVE NO IDEA WHAT YOUR WIFE DID.

Shane checked the number – it was unknown. He was about to call it, but stopped with his thumb over the green button. The detective had told him that there'd be a lot of weirdos curious about this case. If he replied, they'd think that he was interested in their drivel.

The doorbell sounded. Shane looked to the window. Too late for the postman. Too early for Jenny's return.

7

2.15 pm: With the city centre choked, the taxi loitered in the street, clicking steadily through the euros. In the backseat, Jenny turned to page ten of the *Irish Times Magazine* to read the interview she'd given last month that had just been published. It was perfect – one of those shamelessly flattering profiles designed to induce envious loathing in even the most mild-mannered reader. Unlike Shane, she didn't really mind reading about herself. It was kind of titillating to think of people discussing her without her knowing; how Jenny's name could shoot around the country without touching her.

She could already see her mother at home reading the article, trying to decide whether the positive boost her youngest daughter's success gave the family name outweighed the sickening jealousy it would cause her beloved Joan. In the article, Jenny made sure to speak about her father – how a passion for interior design was such a lovely thing for him to have left her. She spoke of how her father had brought her as a child every Saturday to the antique shops as he browsed for a forgotten beauty. It was *their* time together. He'd never brought any of the others antique hunting – a fact her mother would often point out, seemingly for no other reason but to cause an awkward silence during family meals. Jenny had been her father's favourite, even though she'd never sought to be. For some reason, her presence had calmed him.

Going online, she quickly linked the article across all her platforms. The moment the story of her burglary broke, she had started to pick up about fifty new Instagram followers an hour and her blog stats went stratospheric. Jenny pictured the dead girl. She didn't hate her. Jenny assumed Deirdre hadn't intentionally tried to kill her husband. But she did wish that Deirdre had been a man. Then, whenever she reflected on the fact that the burglar was dead, she would have been able to think *So what? One less violent, male joyrider on the road.* Jenny valued clarity.

Despite herself, there was an instinctual response that the world was somehow poorer now that a pretty girl no longer existed. When a beautiful woman died, it was nearly impossible to believe that she had, perhaps, deserved to. Jenny had heard an ambulance man mutter, 'What a waste.' When the police arrived, they sighed and shook their heads, as if the woman who had almost killed her husband had been an innocent victim of a freak accident.

At least Shane didn't feel culpable in any way. In fact, over the weekend there hadn't been a single moment when he'd blamed himself for chasing the burglar. Instead, he had focused on the other thing – his belief that he'd seen a man on the laneway; his certainty that *he* definitely existed, that *he* was out there somewhere.

Shane will get to grips with what really happened soon.

The thought of Shane turning down the investment opportunity jabbed at her again. Because of that, she would soon need to account for her unaccountable actions. Because of that, she was going to have another secret; and she already had too many of those in her life.

Her phone buzzed: a text from 'Mum'. Even after all this time, an unexpected communique from Vera triggered an immediate sparkle of happiness within her. But the fizz of pleasure was always short-lived. No doubt, Vera's text would be an excuse, in lieu of an apology, for not calling about Shane and the break-in.

Has Mum ever apologised to me? Jenny knew all her mother's alibis. This one would be something like Vera being needed to drop one of Joan's twenty-something-year-old incompetent adult kids to the dentist and so she hadn't had the time to contemplate the mere death and burglary that had occurred in Jenny's world.

Sitting up straight in the back of the taxi, she opened the message.

Jennifer, I know you're fine, thank God. Joan told me everything and I read the news. I always pray for you, and I am so happy that He has been hearing me and kept you safe. Now – I know you must be wondering about my asking you to vacate the house. The time has come for us to talk about it. A few months ago, it was the anniversary – exactly twenty-five years ago since you did that awful, awful thing. I had hoped to see you face up to your demons before I die. But you have not done so. We are your family. ALL OF US. Mumma. xxx

Why has Mum brought this up? Vera had addressed something they had not spoken about in twenty-five years – though the subject was always there, in the air, shimmering between them like unremarked-upon heat. *Forget about it. It's in the past.* That, of course, was an empty platitude. The fact was the past was in her head – where it stayed.

Jenny re-read Vera's text. Her head was full of flashbacks from her eighteenth year, and she wondered what grotesque function of the unconscious had decided to vomit them forth. *Mum called it – an anniversary? Maybe she and Joan commemorated it in some ridiculous way because they've nothing else going on in their lives. It's just more family bullshit. And I'm supposed to care? Well, I have a life.*

The taxi wasn't moving any time soon. Ahead were the smeared reds of brake lights as the city core gridlocked. It looked strange in the afternoon – a sight that belonged to the night. She checked the time – 2.28 pm. Where was the day going? She was already running out of hours. Jenny paid the driver and exited the stranded vehicle.

A block away, sightseers and the mere curious crowded the front of LaLucia. Most of the women hanging around were much younger than Jenny. *My prime, when was that? When I was eighteen? Twenty-five? Thirty?* Now that she was forty-three, many in the industry already considered her past it and any day now her clients would, too. Jenny touched her shoulder-length blonde hair for reassurance. She'd bleached it for a quarter of a century and now didn't even know what her real colour was. Light brown, maybe? She never wanted to go back – people look at you differently when you burn the colour out of your hair.

But being an interior designer made her feel truly young – or rather, young again. After all, she'd wasted her first youth. Thoroughly. Looking up at the façade of the department store, she realised that because of everything that had happened in the last seventy-two hours – Shane's rejection of the investment opportunity, the crash, Deirdre's death, the detective, her mother's text – because of all that, she'd yet to step back and take stock as to what was happening to her career.

This is it. The precise moment when I realise that I'm making it.

She minnowed her way towards the security team at the velvet rope and declared, 'Jenny Donaldson, interior designer.' Her voice betrayed the pride she felt in her work.

Stepping out of the crush into glorious space, the rope was replaced behind her with a condemnatory click. Upon entering the spread of the refurbished store, the atmosphere hit her like a surge of electricity. Here, the scene was pure gold, with the chairwoman of the LaLucia empire, Ellie Senzo, standing before the make-up counter, surrounded by handsome men – including a famous actor – who were all totally focused on her… because all she had to do for attention was enter a room. When Jenny had been making an on-site inspection, she'd been briefly introduced to Ellie, who had asked her about her father, whom she'd met in Toronto thirty years before. When Jenny told Ellie about her plans for the home and kitchenware department, she'd detected a faint trace of admiration radiating from the French woman. But after the initial buzz, Jenny had faced up to the fact that it had been for her father.

Jenny scanned the invited crowd to see who she knew. Then she noticed him – about twenty feet away, standing halfway up the showy staircase, an arm resting on the thick wooden banister. Pensive and dressed in black like Prince Hamlet, he looked at Jenny, snapped his phone closed and stared down on her.

He was in black jeans and a coolly distressed thin black leather jacket. His face was obscured by a black beard and… was he bald? No. His head was shaved and there were small white earphones dangling from his head – presumably because he'd just arrived. He stayed there, staring, making his bulk a weapon so that people on the stairs had to move aside to avoid him.

Is he glaring at me? She checked the time, 2.38 pm. Not an hour she normally associated with danger.

8

2.38 pm: Opening the front door, Shane failed to hide the disappointment that arose from multiple springs; it wasn't his wife, it wasn't an interesting delivery – but most unsatisfactorily, it *was* Jenny's financial advisor, Otto.

Otto looked out from behind glasses that were fitted onto a sharp long nose. He was broad and over six feet tall – yards of pinstripe. His dark, side-parted hair was probably in the same style he'd had when his mother had brushed it in Vienna, and his small squinting eyes gave an otherwise macho build a glaze of endearing boyishness. But he was in the difficult first half of his fifties, an age when even romantics must admit that youth is gone.

'How are you?' Otto asked, taking Shane's vague nod as an invitation to shake his hand. Shane tried not to stare at the Austrian's watch, which was like seeing a third-world economy strapped to someone's wrist. It was all gold and diamonds, yet still masculine.

'Fine,' Shane answered, before hurrying the conversation on to what he hoped would be its rapid conclusion. 'So...?'

Otto revealed a bouquet of white roses from behind his back.

'Really?' Shane took them and remained holding the door half open. 'Well thanks. Very nice. Appreciate it.'

'You see, Leona messed up your flower delivery to the hospital yesterday.'

'Who's Leona?' Shane held the bouquet down by his side as though it was a tennis racket.

'The girl I'm going to sack for messing up the flower delivery to the hospital yesterday.'

'Ah c'mon, Otto. No need to do that.'

'I am joking... as in, erasing the tension. Anyway, I was wondering if I could come in and have a word with you?'

'Nah, the place is a bit of a state and—'

'For fuck's actual sake, I just want a word. It's not an inspection.'

Shane sighed and brought him in. Entering the study, Otto, with hands on hips, effortlessly assumed that creamy, entitled bearing of old money. He was the type of man who owned a huge house packed with art and hung out with ministers and lords when over in London. You couldn't but want to impress him and because of that, Shane was determined not to be impressed *by* him; and so he dropped the flowers onto the counter with such carelessness, Otto had to realise that it was just a brief stopover on their way to the bin.

On the drinks cabinet was a silver picture frame containing a photo of a ten-year-old Jenny next to a tall, heavy, besuited man. In the picture she had thick eyebrows, high forehead and a sullen expression. It was clear that one day she would be beautiful – just not yet.

Otto said, 'Well, her old man had taste. These places get torn down every day and the world gets worse because of that. And the furniture. I mean, look at that chessboard. And your writing desk. The features... it's like *this* is why people start wars.'

Shane knew that Otto was attempting to compliment him, but he was really complimenting Jenny's father. 'Well Jenny is the collector. Me – I'm the... what's the opposite to collector? The thrower-outer?'

Otto laughed and asked him how his research was going.

'Fine.'

Otto enquired, 'And how are you feeling?'

'Fine.'

Shane's stress levels were also 'fine'. His kitchen door was 'fine', too.

'And the dead girl... it *was* a girl, yes? Original. I mean... you know what I mean.'

'Look, Otto, I do appreciate the flowers and you popping in. But I need to get back to this stuff...' Shane gestured to his closed laptop.

'You know, Shane, it's almost as if you're not delighted to see me.'

Fully aware of the real point of this visit, Shane said, 'I'm not happy, sad or angry to see you. I simply don't care. You don't even ripple.'

For a second, he held his breath. It felt wrong to speak to anyone like that. But particularly Otto. He couldn't shake off their past. Twenty-five years ago. A quarter of a century. He wondered if his personal history with his wife's accountant had coloured his decision not to invest in his project. Jenny insisted it had. But Shane was sure it hadn't... *almost* sure.

Shane uprighted two glasses on the drinks counter and poured himself his favourite red. Positioning the bottle over the second glass, he waited for Otto's hand to block the pour, as he knew it would. 'Not drinking? Too early?'

'Teetotal, I'm afraid.'

'I keep forgetting you don't drink,' Shane said, though of course he'd never forgotten. He just wanted Otto to think that he wasn't important enough for him to think about. Then, raising his glass, he muttered, '*In vino veritas*,' before taking a long, healthy swallow.

Otto said, 'I made an offer to Jenny. She liked that offer. I'm here to talk about it.'

'You're wasting your time.' Nothing Otto could say would shake Shane's belief that a man can make a fortune with a minimal amount of work – but only if he is a gambler. Because you need to take risks to make serious money with no work. You need to risk it all. Like Jenny had been willing to do. 'And don't blah-blah me about your reputation: Otto – the Rain Man of stats. Got it. Still not happening. So… anything else?'

'C'mon, Shane. This deal will turn your savings of four hundred thousand into well over one million in a year.'

'Unless there's another crash. Aren't you worried about that?'

'No. Yes. I mean, *of course* there's going to be another crash. And it'll be so bad that there won't be a single decent restaurant left untouched in the whole country. But, by then, we'll have all left the crime scene.'

'*That's* your pitch?' Otto's brisk money-making sentences had always bothered Shane in a way that they never bothered Jenny. She was used to his type, from entertaining her father's friends who'd also been powerful, entitled and encased in rich men's secretiveness.

Otto shrugged the shrug of the extremely wealthy. 'Yes. Pretty much.'

'Actually, it's perversely impressive.'

'Shane, there is no other property that can offer the space and advantages this has. Its location is perfect. Its footprint is massive. An office block that would be just safety deposit boxes for the Russians and Chinese.' Then, as if reading Shane's mind, Otto added, 'Look, the feeling of lumping everything on one horse isn't ideal. But when was the last time *anything* was ideal?'

The last time everything was ideal was just before you put this idea into my wife's head, you wanker. 'Otto, your world is one in which anything but extreme wealth is seen as an intrinsic moral failure. That's fine. I'm not judging you. But understand this: I'm not in that world. Neither is Jenny.'

'OK. You're not doing it. Full stop. Debate is the larval state of truth. Let's skip it. And guess what? I'm actually glad you know what you're doing. Because I like your Jenny. I liked her when I first knew her, all those years ago. I liked her when she later sought me out to start her business. And I like her now as a client and yes, as a friend. And I like you, Shane. I like your certainty. Because you're forty-four, and life doesn't start again at forty-four.'

Otto had effortlessly slipped into that homiletic style that Shane disliked so much. How upright, formal and reasonable he looked; like the self-assured manager of a five-star hotel. 'The key to these things is peace of mind. If you don't have that, then…' He paused and behind his glasses, squinted. 'What's up? Something's off. And it's nothing to do with my investment opportunity.'

Shane thought of the second burglar in the laneway, the card that had come with the lilies, the guy with the shaved head outside his house and then the strange text message he'd received. He certainly wasn't going to tell Otto about any of those things and be called paranoid again.

Otto said, 'Look, since we don't know each other that well and we move in different crowds, feel free to tell me. You've nothing to lose.'

Shane smiled. What Otto really meant was that *he* moved in a different crowd. Or rather, *he* moved in a crowd and Shane didn't. 'Otto, know what stresses me out right now? More than the break-in or the dead girl? It's the fact that Jenny's family is right back in our lives. *That's* what stresses me out.'

Otto's eyes narrowed, as they always did when something interesting or inappropriate was being said to him. 'The mother hates you, right? Because of what you did to—'

Shane interrupted with a wave of his hand. 'Yeah. All that. But it's pretty much in the past. This is about now. Getting our marching orders from this house… it makes Vera an invisible presence in every room. A silent third party in every conversation. She's driving me crazy. But Jenny won't mention her, because Jenny never talks to me about her mother unless Vera has done something spectacularly awful to her – which is about once every three months.'

'So, when Jenny talks to her mother, you consider Jenny disloyal?'

That Otto had put his finger right on it, annoyed him. It was as if Otto had screamed his name inside the house. The fact was, he *was* angry and disappointed with his wife's unending quest to get back what her family had taken from her. Sometimes, it felt that her commitment to the battle, her fascination with it, her enthrallment with them, was deeper than anything her psyche directed towards him.

But Shane said, 'Jenny has a right to have a relationship with her mother.'

'Maybe the mother will die soon.'

'Her kind don't die easily.' Shane wasn't even sure if that possibility was a good thing. How would Jenny react? Would it mess her up even more than Vera had when she was alive?

'Maybe a bus will hit her.'

'Ah, the bus. *That* bus. The bus that goes around hitting people.'

Ducking Shane's sarcasm with a laugh, Otto clarified with, 'What I mean is, she might die and correct the injustices that have gone before. Blood is thicker than water.'

'Blood's thicker than water? True. But with this lot, money's thicker than blood.'

'But can an old woman really be that bad?'

'Put it this way, Otto, whatever good things you've heard about her aren't true. And whatever bad things… they're just the tip of the iceberg.' Shane was beginning to begrudgingly enjoy having someone familiar with the situation to offload onto.

'I know she disinherited—'

'She didn't *disinherit* Jenny. She stole from her and gave it to Joan, who hates Jenny and is jealous of Jenny. Joan has never done anything for herself in her life. Despite being middle-aged, Joan still sees her mother as a nurturing entity, the goddess Vishnu, the leader of the pack from whose breast she continues to suckle; the infallible source of all her happiness. And Joan will never forgive Jenny for doing her own thing; for stepping away from their glorious mother; for actually doing something constructive with her life, without their mother's help and without their mother's permission. Sometimes I think the reason Joan really hates her is because Jenny has done what she's unconsciously always wanted to do – free herself of her mother's regime.'

Shane had seen for himself how Vera had never had any great ambitions for her two girls. She'd considered them as a collective that should concentrate on keeping their weight down, getting married and giving her grandsons. And yet, with such low expectations, they had both still failed her. Jenny was childless and Joan had only produced granddaughters, rather than the grandson Vera craved.

Otto said, 'Well, since Vera gained control of the family estate, she can leave it to whoever she likes.'

'She was just supposed to mind it for tax reasons and *then* distribute it equally.'

'*Supposed* to.'

'But she bought Joan a penthouse with the funds after her separation. She then used the funds to renovate it, even though it was already fantastic. She used the money to have all three of Joan's kids put through college. And she keeps Jenny on in the background, watching all this, seeing what is hers being flushed away. You know, Jenny asked for a single piece of jewellery? These pearl earrings she'd always liked when she was a kid. But the mother just laughed as if she was mad, and wanted to know if she also wanted her old underwear.'

'Lovely – words to be treasured forever.'

'Vera said that her favourite granddaughter would get the earrings.'

'For Jenny to be treated like that… to take that shit…' Otto struggled for words. 'The best thing I ever did was tell my father to go and fuck himself. We got on better after that.'

Shane looked at Otto as if he was insane. 'You can't do that with a textbook narcissist who owns your house and controls what's left of your inheritance. Not if you still want to live in that house and ever see a cent of your inheritance. You've just got to take it. That's why Vera continues to see Jenny every week. It's to control her. Vera loved us being in this house. It gave her access to Jenny, which allowed Vera to make sure she wasn't doing too well. And it also gave her the power to throw Jenny out. Which she's now doing.'

'Think she needs the money?'

'Nope. Jenny says there should still be a few million left. So why is she kicking us out when we're her favourite toy?'

'What does Jenny think of her mother?'

'I've given Jenny printouts about narcissist mothers. But the most Jenny concedes is that Vera is just difficult… and poisoned against her by Joan. Jenny obviously still loves the woman; the way a lot of abused people love their abusers.'

Shane had always thought that there was an unhealthy connection between Vera and Jenny. Something in which the axe had yet to be buried. It was in the looks they'd given each other over the years. It was something that Shane didn't know yet and, maybe, never would.

'So, when Vera gave us a year to get out, it crushed Jenny because she'd always believed that Vera would eventually honour her husband's intention to give her the house. But I knew it was never going to happen – not while the golden child, Joan, still lives and breathes. Jenny has never accepted that Vera will never normalise, will never lighten up. Vera, by her very nature, will only get worse. She'll only get more extreme. She will find her way and then get her way.'

'You must hate Vera for everything she's done to Jenny and *then* throwing you out.'

'No – I don't hate Vera. Or any of them. My savings have reached the point – as you damn well know – where we've enough for a deposit on our own apartment in a neighbourhood near enough to Clareville—'

'But *not* Clareville.'

'If it gets Vera out of our lives forever, then I'm glad the house is being sold.'

'And is that what you want?'

Shane disliked questions like that. 'Is *what* what I want?'

'Getting Vera out of your life. Or do you want to know what *really* happened between Jenny and her? To know why Vera does what she does to Jenny? Or maybe you want Vera out of your life because you realise that you don't want to know and—'

'Of *course* I want to know. I mean, how bad can it be? It's not as if Jenny's hiding that her mother was a member of the Waffen-SS.'

'But to know everything about someone makes them boring. Dangerous for a marriage. And yet, paradoxically, secrets are only fun when you know them. Shane, the smart thing is to ignore it. Pretend there isn't a secret. That's what makes marriages last – people figuring out ways to keep their distance from each other without keeping their distance from each other.'

Shane wasn't used to Otto speaking to him warmly and didn't know how to react to this apparent openness and blunt honesty.

Otto continued. 'Stressful times can be a breakthrough. I had a nervous breakdown in my mid-twenties. I only really snapped out of it when I finally woke up and realised that it couldn't possibly get any worse, so who cares? In other words, I'd crossed the tipping point into "fuck it" territory. That's a great land to live in. And just like that – my recovery, my ambition, my business plan – it all came on me like a sudden urge to piss. So, I took risks again and was no longer afraid of failure. From there, I started my own business from nothing.'

Shane had to stop himself from laughing. If Otto, the son of a German industrialist, had started his business from nothing, then Otto's 'nothing' was somewhat more substantial than most other people's.

'Shane, you've little to worry about. Most couples married for as long as you are, are doing it for the kids. But you guys actually seem to like each other. You have it good. Get me?'

Shane thought of all the children he didn't have.

'Look, forget about Jenny's sister and her shit-stirring toxic mother. If Vera is the textbook narcissist you say she is, then she'll have done everything in her power to switch Jenny's attention from you to her. Just like she probably did with Joan's marriage. Joan's separated, right?'

Shane's phone began vibrating and he checked the message.

BE CAREFUL WHAT YOU SAY TO HIM

What the hell? Shane looked out the window as if expecting to see a bearded man in a leather jacket staring in. There was no one there. He checked the number. Unknown.

Shane looked at Otto. He had one long white hair in his left eyebrow. It was very unlike him not to have got rid of it. The air instantly throbbed with agitated atoms. The atmosphere had changed.

'Well?' Otto asked. 'You look as if you've just got bad news?'

'It's nothing,' Shane muttered. He looked out the window again. Was somebody outside – spying – warning him? But warning him of what? A mother rolled her buggy along the far pavement. There were a few empty parked cars. Nothing else. 'Just give me a minute.' He dialled the number. The tone pulsed four times before flatlining.

Otto licked his lips. Shane knew that people who have things to hide are liars, and that all liars are anxious. Some tremble. Some talk too fast. Some only offer monosyllabic answers. Others get a dry mouth. *I'm losing my mind.* It had to be a mistake. Or, at worst, it was one of the weirdos that Detective Murray had warned about, trying to press his buttons; someone who had no idea that Shane was standing in his living room talking to anyone.

Shane put away his phone. He just wanted Otto to go now. 'Sorry but I've got to… get back to the work.'

'Sure. We're done here anyway. But remember what Lovecraft said – "You can always kill yourself next year." God speed, brother.'

After they parted at the hall door, Shane returned to the study, sat at his desk and breathed out long and hard. The morning was well gone and already the afternoon was slipping away from him. His phone buzzed with the arrival of another text.

DON'T TRUST HIM

Shane stared out the window. *Please let there be somebody out there. That shaven-headed weirdo with the beard. If he's there, then I'll go out and face him.*

He remembered his one significant violent encounter: a night that had changed his life forever in ways that he could never have imagined. Twenty-six years had passed since then. *Is it really that long ago?*

9

Twenty-Six Years Ago

Shane, seventeen years old, walked into the lounge of an inner-city bar to meet a friend, having no idea that what was about to happen would still be shaping his life almost three decades later.

The Ploughman, infamous for serving underage patrons, was packed with teenagers. Most of the guys reeked of skunk and cigarettes, and had hoodies pulled over their heads so that their faces were in shadow, like scummy monks. The girls were underdressed and goose-fleshed, with cries as shrill as seagulls. The one sitting nearest Shane stretched lazily across the sofa, her ribs lining up beneath her pink belly-top like a row of slim book spines.

As Shane worked up the nerve to order a pint, a new group entered the lounge. There were five of them, but the alpha was easily identifiable; his noise footprint was large, with a cloud of sycophantic laughter puffing up around him. Next was his trusted lieutenant, and then the soldier ants. They stood out for many reasons. In their early twenties, they were older than everyone else. They were tall, muscular and wearing the black-crested blazers of a prestigious rugby club. They didn't care that people were looking at them – they expected to be marked with consequence in a pub like this. It was why they were there.

The rugby lads crowded the space that Shane had eyed, from which to order his pint. Now he didn't know where to stand. He didn't belong with the track-suited regulars because he didn't live for football and lager and had ambitions to go to university. But he also didn't belong with the older rugby guys. Even at seventeen, he resented how such young men had already grown so comfortable with money that they genuinely believed that they were entitled to it. He disliked how this belief gave them such a glow of vigour that they actually radiated a little.

A sixth member of the rugby crew arrived, walked straight to the alpha and asked, 'So how's it hanging, Hugh?'

Hugh clapped him chum-chummily on the cheek and, as if addressing an audience, loudly answered, 'Long and hard. Long. And. *Fucking*. Hard.'

'Amen.' The new arrival clinked the leader's glass with his bottle.

Hugh then pulled one of the girls off the sofa and started kissing her. His twenty-something-year-old tongue lapped at the pool of her adolescent mouth, his hands running up and down her back and ass. She pushed Hugh away. Hugh pushed her back. Her heels hit the corner of the sofa and she toppled over.

As Shane helped her up, the group of rugby friends turned to inspect him. After a moment they looked away, having seemingly failed to see anything at all. Facing Hugh's broad back, Shane muttered, 'What a prick.'

And just like that, a pool of silence gently spread around him. Hugh slowly turned, smiled and said, 'A wise man does not step between the beast and his meat, you fucking tosspot. Now run along before I decide not to be so friendly.'

Shane reddened as he stood inadequately before this muscled man, who demonstrated an enunciation that suggested locales of finicky privilege and robust breeding that he only knew about from the socialite pages he browsed at the barbers, when hard up for prose.

'Are you deaf?' Hugh then asked. 'I mean, *why* are you still here, before me, like some lost little kitty? Or can your pea-brain not cope with adult instruction?'

Shane reddened but forced himself to keep his gaze on those unpleasant brown eyes. *I can't walk away. That would be... that would be... that would not be cool.* Knowing that he was probably making the first big mistake of his life, Shane said, 'Big man, pushing girls around – you wanker.'

Hugh's mates, smelling blood in the water, pondered the drama unfolding before them. A thawing boredom was being replaced with cruel expectancy as they waited to see what would happen next, hoping it would be something that they'd be discussing for days to come.

Hugh spread his arms. It was an impressive sight; a six-foot-tall, muscled gladiator accepting the crowd's acclaim. He said, 'In Blackrock, we've a saying for dickheads who get themselves into your particular predicament. It's called – Being Completely and Utterly Fucked.'

But, betraying his anxiety, Hugh swallowed and, instead of thinking, he charged, Italian leather thumping against the floorboards.

Hugh smashed into Shane with the whack of skin and muscle colliding. Shane staggered backwards through a maze of limbs belonging to a gang of engrossed spectators. Colliding against the wall, Hugh shoved Shane again, ricocheting him off it before grabbing his hair and smashing the back of his head against the door frame.

Shane felt as if he was in the midst of an exploding bomb. He half expected to see his own legs flying past his eyes. A ticker tape of data reeled across his mind – *Am I bleeding? Could I be brain damaged? Is the wall damaged? Will I have to pay for it? I can't afford it. If I can't pay for it, could I go to jail even though I'm only seventeen and he's what – twenty-two? Taking a beating is better than running, isn't it?*

Suddenly, Shane was fighting back. With all his strength and determination, he pushed his entire being towards Hugh and both men bolted each other into headlocks. Hugh's low-tide breath gassed Shane's face, warming his skin. For a moment, Shane saw Hugh's eyes up close, and he recognised regret and embarrassment within them. Hugh began throwing punches, his fists pounding into ribs and stomach like two bags of cue balls. Shane lowered himself closer to the carpet, pretending to shield his midriff. Then he made his play.

In a blur of movement, he freed his right hand from around Hugh's waist and slammed a fist into the middle of his forehead. Hugh's body snapped up straight, air exiting his nose, his eyes wide and shocked. Reality dawned on Hugh's older face. He was not merely about to lose a competition in front of his peers. This was the end of everything.

Shane's body pulsed with a surge of renewed strength. He lunged and thumped Hugh in the stomach, driving all breath out. Then, he hit him one more time with a perfect right hook that resounded with a horrible crack. Hugh staggered in reverse, almost comically, as if being vanquished in slow motion. He fell backwards to the floor, his arms flopping outwards.

Despite everything, Shane pitied him. It would be a long time before Hugh could look at his friends again without knowing exactly what they were thinking.

But someone like that deserves to be on the floor after having the crap kicked out of him by a seventeen-year-old in front of all his rugby mates. Shane just wished he hadn't been the one who had to put him there.

As two barmen barged their way through the crowd, Shane, trying not to shake visibly, walked around Hugh towards the exit, very aware that what had just occurred was something he would remember for years to come.

Of course, he had no idea just how much it would actually affect him. How it would affect his entire life, and Hugh's.

10

Now

2.39 pm: Jenny forced herself to stare back up at the man on the stairs. *I'm not scared. The break-in will not change my life.* Jenny had grown up when little girls could still cycle the streets alone. She felt sorry for young women these days, who sensed the need to pack rape whistles and mace in their bags along with lipstick and phones.

Despite her secrets, despite what she was planning to do behind his back, Jenny wished that Shane was beside her now. She suddenly missed him terribly: his easy company, his unruffled demeanour, his ability to calm her with a nonchalant shrug that said, 'It's no biggie. We'll deal with it.' Sometimes, she regretted not having a baby with him. Sometimes, it felt like the biggest disappointment of her life.

Recently she'd watched Shane sweep a crying child from the ground with one hand while he lifted her bike with the other. As he calmed her, Jenny had been overcome with a kind of ravenous hunger that had rooted deep in her abdomen. She'd had to lean against the wall in surprise.

There was a tap on her shoulder. Jenny put her best face on, turned and smiled into the face of a glamorous brunette who was fighting fifty with Botox, fake eyelashes and a weekly spray-on tan. It was Sandra Gleeson, the TV presenter for the show *Teatime Ireland.*

'You're Jenny, the interior designer, yeah?'

'Yep.'

'You're the one who was in the papers over the weekend with her husband, the writer?'

'Yep.'

'Shane Smith. *The* Shane Smith,' she repeated, making Jenny wonder if Sandra had a better idea who Shane was than she did. Sandra continued: 'Look at you – after everything that happened and you are still, truly, the most beautiful woman in the room.'

Jenny smiled and then she lied, too. 'Love the cerise lipstick. Suits your complexion.' Looking beyond Sandra to the man on the staircase, she stared up at him, to let him know that she was aware of his presence, that she knew he was looking, and that she wanted him to stop. However, instead of looking away, his head jutted forward, as if responding to a challenge that she had just laid down. He released the banister and straightened, demonstrating his full height, over six feet of it.

Sandra noticed her noticing and asked, 'Who's that up there?'

'Don't know,' Jenny muttered.

'Well, he's nobody then.' Sandra clapped her hands. 'Right, up for an interview?'

'Of course.'

'Great. I thought Ellie wouldn't want to contaminate the product with death and shit, but she ordered me in this direction. Now, remember, my audience love flash-flash glamorama. One of the biggest ball-aches I have to deal with is people spewing the official press release.'

'No probs.' Jenny looked back to the staircase. She'd intended to ignore him, but couldn't. There was something about him so threatening and off, that she needed to know exactly where he was while she was in the same vicinity.

As Sandra positioned her before a white wall beneath a modernist clock, Jenny thought, *this is an important opportunity. Focus.* Gazing into the cameraman's lens, she explained: 'I imported several Vablum ornamental antiques to hang above the kitchenware space. You know what a Vablum antique is?'

'Sure,' said Sandra.

That was too bad, as Jenny longed to explain it to her on TV. 'Well, good. So, the quartz clock I picked – hanging above my head – is beyond fashion. Notice the creaminess of the dial, the sweeping space between the Arabic numerals communicating that everything is easy and spacious and free. My father loved clocks and watches. He was the one who made me appreciate the significance of Vablum scarce goods, such as this one.'

Why do I keep mentioning Vablum goods? It's teatime TV. You have to be of a certain net worth to even understand what that is. He's still there, on the stairs. Go away. Go. The fuck. Away.

'Aaaaand cut. Fabby! It's a total smoke show, Jenny. And it's amazing how you look all *not* damaged. *Not* traumatised. And that burglar… the… the… it was a girl! Wow. What a weekend you've had – Mercury must be in retrograde. Now, I'll do an intro in the studio. Don't worry, we won't go full dark, no stars. It'll be all how amazing you look despite the drams.' Sandra and her camera guy were already walking away. 'Bye, hun.'

Jenny was looking for the leather-jacketed stranger. He was now at the bottom of the staircase, rubbing his beard. Jenny didn't like how his shaved head towered over people and she didn't like how she seemed to be the only thing on his mind. For Jenny, her own hammering heart was the loudest sound in the building. *What in the world possesses you to be so stupid?* – her mother's favourite scold, whisper-hot, in her ear.

He was now crossing the shop floor, hurtling in a straight line towards Jenny, like a stone released from a catapult.

11

2.55 pm: Shane stepped away from the window. Otto had gone and no one else was out there; specifically, the guy with the beard and the shaved head. He looked down at the last message on his phone – **DON'T TRUST HIM**. 'Jesus,' he said forcefully, as if by disbelieving hard enough, the letters would rearrange and say something else. His palms grew clammy. *I shouldn't have called the number. Now they know I'm reading their crap*. He flicked through the phone's options, looking for 'block caller'.

Three days ago, on Friday morning, he'd woken up as a youngish man, bustling through the first half of his life. Now, suddenly, just like that, Shane was firmly ensconced in his life's second act. There had been no gradual realisation, no slow adjustment. Instead, it had happened as quickly as walking from one room into another. Without warning, so many good things were ending – the avoidance of his in-laws, financial security, the assumption that his marriage was indestructible.

The doorbell sounded.

Shane rose so quickly, it was like he was levitating. He checked his watch. He'd been sitting, ruminating, for over ten minutes. *Where's the day going?* Opening the front door, he instantly retreated two feet as if a gust of wind had smacked into him. A slight brunette stood in the porch. Clearly underweight, her tailored navy suit jacket was fastened by a single button across her tiny waist like a punishment. It was hard to tell her age because of the Ray-Bans. They were statement shades, favoured by those who wanted to appear aloof and important.

'Shane.' She spoke his name like it was an incurable medical condition.

'Joan. Hallo. How are you?' He adopted a loose chatty manner, as if he were making small talk at a party, beer in hand, as he reckoned it had the potential to irritate her the most.

'Where is she?' The jacket pulled uncomfortably tight across her shoulders.

'*She's* not in – regardless of how hard you knock.'

'Mom's so hurt. Why does she treat her own mother so cruelly? What's the matter with you? You're happy that Jenny is doing this?'

'I don't know what you're talking about.'

Joan placed her hand on the doorframe. 'Mom has been calling her all morning. But Jenny won't answer.'

'That sounds like a *you* problem. Not a *me* problem.' The mere fact that she had her fingers on the inside of his house felt unpleasant, like a territorial violation.

'And you sound just like Jenny. Cause a mess and then expect everyone else to clean it up after you. Just like her disaster twenty-five years ago. "Not my problem – it's yours now."'

'What disaster twenty-five years ago? What are you talking about?'

'Oh, my God – you really don't know?'

'Don't know *what*?' He didn't like the way she was examining him. It was as if she was peeling back his face.

'Wow.' Joan laughed – excessively. 'You're telling the truth. She never told you. And here's the world thinking we had the perfect couple. Oh, that's just brilliant. *Faaaaantastic.*' She clapped her hands. 'Christ, I actually feel sorry for you. I… feel sorry… for *you*? It's bloody farcical.'

Shane was embarrassed and that made him resentful. He blamed Joan for bringing her mental frailties, her hysteria, her fixations and baggage, all the way to his house; for having once again spoilt his day with her neurotic presence.

'Joan, I've had enough of your type of crazy. So, either tell me about this so-called disaster or get the hell away from my door.'

'Oh, I'll tell you all right. With the greatest of pleasure. But I won't do it here on the doorstep to *Mom's* property. I'll tell you inside.' She then spoke the next sentence carefully, as if the words were very precious and she might drop them and they'd break. '*Because* you'll need to be sitting down when you hear it.'

12

2.56 pm: Jenny tensed up. He was twelve feet away. What did he want? What was he going to do? Up close she could see that it was not in fact an artfully distressed thin leather jacket, but rather the kind that had been slept on and had several former owners.

Now he was eight feet away and she could already tell that there was something off about him, an aura of decay that was strange for a man in his thirties. His skin was like a spread of nicotine stain: the colour that her father had gone on the day he'd died. The top buttons of his shirt were open, and tattoos bloomed up from his chest – hieroglyphs as if to ward off bad energy. Yet he radiated so much of it, she needed to get away from him. But it was too late.

Standing in front of her, his height was so pronounced that Jenny had to slightly tip her head back, as if looking at a sculpture. He was over six feet tall, and his upper body was clearly worked out, which, along with his beard and head, gave him a ruthless look.

Sensing her alarm, he held up his hands, as if to show that he meant no harm – which just made her feel like he definitely did. A scar ran across his right palm. It was jagged, not clean; the kind that resulted from a knife wound. There was a story there. She noticed two more scars on his forehead. Even though they were small, they certainly gave him character – as if his body was a rich map of violent encounters with dangerous animals and brutal men.

He smiled, bathing in her unease. Then, as if deciding to grant mercy, he said, 'Nice to finally meet you.' Cigarette tar coated his voice and he had an accent that she could not place. There was a North American inflection and something European, too – an international accent; the voice of a man who had lived in many places.

Jenny offered the well-practised smile of someone who thought this man was not important enough for her to care who he was. 'It's always nice to meet me. Actually, how do you know me? I saw you staring from over there.'

'Was I?' He scratched his beard and his big hands reminded Jenny of her father's.

She said, 'You *know* you were.'

'Well, look at that – I'm afraid you've caught me out.' His deep voice, now like a PA system, didn't sound afraid at all. 'See, your pictures are always filtered and so the real-life Jenny, while not a disappointment, is just too flesh-and-blood to be instantly recognisable.'

Jenny considered his comment and then, having reached a decision, looked at him with penetrating curiosity. He had brown eyes, like her brother's. She liked them, despite herself. 'You've got my attention. What can I do for you?'

He almost seemed disappointed to be finally bringing a point to the conversation. 'Well, I was wondering how you feel, having witnessed death at such close quarters the other night.'

She covered her mouth to cork the hole of outrage that had appeared. Then she said, 'A person died. How do you think it makes me feel?'

'Well, there's not much I haven't done…' *Interesting move,* she thought. A boast disguised as a confession; or even a threat disguised as a confession. He continued: 'So when a person dies, I feel that the person is dead.' His eyes held hers. 'People die all the time and when they do, most believe they're leaving this world too soon.'

She waved away the offer of champagne from a passing hostess. It was time to put a full stop to this. 'Well, it's good that we've made friends with each other. It's been emotional.'

'We're not friends. You're lying to me half the time and I'm lying to you all the time.'

'Huh?'

'You're only talking to me because we have the same chemicals reacting against each other in our blood: shame, anger, greed. A need for revenge.'

With his already impressive bulk almost taking up the width of the aisle, he stepped forward. His tattooed torso strained against his shirt. 'You feel that?' He was suddenly radiating such naked aggression, that even his tight haircut seemed a strategic choice so that his victims would have nothing to grab onto. '*That's* chemistry.'

'Jesus. What's the matter with you? We're done here.'

'No, we're not.' His hand landed on her shoulder. It weighed as much as a large steak.

Shrugging him off, her wide eyes made it clear that she was about to cause a scene. She hated the fact that some men were so comfortable physically intimidating other men, women and animals. They did it too easily. It made her doubt herself, as if feminism was just a marketing strategy for women to buffer themselves in a man's world.

Calmly he said, 'Think of everything you hold precious, Jenny. What are they?'

My secrets. My husband. My house. She couldn't tear her eyes away from his. Jenny had the uncomfortable sense that, when this man looked at her, he saw the things within her that she tried to hide.

'By nightfall today, I will fucking destroy you. Understand?' Then, with a smirk, he added, 'Tick-tock, Clarice. That's just six hours.'

Jenny startled, as if she'd been punched in the throat. Into the chalice of her cupped hands, she muttered, 'What did you say?'

'Destroy,' he repeated, drawing out the word for so long, Jenny felt it might break.

As he walked away, her eyes began to well but, just as suddenly, she turned off the tears with sheer will. Jenny had always believed that over-emoting was a selfish trait. People cried in public because they wanted to be seen to cry.

He was moving towards the main exit. Jenny began to move too. Who was he? Why her? *What did I ever do to him?*

Her brain was suddenly throwing up memories of twenty-five years ago, like computer glitches. She wondered if she'd committed another terrible mistake. Was this the beginning of the unravelling? In years to come, would she look back and see this precise moment as the instant she threw everything away? And what was 'everything' anyway? 'Everything' was just one thing. 'Everything' was Shane. Wasn't it?

13

Twenty-Five Years Ago

Jenny was eighteen. It was a freezing February but, in her family home, full of the type of dazzling light that only money can radiate, there wasn't a single draught. Soaking up the greenhouse heat of the living room, Jenny lay on the thick carpet, bare feet stretched out, spine propped up by the front of the L-shaped sofa. She gripped small barbells, flexing muscles which had already been worked out that morning, before college. She had been a member of the gym since the age of fourteen, her mother having encouraged her early to battle with the preordained.

Her brother sat on the armchair, ignoring his sister but watching the same TV show. At twenty-three, he was good-looking in a dashing way. His relationship with his little sister mostly consisted of him barking a few commands at her during the day, and sometimes Jenny would obey and other times she wouldn't. When she didn't obey, he would look at her as if she was an idiot and say, 'You bitch,' and complain to their mother, who would purse her lips and put Jenny in her place. Jenny hated the way he said 'bitch'; she felt it revealed aspects of his character she'd prefer not to know.

Back then, her brother was Vera's golden child. He was male, and that was all that Vera had ever wanted – boys. From the moment her brother was born, he was taught – by Vera – that he was special: smarter, holier, stronger and braver than everyone else. But the fact was, no teacher had ever called Vera after class to suggest that he had the slightest hint of any talent that would make him stand out, never mind to confirm her belief that her son was a gifted child.

An American soap was on, and although Jenny was enjoying it, she felt somewhat ashamed because she no longer wanted to exude intellectual mediocrity. Her reading list, piled on her desk, was now full of Foucault, Postman and Lacan. She was intending to major in Economics but for the first year of her degree she was also taking The Psychology of Modern Literature. This attempt to expand her interests had impressed her father, who knew that most of her peers from her extraordinarily expensive secondary school were merely being groomed to become minor executives in their father's company or competent, appealing wives to important men.

In the business wing of the university, money and beauty were the prerequisites for popularity and Jenny had both. All the pretty girls and rugby jocks orbited around her, like leeches searching for a vein. But in the arts wing, the fundamentals were money *and* enigmatic talent. These rules seemed to apply to everyone except the one guy she really fancied – Shane Smith – who had talent but no money. Shane was also the one guy she shouldn't fancy. In fact, he was the one guy that she was emphatically *not allowed* to fancy.

Jenny had not spoken to him, but she'd noticed him noticing her. It seemed as if Shane had come from nowhere. When one of the guys had asked him where he'd gone to school, he'd said, 'city centre', as if that was an answer. Though Jenny knew where he'd gone to school and, most importantly, she knew who he'd fought with last year. Everyone did.

By making it obvious that he didn't appreciate being waist deep in rich kids, it had impressed Jenny how coolly Shane absorbed the awkward silences that he caused at will. Many people claimed that they didn't care what people thought of them, but Shane was the only one whom she could believe. He was smart, too; the type who, when the lecture was over and the teacher asked if there were any more questions, actually had more questions.

Lorcan Donaldson, Jenny's father, entered the room, phone to ear, glass of Merlot in hand, pinstripe suit unbuttoned to reveal a businessman's bountiful belly. 'That's Ted for ya – in for a penny, in for twenty million.' At seventy-four, Lorcan remained the irremovable chairman of Dublin's most historically sacrosanct, but fogeyish, pensions brokerage.

'Keep it down, Dad. My gosh,' Jenny said, though she enjoyed the sound of her father's good cheer that had, so far, lasted all the way through Christmas and four or five weeks beyond.

'You got it, sweetie,' Lorcan acquiesced but continued talking at only a slightly lowered volume. 'Sorry, John. Where were we?'

The doorbell rang.

Her brother's eyes didn't move from the television, from which he was hypnotised by some fat American kid going berserk with excitement. 'Get it, Jen.'

Jenny looked up at her father and he looked down at his daughter. They both shrugged. Then Lorcan walked out into the foyer-like hallway, still talking on the phone. 'When the other one isn't around, I can always depend on Jenny to be the boss of me…'

By 'other one', Lorcan meant Joan and not his wife. With Jenny's parents it was the typical case of finally packing the youngest – Jenny – off to secondary school and then having the time to face up to the reality that they actually hated each other and had done so for years. Her father despised Vera more than she despised him – but he disguised it better. Now, Lorcan just avoided her; the house was big enough to make that possible. But Vera would often search him out with her unwanted presence, enjoying the discomfort she caused, revelling in her power to be destructive just by being there. Normal people would've called it a day shortly after Jenny was born. But her family were into the kind of old-school Catholicism that was – to most people, even in Jenny's youth – disconcertingly antiquated and would later become glibly irrelevant to the point of being considered superstitious gibberish.

A few moments later, the living room door opened. It was Shane. He was dressed in the same clothes he'd worn that day in college – black jeans, oxblood Doc Martens and his *Less Talk – More Rocks* logo-blaring T-shirt. The dimmed light from the many lamps embroidered his matinee idol good looks and he moved into the room with a shoulder sway that told Jenny, 'This guy can dance'.

'What's going on?' he asked.

Jenny, still sitting on the floor with arms outstretched clutching barbells, repeated, 'What's going on?'

Her brother, who had picked up his phone and was looking over the bright display, suddenly leapt to his feet, legs spread in something like a sparring pose.

Calmly, Shane said, 'Hugh, I apologise for what happened in that bar last year. I didn't want to fight and I'm sure you didn't mean to—'

Hugh said, 'What *the fuck* are you doing in my house?'

'What am I doing in *your* house?'

'I said it loudly enough.'

Jenny dropped the barbells to the floor. They landed with dull thuds.

Hugh said, 'You are *not* fucking welcome here. You understand?'

Shane didn't redden or look away.

Hugh said, 'Why don't you say it loud, just so we're clear.'

'I'm here to see Jenny and—'

'Out. Get out!'

In one fluid yoga-like movement, Jenny rose to her feet and was just about to speak when a smiling Shane said, 'Chill, man. You and me – that's all over. A year ago. Can't I—'

'Jesus Christ!' Hugh marched towards Shane, but just when it looked like he was going to shoulder him, he squeezed his body tight so that his arm barely nudged Shane's, and he kept on going into the hall.

'Damn. Sorry, Jenny. I didn't mean to cause a scene.' Shane was leaning against the white wall as though he was propping up the entire building, and Jenny thought how horrified her mother would be, if she knew someone was touching her spotless paint. But Vera was upstairs in her bedroom suite and would not be seen until morning.

Shane continued; 'I just thought… well, we're gonna be together for the year and the next two after that… and I like you, Jenny. I mean, I really like you… and I think that you like me… so, it would be cool if we could hang tonight. What d'you think?' Like someone at a funeral, he joined his fingers before his groin.

'Yeah, that'd be cool.'

'Look, your brother and me… I didn't mean to—'

'Oh, my God, what kind of a host am I? Let me get you something.'

She glanced out into the hallway and was relieved to see that her brother wasn't waiting. *How embarrassing*. She needed to move this along and see where it was going before it all blew up in their faces.

Shane's eyes widened at her refusal to acknowledge the drama that had just occurred. Was that how it worked in this big bright house? Act like everything is OK until everything *is* OK? 'Erm… a beer would be nice. In fact, beer is necessary to my existence right now.'

'Dad doesn't like me drinking. In the house, that is. You know how it is.'

Just then, Lorcan returned. He threaded his way across the thick cream carpet in his size ten Italian leather shoes and stopped in front of Shane. Sipping his wine, and without looking at his daughter, Lorcan asked, 'Jen, where's Hugh gone?'

'Upstairs.' She noticed that her hand was slightly shaking.

'So, who is this?'

'It's Shane Smith. He's my friend. From college.'

Shane cleared his throat and said, 'Mr Donaldson, pleased to meet you.'

'Hugh seems annoyed.'

Jenny blurted out, 'Hugh doesn't like Shane. A stupid boy-thing from ages ago. A silly argument over nothing. Shane apologised just now, but Hugh was having none of it. And Hugh is twenty-three – *five* years older than Shane! My gosh, you'd think it was the other way around the way Hugh had his little tantrum. He's probably run upstairs to Mum.'

Lorcan said, 'Jen, that's not fair,' but didn't seem to doubt the probability.

Shane said, 'Mr Donaldson, I'm just here because I was hoping your daughter would come with me tonight to an exhibit at the Irish Museum of Modern Art.'

'Wow. Super amazing.' Jenny's hand rose to her mouth to block a squeal of delight.

Lorcan kept Shane's stare.

Shane said, 'Mr Donaldson, I decided that if I was to ask your daughter out, then I first needed to apologise to Hugh and I then needed to ask your permission. I don't know Jenny that well. But I want to. I called in, because I thought it was the correct thing to do.'

A door slammed somewhere upstairs. Hugh. *He's in Mum's room, right now.* Jenny envied the way their mother's love came so easily to her brother.

Lorcan drained his wine and said, 'You're an honourable lad, Shane. You did good coming here like that. Can't have been easy. Shows guts. Shows class. Enjoy your night, kids.' With a manly slap to Shane's shoulder, Lorcan left the room.

That was it. Shane was the only man under fifty she'd ever seen be unintimidated by her father.

Until then, Jenny had thought about love as something captured by hearts and flowers. But from that moment, she knew the truth. Love was a bolt of lightning.

14

Now

3.01 pm: The phone was ringing next to Jenny's ear. She hadn't realised she'd been holding it up to her head while passing beneath the exit portico. Detective Murray's voicemail kicked in and when the tone sounded to leave a message, she disconnected. *What can I say? 'Someone was mean to me – please send in the SWAT team?' Jesus, grow a pair, Jenny. He's just a weirdo. The city's full of them.* The phone seemed fragile, as if her hand might crush it.

Outside, Jenny approached one of the security team. 'A big guy with a beard, tight haircut, mid-thirties, just exited. Where'd he go?'

The bouncer shrugged, gesturing vaguely to the street where two limos were parked snout-to-snout. 'Out there somewhere.'

Sometimes, she wished that she could be like her mother. Insolence from doormen and waiters, even in homeopathic doses, was something Vera would not tolerate. But she didn't have time to try and act like her mother. Anyway, *he* was gone and that was what mattered. As Jenny checked the time on her phone – 3.02 pm – it buzzed, and the screen notified her of an unknown caller. Answering, she said, 'Finally. You were meant to meet me here already… Uh-huh… Is it nearby? … Good. See you there in five minutes.'

Jenny walked on, blinking into the sunlight of the main road, and felt like an animal limping away, a lame rodent that needed its neck wrung. She felt punctured from allowing the world to seize and dispirit her so quickly. One word filled her brain – glum. It was another of Vera's adjectives to describe her youngest. Jenny hated that word. To be glum was to be aggressively sad; to be dejected in a way that annoyed other people, particularly her mother.

Jenny turned onto a smaller side street, with little footfall. She noticed what *wasn't* there: neon signs, cafes and restaurants, the fur and diamonds of a big city. She leaned against a shop window to take a moment to clear her head. At her feet was an abandoned bottle of milk, next to the exit of a down pipe. The liquid had segregated into layers, like a sedimentary cliff face. She tried not to picture what her father must look like, after so many years of putrefaction. Jenny suddenly missed him terribly. A childish yearning within her assumed that if her father was still alive then that bearded man would not have dared try to intimidate her like he'd done.

With no one around, Jenny was suddenly very aware of a fact, expediently ignored by most women, that if they were going somewhere unaccompanied or doing anything alone, they would be easy to hurt. Since the crash on Friday, she'd been feeling lucky; but she also knew that kind of luck had to be balanced out.

Something bad is coming.

Jenny pictured the young woman's face, unveiled as she pulled off the balaclava. She remembered what the bearded stranger had said – 'When a person dies, I feel that the person is dead.' She thought of her mother selling her house and of Joan spending her money. Perspiration trickled under her arms. Jenny felt her pulse trending through her torso. Quickly, the palpitations combined with a tightness of the chest. The oxygen felt warm, stale and heavy. The pressure in her chest intensified as if elastic bands were compressing her ribs. She inhaled again and again, short sharp intakes. *Jesus Christ.* She concentrated on her lungs, reminding herself to breathe, to keep breathing, to never stop breathing. *I work out three days a week. I don't smoke. I eat sushi. I'm only forty-three. I'm female. Females have to grow old to die.*

Just like that, she was back in the street, calming down, regaining her breath. *Welcome back Mister Panic Attack, my old friend. It's been twenty-five years.* It startled her, how familiar the sensation felt.

Halfway down the road was a metal door, the breeze bouncing it against the frame. There was a sign saying **Keep Out – Private Property**; yet kaleidoscopic gang graffiti on the door demonstrated just how many *hadn't* kept out. On the other side of the metal door was a second entrance – a wooden one. Jenny pushed it open and entered Cassidy's Bar – not a pub destined to feature in any *Beautiful Ireland Guide.*

A mute TV showed horse racing and the overweight barman gripped the edge of the counter while looking up at the screen. There was a blackboard above the cash till; white chalk listed upcoming football fixtures. A digital clock read 3.07 pm. Besides a single male perched on a stool at the bar, there was a handful of customers scattered about the lounge. Those that were talking did so with pre-dawn voices; most were shrunken or bent, shaped by that indomitable foe, age.

She carried on up to the bar.

Positioning half a buttock on a stool, she said, 'Thank God you're here. You wouldn't believe what just—'

'I told you I would be.'

'I thought you'd change your mind.'

'I don't do that.' Leaning across from his stool, Otto's lips fell on hers.

15

3.25 pm: When dealing with his in-laws, Shane tried to employ the three Ds of pruning that his father had taught him: cut off anything that is diseased, decaying or damaged. Psychologically, Joan was all three. *So, why am I bringing her into my home?* He then heard his own self-punishing voice in his head, admonishing him; *You took the bait again. You've stirred up more family drama.*

Joan strode through the hall, hips swaying with the click-click-clacking of her heels. She had the sort of absurd figure that was held up as an unrealistic example to young girls. *When was the last time she ate?* Joan left her shades on, as she always did, because she claimed to be sensitive to electric light; though Jenny said it was because she was always hungover. He'd seen Joan at family meals in the early days; and later at weddings and funerals – watching her drink was like watching a vampire feed. The more she had, the more alive she became. In that way, the smooth chicness of the shades was at odds with the sad story told by the lined and loose skin that surrounded them. Joan had been abandoned by her husband and dismissed by her children, leaving her with nothing in her life besides her seventy-five-year-old mother.

When Shane had started dating Jenny, Hugh moved to London to start his super-stellar career in the UK outpost of his father's firm. Thus, Shane could call in to see Jenny without fear of drama. When he did, he'd still dread being alone with Joan. She seemed to be a woman entirely claimed by her neurosis. Small talk and normal social skills were silly things that she didn't bother with and, thus, two tense minutes in her company passed as fast as the ice age. Shane had wondered if Joan was actually depressed, but Jenny had laughed. '*Joan*? Depressed? She doesn't have the attention span to be depressed. She just hates that I have a boyfriend and she doesn't. And since Mum disapproves of you after what you did to her prince, Joan is required to hate you too. Fiercely.'

As Joan examined the study, she blanked him so successfully, it felt like she was blind behind her shades. Finally, in her cut-glass, almost antique, accent, she said, 'God, I know Mom's given you your marching orders, but you should still make a bit of an effort to keep the place better. Papers everywhere. Stuff out of place. But look, it's none of my business, I suppose. And I don't want you convincing yourself that you're all hurt and—'

'Have you just come into my home to insult—'

'Shane,' Joan said, as though she was making a sad declaration of fact. 'Let me explain things. Everything you have is my mother's. Everything you have is from the generosity of my family. This house – it's Mom's. She *allows* you to stay here. She *grants* you that freedom. Well… for the rest of the year, anyway.'

Shane's confidence wobbled. She'd put him on the back foot and when people were on the back foot, they found silence awkward. He rubbed the back of his head. That tension and stiffness in his neck – it had been there since the crash. It was as if his anxiety had seized upon his muscle aches, found them to its liking and declared them permanent.

Someone walked by on the road. Shane expected to see a bearded man. But it was just a guy in a suit. *Everything's OK. After the crash... the texts, the note with the flowers... and with Joan here now... I'm just getting paranoid.* But Shane believed that the problem with the world was that there was a lot of darkness out there that could *not* be explained away with films, TV and books – specifically *his* books, no matter how hard he tried.

Joan almost smiled. She could tell that her presence made him uncomfortable, and that type of knowledge was power. 'Oh, there's *our* chess set. Daddy had it carved in Uganda. See, the King's crowns have our family crest.' Joan always found ways to either enlighten or remind those in her presence of the stock she came from. Whenever she introduced herself, she never just gave her Christian name. Instead, she said, 'Joan Donaldson.' Even her children eventually took *her* surname instead of their father's. Vera, no doubt, loved that.

Shane's patience was already at stretching point. First Otto and then Joan, who was almost fifty and still thought 'normal' was having a vault full of money; still thought 'normal' was getting what you want all the time.

Joan picked up an A4 printed sheet from Shane's desk and began reading aloud:

Social media was Samantha's real world; her day-to-day existence being just a rehearsal for her online fabulousness. Samantha's life had been one big cuddly squeeze and her online persona just wanted to spread the warm ooze about.

Looking at Shane, she said, 'Sounds like you're writing my sister's biography.' Joan then sniggered – and because she was too old to snigger, she appeared petty and childish.

'Put. It. Down.'

'Wow – where did that come from? I was just joking. People see you as a loyal, nice doggy. But it wouldn't surprise me if underneath it all you can turn into a vicious Rottweiler. Relax.' She released the sheet like it was a live grenade or a venomous snake, and it see-sawed to the desk. Shane gestured for her to move away from his desk and slammed the lid of his laptop down – though making sure to decelerate at the last second so that it actually closed somewhat gently.

Poor Jenny – I only have to face this crap about once a year. But she has to deal with Joan every few weeks, and her mother every few days. He admired Jenny's stoicism. She took Joan's unrelenting bitterness and put her faith in karma balancing the scales. Jenny would say, 'Look at Joan's husband. He's gone. Look at her messed-up kids. They're all medicated or hate her. *That's* karma.' But Shane didn't believe that. Karma was just a lie that people told themselves, so they didn't have to force themselves to fight back. You have to be the *agent* of karma if you want it to take someone down.

And how he wanted to take down Joan and Vera.

Shane said, 'Look, I didn't know we were going to do the whole hostile thing today. See, I assumed you'd back off for longer than usual, given that I was nearly killed, and our house was broken into. So, can't we just skip it?'

Joan lifted her shades. Sharp eyes stared back – as brown and clear as Jenny's – conveying that she was impatient and annoyed at having been forced to listen to this inane weather report from another person's life. 'God, I don't know why I'm saying this… But you have no idea who or what Jennifer is.'

Incredibly, Shane found himself inching towards her. 'Go on.'

Joan patted his hand, as if regretting having to tell a child these terrible things. 'Let me spell it out. Your precious wife has kept big secrets from you. No one knows but Jennifer, Mom and I – her *family*. Of course, we'd assumed that you knew. But… she never told you.' Joan looked straight at him, a hard stare that she cut off after a few seconds. Then she lowered her voice and asked, 'Are you positive that you don't want to sit?'

Suddenly there was a noise from the hallway. Keys in the door. For a peculiar moment Shane felt like he was about to be caught *in flagrante delicto* by his wife with her sister.

He muttered, 'She's home.'

The study door opened, and Jenny entered, beaming. For a few shocked moments, her smile struggled to stay lit like a fading coal. Withdrawing a tissue from her pocket, she balled it in her fist like a stress ball; offended, angry. She then blinked three times, seemingly making a wish for her sister to disappear.

It didn't work.

The two Donaldsons faced each other, and they stared like fighting dogs across a pit. Shane's gaze moved between them, and he reminded himself to be very, very careful.

Joan cleared her voice 'As I was saying, Shane, there's something you should know about my little sister.'

Shane folded his arms, feeling an odd sense of unease. He was aware that in the future he would remember this moment forever, because of what was about to happen.

16

3.35 pm: When Jenny closed the front door, she'd wondered if that was her sister's voice. But it couldn't be. She didn't want Joan calling in. The voices turned to whispers. She didn't want Joan in her house. She opened the study door. Joan was in her house.

Now, Jenny took a moment to soak Joan up. Joan wasn't the most capable or most personable of Vera's children, but from her earliest years she'd taken the crucial slot in the Donaldson house as the thinnest. It was something she knew her mother would always appreciate. To achieve that goal, she gave herself an eating disorder that, of course, no one in the family ever directly commented on. No doubt, the disorder also gave her a sense of control – which was important, considering she'd handed over all other control of her life to her mother. Jenny remembered her sister going to the bathroom before the conclusion of every meal and then returning to the table, where the only comment would be the occasional, 'You shouldn't eat so fast,' from someone. Joan always had gum on her.

Joan nodded as if Jenny was a barely remembered bore whom she was surprised to find standing at the edge of *her* party.

Jenny asked, 'Why are you here?' Light reflected off a spectacular diamond on her sister's finger. *How many fucking carats is that thing?* 'Actually, scrap that. I don't care. Just get out. How could you come here on the day my husband gets out of hospital after nearly being killed and… and… our home being burgled?'

Joan sucked in her lip to let Jenny know two things: one, that she was trying to exhibit appropriate sympathy and two, that she was obviously faking it. Then she said, 'Oh God, just how much do you expect to milk from your little adventure?'

Jenny took a hesitant step towards her sister. 'Wow – it must've killed you to know that we were being talked about on the news and written about in the papers all weekend. It would've reminded you that I'm the only one in our family, besides Dad, that actually did something *constructive* with their life. I mean… with the opportunities that were handed to you on a plate – money, prestige, contacts – you still managed to end up as this sad fucking wreck of humanity that stands before me. But at least you're sober and managing to keep your voice down. Baby steps, Joan, yeah?'

Joan's small ears had turned red, like angry embryos. Speaking with the gritted tone of a person who believed she had a great deal of patience, she asked, 'And what achievements of yours are we talking about? As far as I'm aware, you designed a very singular department for LaLucia? But listening to you on the radio, you'd swear you'd got yourself a seat on the bloody board. And as for your social media feeds – well, I'm sure when you read your own Facebook page, you actually wish you were that person.'

'So, you *did* listen to me on the radio, and you *do* snoop on my social media. Brilliant. Thanks. You're even more wretched than I thought possible. Now, for the last time, get out of my house.'

Jenny didn't even want to share her air.

Joan didn't move. 'I suppose we all pay for Jenny's sins.' Then, bringing some subterranean string of thoughts close to the surface, she looked at Shane and said, 'Even you must realise that by now?' However, with a flick of her hair, she malleted that bud of revelation back to where it had come from.

Shane prompted Joan. 'You have something to tell me that's so shocking I need to be seated? I'll stand, thank you.'

Jenny shuddered as another life closed in on her.

Joan smiled. 'Oh yes. That. I almost forgot. Jennifer, don't you think it's about time Shane knew the truth?'

'Get out.' It wasn't a scream. It was the cold, over-enunciated command one gave to automated phone systems.

'He *is* your husband. Almost your childhood sweetheart. If you're both so in love, surely you share everything? Are you going to tell him, or shall I?'

All the nerves in Jenny's body became eyes – reading the situation, moment by moment. It was as if her sister was talking about another woman, someone who had died a long time ago in another place, far across the ocean. The problem being that this dead woman's problems were still hanging around – as if they hadn't buried her deep enough.

Jabbing her father's corkscrew into the lid of a Cabernet Sauvignon on the drinks cabinet, she expertly worked the cork free. Then, sloshing some – and a bit more – into a balloon glass, she raised it to her lips, taking just enough time to signal her complete lack of interest in what Joan had said.

Baring her teeth as the wine hit the back of her throat, Jenny thought, *some people are just bad. Everything they want to do is bad.*

If it didn't start bad with them, they'll turn it bad. People like Joan are polluted, their depths contaminated.

Jenny flung the glass at her sister.

It was the first time she'd ever done anything like that. Joan was too shocked to either duck or jump to the side. The glass flew by her head and exploded against the library wall behind Shane. Most of the wine dashed to the wooden floor, splashing up against Joan's shoes and trousers. Some drops landed on Shane's desk and the rest dribbled down the spines of several hardbacks. For Jenny, her rage felt righteous and strong, as if all her misery had been transformed into a powerful currency.

Shane raised one arm, exposing a sweat patch the size of a dinner plate, and pointed his palm at Jenny, conveying, ENOUGH!

Joan looked down to her feet, almost embarrassed, the way someone would if an elderly relative were causing a scene. She removed a tissue from her trouser pocket and wiped each of her shoes clean of spattered wine, then dropped the tissue into the wastepaper bin.

Calmly, Jenny said, 'I won't miss with the bottle.'

Joan swallowed and then cleared her voice. 'I came here to see *you*, actually. Mom has been calling you all morning and—'

'Mum didn't call. But she did text. Once.' It never even occurred to Jenny to ask her sister what Vera wanted. If she'd sent Joan, then either Joan didn't know or she'd never tell. Triangulation – that was how her family communicated. Instead of talking to each other directly about important topics, everything had to go through a third party – and that party must always be Vera. It meant that their mother was the family interpreter.

Joan said, 'Call. Text. Whatever. Mom wants to talk to you. She needs to. It's important. She sent me here to make sure you—'

'Message received. Get out.'

'I try and I try, and it always ends like this. I just want to... Oh, fuck you, Jennifer. Fuck. You.' The expletives carried the added weight of those uttered by people who rarely curse.

As Joan's heels clicked through the hall, Jenny unreasonably felt that somehow the bearded stranger back at LaLucia was the physical manifestation of all the nefarious elements that had invaded her life, to such a degree that they did not even feel her thumb on the scale.

The front door opened and then slammed. Jenny exhaled. Joan was gone. Disaster averted. For now. Jenny lived a charmed life, and she wasn't going to apologise for it.

'What's going on?' Shane's voice was low, his tone solemn.

She stood there, looking at him, admiring how her husband had the vigour of a young man and yet the cunning of an older man. It made it hard to imagine him ever being vulnerable. Suddenly, she realised that she was waiting for Shane to take over, to make it all better. In the past she'd always been able to go straight to Shane and tell him about whatever was worrying her – whether it was work or family – and she would immediately relax, knowing that she had a real friend; someone who unquestionably would jump into that dog pit with her and who was cheering her on as she tried to clamber out of it. But now, for the first time in their marriage, she was alone with these problems. She was the only one who could fix this.

Jenny knew that twenty-five years ago, Shane had fallen for her because she was naïve and even ignorant and that meant that he'd been able to look after her and teach her – and that had made him feel like a man. She was no longer that person, but Shane was still playing the same role – and she still loved him and never wanted him to change. Jenny just had to make sure that he didn't notice who she now was. More importantly, she had to make sure that he never found out what her sister was talking about. The only way to do that was to give him something else; something lesser – to sacrifice a different secret.

In other words, to get out of this mess, things would first have to get worse.

'Shane,' she said. 'I've done something awful.'

17

3.45 pm: Rounding the desk to his black leather executive chair, Shane's phone, next to the laptop, buzzed the arrival of a text. He glanced down. Unknown number. *Again*?

IT'S TOO LATE. YOU'RE IN IT NOW. THERE'S NO WAY OUT.

'Just a minute,' he muttered and tapped out, **WHO IS THIS.**

Shane looked across the desk to his wife, who was still standing in the middle of the room, holding the broken stem of the wine glass. He was not going to add to her worries by telling her about the note that had accompanied the flowers and the bearded stranger he'd spotted outside the house and then, of course, these stupid anonymous texts that may imply that he was being watched. Besides, he didn't need the possibility that, like Detective Murray, she would continue to doubt him.

A second text arrived.

YOU WON'T BE LIKE YOU WERE BEFORE EVER AGAIN.

Looking out of the window he wondered, who was this great and all-powerful Oz that was watching him? Shane turned from the view, put away his phone and sat into his chair. He warned himself: *No one's spying on you. It's a coincidence. Paranoia is just another term for being afraid. Get your shit together.* Folding his hands behind his head, he watched Jenny as if she were his habit, his due; and he did one of those things he was very good at – he listened.

Jenny began to speak from the middle of the room. A few minutes later, she was still talking while seated in the two-seater sofa opposite Shane's desk. Despite the preposterousness of what he was hearing, he remained calm. It was as if he was watching the secret life of his wife being revealed, like trouser pockets being pulled inside out.

When Jenny was finished, Shane greeted this new information with a long, long silence. It was as if he was still listening to what he'd just heard. Incredibly, the secret that Joan had spoken of was no longer the primary focus of his mind. Instead, something much more important now occupied it. Shane stood and went to the drinks cabinet. Twisting open the lid to a Jameson, he poured a glass and swallowed it in one gulp.

Then he poured himself another.

He'd survived a burglar trying to kill him. He'd watched that burglar die right before his face. There was the possibility that there was another man out there wanting revenge; a possibility that no one but he deemed imaginable. There were even threatening texts from someone who seemed to know his every move. Now, inconceivably, there was this *betrayal*. He hadn't thought it possible to squeeze more bad luck into seventy-two hours.

Jenny said, 'I feel terrible. I didn't want to hurt you.'

He gave her a wintry smile. 'You want *me* to feel sorry for *you*? Really?'

Jenny went to reply but no sound emerged. Sad and defeated, she was like an adolescent who had let her house get trashed while her parents had been away.

'So, despite our agreement; despite it not being your money; despite most of it being mine... you, behind my back, and against my expressed wishes... you've given it to Otto?'

'I *invested* it with Otto.'

'You gave that asshole all our savings when, after weeks of talking about it, arguing about it, fighting about it and making up after it, we decided that we weren't going to do it?'

'I'm just sick of everything in our future being about mortgages for a tiny apartment, and moving costs and decorating expenses and what we can or can't afford.'

'It's called *real life*,' Shane snapped. Sometimes it felt like he was married to a spoilt child who wanted to be ultra-happy all the time; a child who didn't understand that you can't even be normal-happy all the time.

'Look, it was—'

'*You* don't get to talk anymore.'

Jenny made a steeple of her hands that half concealed her face. Shane couldn't read her expression and he assumed that was the point. His wife was betting their savings on a dream. The dream being that Otto, via alchemy, would transform their four hundred thousand into over one million euros within twelve months. And all because Jenny wanted to anonymously purchase Clareville from Vera. Once the deposit was paid, Otto would again appear to heroically secure the mortgage by guaranteeing it against her future options and dividends from his investment portfolio. It was reckless and it was naïve.

'Jenny, all our savings would have to be in it, so it's a stupid investment. And we agreed – we're not stupid. But look what you just did. Behind my back. I mean – what *the fuck*?'

'But we'll get every cent back in twelve months. And then some. In fact, we'll be… if not *very* rich, then *very* comfortable.'

'Jenny, you invest what you can afford to lose, and we can't afford to lose anything. You *know* this. Therefore, it's not an investment. It's a gamble. It's gambling everything.'

'We're not going to lose, Shane. Trust me. Trust Otto. We're not both wrong.'

Shane gave a tight smile, a passive aggressive way of communicating that he didn't care what Otto thought. 'We work hard at our careers. So what if people like Otto think making a 'decent living' is akin to having some kind of embarrassing disability? Working hard brings rewards.'

'Hard work – *that's* your plan?' Jenny stared at Shane as if he'd just pissed on the floor. She stood from the two-seater to emphasise the importance of what she was about to say. 'Hard work hasn't made you rich. It hasn't made anyone rich. Hard work makes people ill.'

'Jenny, Otto doesn't need our money. In his world, a million doesn't mean anything. What you want to put into it, wouldn't even register as a decimal error in what those guys are pumping in. People like you and me with our type of money – they consider us less than roadkill. And Otto doesn't give a damn about your obsession with this house either. So, tell me, why is he pushing you so hard on this investment? Huh? Why?'

Jenny replied in a staccato manner – like she was stabbing words with a pitchfork. 'Because – he's trying to give us free fucking money.'

'And if I believed that then, again, the first thing I would ask myself, is, *why*? Jenny, when someone goes out of their way for you, there's always an angle.'

She folded her arms. 'I'm having difficulty understanding why anyone would want less when they could have more. I mean, it's not as if you struggle just to walk around without smashing your head into walls. In other words, Shane, you are not a fucking moron. Jesus, this isn't twenty-five years ago. Do you want to regret *this* for the rest of your life, too?'

'Think carefully about what you're going to say next, Jenny.'

'Remember who I am, Shane. I know exactly what you did way back then. I was there when you did it. And Otto was there as well. So, obviously, he also knows your story. All of it. Including the parts you'd like to forget ever happened.'

Shane's lips straightened. So, she was going to use *that* against him.

Jenny said, 'Your life is not about you only. It's about me too. This is our chance to step away from my family. We can, finally, while still in our forties, be free.'

'There's nothing more boring than being a reaction to your parents, Jenny.'

She looked at him, trying to be hurt, but it was obvious that she knew he was right.

It was true that, unlike Jenny, Shane had never been in line to inherit a few million. Instead, Shane had inherited his father's lawn mower. Also true, he had not been raised by pushy parents with big dreams who had pictured their son as a future prime minister. Instead, they'd tried to keep his expectations low; not because they disapproved of dreams but to avoid the inevitable disappointments that people of their rank – occupiers of the middle pews, halfway up the parish church – were destined to endure. His parents had been ruled by the pragmatism of three Irish recessions and had pictured their son as a diligent office worker with a good pension and a serviceable mortgage. But he had done better than that. Eventually.

Shane threw back the second whiskey; it followed the first, weaving its warm path down Shane's gullet to bond with something inside. His synapses were fizzling with the certitude of it, like an old dependable lover artfully slipping him a hotel key card. There it was – clarity. *I'm not accepting this. I'm going to find Otto and get our money back. Right now. All of this will not even be a footnote in my life.* He looked at his wife and tried to understand how they'd got to this place, but couldn't do it. *I wanted Jenny from the moment I saw her in college. I wanted her when she didn't even know who I was.* Back then, she had looked like the perfect daddy's girl whose father had decided that, although he couldn't protect her from the world, he could gold-plate it. But there had also been a vulnerability to her, like she was the type of young woman who would easily get lost in crowds. When he'd discovered exactly who she was, or rather, whose *sister* she was, it hadn't seemed like bad luck, but rather like fate. He remembered calling into Jenny's house to ask her out. Christ, the balls it had taken. The sheer nerve.

He was going to need those qualities again.

18

Twenty-Five Years Ago

Shane pressed the doorbell and waited and waited and suddenly, Lorcan Donaldson was before him, revealing all his height, brawn and style. Even his shoelaces looked pressed. There was no doubt he was the dog that always ate first. Yet, at the same time, there was an air of desolation about him – as if, even then, he knew that a time of personal disaster was inevitable, and rapidly approaching.

Lorcan brought him through an entrance as palatial as that of a Dublin museum. Inside, the broad hallway retained the atmosphere of a bygone age. Lining the walls were side tables holding ornate lamps and a sofa with gold leaf finish. The large staircase led to a spread of tiger skin nailed to the wall. It was so far away from his own house, that Shane may as well have landed on another planet. He listened and heard the silence, despite the fact that there were five people in the residence – Jenny, Hugh, Joan and their parents. There was definitely a stay-in-your-room, Agatha Christie-type vibe going on.

Resting on the hall sofa was a silver tray containing a platter of half-eaten crackers and cheese, along with assorted dips and accoutrements. Without thinking, Shane picked up the salt shaker from the tray. It was heavy and the lesson it taught was that money weighed a lot. It was here to last. He thought of the salt shaker in his own home. It was red, plastic and cracked. He noticed Lorcan looking at him and immediately put it back down. 'Sorry,' he muttered. 'Nice.' Lorcan grunted and gestured for him to enter the first of the three hallway doors.

Shane arrived in a large drawing room with chandeliers, bunched velvet curtains and antique furniture. His own home's entire footprint could've been contained within this room. Watercolours of the Irish landscape hung from the walls and a turf fire glowed in the huge hearth. It was the first time he'd come across such wealth, and just standing there he realised that real money doesn't walk and talk – it fucking *nukes*.

He'd gambled that Hugh wouldn't be in; but there the wanker was – and immediately he began mouthing off. For a moment, Shane wondered if he'd made a colossal error. He wondered if he should just cross the room and shut him up again. But a moment passed, and Shane knew that he didn't want to feel Hugh's flesh once more breaking open under his fist; because he reckoned that *this* time it would feel good – like the second time he did coke and had known that, if he did it a third time, he'd probably never quit.

Instead, Shane stood there and took it from this over-privileged arsehole who had gone to a school that actually had an official anthem, which everyone sang proudly in Latin; this dickhead who believed he was tough and hard because he was a great out-half. Yet Shane knew that, if Hugh had been obliged to go to *his* school, then he would've been bullied into hanging himself within a week.

But taking it off Hugh didn't matter, because right there in front of him was Jenny, sitting on the floor, back against the sofa, dressed in a Gucci fake-retro suede mini and an expensive, high-necked and antique boho lace blouse. Her legs were long and tanned, her neck slim and delicate within a noose of shells, a perfect Natasha, straight from the pages of *War and Peace*. Her bare feet could have come from a *Vogue* manicure feature, her painted toes like the keys of some unfeasibly elegant instrument. Shane simply stared at that banging body, that was non-stop worked-out muscle, her thighs that looked like machine parts visible beneath her mini. This was the Jenny he had tried not to stare at in lectures; whom he'd followed across the campus.

Shane charted the flow of skin from bare toes to where her mini-skirt had become hitched up to expose half an inch of pale buttock. The sight inked up his mind, reassuring him that he had been correct when he sensed something dark about her; a darkness which suited her better than her nice exterior. It made her more interesting. After all, no one ever sold their soul to an angel.

19

Now

4.12 pm: Jenny watched as Shane rounded the desk, buttoning his jacket. She asked, 'What are you *considering* doing?'

'I'm *considering* failure and the means and ways not to repeat it.'

'Where are you going?'

'To make this right.' He spoke as if each word cost him blood.

'But. But what are you—'

'What am I going to do? I'm going to get our cheque back and then I'm going to fuck Otto with the biggest, baddest stick I can find.'

'But…' Her husband was making all her sentences begin with 'but'. 'That's insane. This isn't you. You never—'

'I just got out of hospital after somebody died in front of my face after trying to kill me. My wife has put all my life's savings, behind my back, on a puffed-up bet. And then Otto – her glorified bookie – stood here in this very room, only two hours ago, acting like my best friend, and yet knowing that he already had our money… But wait.

Joan mentioned twenty-five years ago. What has twenty-five years ago got to do with any of this?'

'Twenty-five years ago is...' She needed to think quickly. 'When we started going out with each other. Remember? Mum and Joan use it as a point of reference for when my life went awry. Joan was fucking with you. Looking for an opportunity to try and blame you for me being disinherited. Just typical Joan behaviour – why merely present her big exposé of the investment, when she can press your buttons, too?'

'But how does Joan know about the investment? And your mother, too?'

Jenny took a step back. 'What do you mean?'

She knew exactly what he meant.

'How are Joan and your mother in a position to tell me about this?'

'Mum... her friends... two or three of them are involved in the investment. Or their husbands are. So, she must've heard from them. Through the grapevine that...' Jenny could feel her confidence swell with each new piece of fiction. 'That we were investing in it, too.' Jenny nodded with satisfaction. It seemed believable to her, aside from the fact that she'd just made it all up.

What Joan and her mother knew and were threatening to reveal was, unbelievably and frighteningly, much more significant than any of this.

Jenny took Shane's hand between both of hers. She remembered holding her father's hands like this. He hadn't been a vain man, but he did like to pamper himself with a weekly manicure and between appointments would be constantly oiling his fingers, because they were always so rough and dry. Jenny would tease him. 'Daddy, don't touch me. You're like a lizard!'

'Shane, I'm sorry.'

He spoke slowly, clearly and patiently. 'You've disappointed me.'

Jenny exhaled. Her father had said that to her, and it had broken her heart. Her mother had said that to her, and it had broken her spirit. But never her husband. Never her best friend. Then again, the fact is that everyone disappoints, eventually.

Shane left the study and moved through the hallway. The front door opened, and she waited for it to slam. It closed with barely a sound.

Next to the window was a large corner beanbag where Shane would often flop in the evening, listening to music or reading or looking at the people drifting by. Standing next to the beanbag, Jenny watched Shane walk away, his jacket suspended from a crooked finger. She had believed their relationship was special, different, that it could withstand anything. All lovers do – and most lovers are wrong.

Jenny surveyed the study, full of her sister's atoms and her husband's anger. Red wine – that fighting fuel for couples nearing their end – still dribbled down the hardbacks. Her plan to get the house was in ruins. She had been determined – *determined* – that it would work. It would be infuriating – even heart-breaking – if there wasn't something bigger, something much worse, closing in on her. There it was – that feeling – the one she had refused to pay attention to over the last few weeks; the feeling that her steady, simple-enough life was about to get blown to bits; as was bound to happen sooner or later to anyone who tried to live a steady, simple-enough life.

Jenny turned away from her husband's desk. She glanced at the framed photograph of her father on the cabinet. His eyes fixed their gaze to hers and they wouldn't let go, even when she continued further into the room. The antique clock next to it read 4.20 pm.

Jenny sighed and readied to steel herself. There was only one course of action. It was time to confront her mother; not just about being evicted from Clareville but about the contents of her text. Incredibly, her mother had referred to what had happened twenty-five years ago. But that was what Vera *never* talked about – even though, by just not talking about it, she managed to make sure that it was always there in the room between them, like oxygen.

Jenny focused hard on what she was about to face. *My past will not steal my present.* Whatever Vera was up to, whatever she wanted, whatever she was planning, she was spinning her web very cleverly. *Here I am – caught between Scylla and Charybdis.*

She took up the wine bottle and necked a long swig. How had everything already gone so wrong, in just a few hours? That morning, Shane hadn't been hurt, LaLucia was hauling her career up the ladder, Otto was going to lock down their investment. It had been a *guaranteed* great day.

She pictured the bearded man in the leather jacket. His image was like a totem of misfortune. She checked her watch – fewer than five hours till sundown. *But he didn't make Mum and Joan interfere with my life. He didn't make me meet Otto this afternoon.* She thought back to what had happened in that bar, less than an hour ago. *Nothing is ever simple.*

20

One Hour Ago

Otto's lips were on hers, his mouth opening, his tongue pushing.

Jenny immediately retreated. 'What the?' she said, as a complete sentence.

'I'm just… I'm just… Celebrating. Hey, the deal is done!'

This mild flirtation had to end today, in this bar. Every time she'd clandestinely met Otto over the past two months, part of her had wilted. But the deal was her big chance.

She tried to tell herself that it wasn't about the money; that it was about her family, about her mother. But at the same time, it was *always* about the money. Jenny had to keep her eye on the prize. She couldn't allow herself to feel regret.

However, being kissed by Otto was not part of the deal. Fine, she'd toyed with him. She flirted with most men she liked. It was part of her repartee. But there was a difference between being coquettish and intimating availability. *That* had not occurred.

Jenny said, 'Screwing clients – it's gratifying to the male ego, apparently. But I thought you were above such things. God, you're pathetic.'

'Are you joking?'

'For future reference you'll know when I'm joking because it'll be fucking funny.'

Otto waved at her last sentence like it was fading smoke. 'It was a misunderstanding.'

'Didn't feel like a misunderstanding.'

'I get it. I get it, right?'

'Who do you think you're dealing with? After what you did to me? Remember? Or did you forget because it's more convenient that way?'

Some of the older patrons glanced over.

'Of course I haven't forgotten. Not for as long as I live. You know that.' He took his glasses off and suddenly his face looked dim and empty without them. 'And that kiss… it wasn't like that.' Otto clearly wanted Jenny to keep her voice down, and he led by example, continuing in a whisper: 'I don't know what I was thinking just now. Maybe it's because I recently realised that I love you. And because I love you, I want what's right for you.'

'You don't love me. If you did, you wouldn't say you want what's "right for me". With love, you only recognise yourself. Like, do you think I ever gave one moment's thought as to whether I was right for Shane? Of course not. He was right for me. The end.'

Otto put his glasses back on. It was clear he was angry, because he was so obviously trying hard *not* to be angry. Picking up his drink too quickly, a wave of orange juice landed on his shoe. And just like that, Otto's hatred flowed at flood level. He slammed the glass onto the counter and shouted, 'Jesus Christ!'

Jenny didn't look around. Everyone heard and, no doubt, everyone was looking. It was better to act disinterested and hope that her indifference was contagious. She said, 'You need to learn how to relax and act like a fucking human being. Otherwise, you'll discover that you have no real friends and instead are just surrounded by people who are paid to tolerate you. Now, Otto, I want you to calm down. Can you do that for me?'

Otto agreed to calm down which, of course, made him tenser.

Lighten the mood. 'What were you thinking? I mean, I'm not even your type.'

He stared at her. 'Yes, you are.'

Jenny's eyes narrowed. 'Really? And what type would that be?'

'You're in excellent shape and—'

'What are you, my fitness instructor?'

'*And*… you're the type that appeals to men who prefer their women to be able to hold a conversation. In that, you're smart. Nearly as smart as me.'

'You old charmer, you.'

'Sure, I suspected I was punching, but I thought we had something. Besides history.'

'Can someone that rich be punching?'

The rumour of a smile spread from the corner of his mouth. He was beginning to relax. He was beginning to see that he could run with this; that everything had not been ruined. He said, 'Let me get you champagne.'

She shook her head.

'No? What's the matter? Are you on strike against money?' When Otto crossed his legs, he did so in a feminine manner – like an actress being interviewed on television. Once again, he looked healthy, prosperous and disreputable. It was his charisma that made him handsome. Without it, he would seem mole-like in an exemplary dull accountant way.

Otto asked, 'So was LaLucia loaded with high-net-worth individuals? The types that like to play on their yacht every weekend – you know, the one they bought last year because it was so sparkly when they walked by it in the midday Ibiza sun.'

Jenny pointed her chin towards the barman, whose attention it wasn't hard to get after the outburst, and ordered a pint. Then she said, 'It was fine, until I was harassed by a weird stalker guy who hates me because of my Insta feed or something.'

Otto put down his drink. 'Jesus. You OK?'

'Yeah, it was just weird.'

'Have you a weapon? Like, do you carry?'

'I wasn't thinking of *that*...'

'If you're being stalked, I'd advise you to think of that.'

'Well, hassled just once by a complete knob doesn't make him a stalker, I suppose. Just felt "stalkery." Anyway, it's over. Forget it.' She hadn't realised how uncomfortable talking about it would make her feel.

'No. Go on. What did he want? There's something you're not telling me.'

'There's lots of things I'm not telling you. Because I'm a private person, Otto.'

'Jesus, I'm just showing concern.'

'No need. I'm fine and it's over.' The barman placed the pint before her and Jenny took a sip, resisting the desire to knock it back in a single draught. She asked, 'Anyway, how did it go with Shane?'

'He reluctantly talked about it for maybe five seconds. Your plan for him to have a last-minute change of heart was mission-completely-and-utterly-fucking-impossible. Sorry – I tried.'

'Shane is just being true to himself.' She didn't know why she was trying to explain her husband's reasoning to Otto, as he utterly believed that those who rejected pure capitalism were providing an implicit admission that they lacked the balls and energy required to succeed in this world. 'Shane was never a guy who tried hard to please people all the time.'

'Well, I wouldn't mind if he tried harder to please people, actually. In fact, he could try a fuckload harder.'

'Shane and I always said that both of us have a veto to say no… because we always agree. Eventually.'

'That's boyfriend/girlfriend stuff. It's not the real world.'

'It's *our* world,' she muttered.

'Then it's a case of "Welcome to the world of Adulting." Come on in! It's been expecting you for about twenty years. Now – your money went *ka-ching!* into my account today. I'll lodge it into the fund tomorrow. Congratulations. You now own very much *less* than one per cent of an office block that will arise from its huge footprint next year. Feel good?'

Jenny had no fear that the investment would fail. It wasn't just her faith in Otto, it was also due to an obsessive childish belief that if she wanted it enough then it should, could and would happen. *Oh God, the look that will be on Mum and Joan's faces when they discover that we've anonymously bought the house. The dismay they'll feel when they realise that they're powerless; that I'm free of them; that I win.* She was beginning to see how far she'd go to get what she wanted – and it was exhilarating; beyond anything she'd experienced.

'I feel confident,' Jenny answered. 'And I do appreciate you doing this for me. For us. Shane and me. It's very… kind.'

Otto adjusted his glasses; he was a man used to accepting praise.

She added, 'And yet, I still can't believe I'm going ahead with this.'

'Don't make excuses for what you want. It's weak.' His knees spread, as if the girth of his testicles required the width of a motorway.

Jenny thought of all the ways she was betraying her husband: lying, scheming, taking their savings – most of which were Shane's – and handing them over to the man he disdained. *You have to do this to win. This is what winners do. They make sacrifices.* In this world you must pick the strong and the clever, not the strong and the kind, to come out on top.

Now that they were in their forties, how many doors did Shane think were still ajar for them? Especially given how few they'd managed to squeeze through so far. Shane liked to take out his boat over the weekend, but it was Otto who owned an acre of lakeshore land with fantastic fishing, privacy and clean air. It was Otto who had a wonderful A-frame three-storey country house where he screwed the models and actresses he brought up with him from Dublin. Fine, Shane was super-accomplished in his area of expertise; but on the real-life scoreboard, he'd never registered anything near serious money. There were a lot of men like Shane in neighbourhoods near Clareville, except twenty or thirty years older. She'd seen them in their shabby clothes, browsing the antique shops or in the newsagents to pick up their highbrow journal. They'd all swept by some critical juncture in their lives a while back – a poor career choice, a risk never taken. Now, they were out of options, their potential wasted, their boat well and truly sunk.

Otto was staring at the other side of the bar, where a window overlooked the street. Did he recognise someone passing outside? Jenny followed his gaze. There was no one out there.

Turning his attention back to her, he said, 'OK. Well, it's good that we now know where all our pieces are on the board. And again – sorry about that… *incident*, a few minutes ago.'

'Don't worry about it,' Jenny replied, trying to make it sound as if she'd just remembered. Then she quickly added, 'I probably over-reacted. Oh wait – no, I didn't. You were just being a dick.'

He held her gaze and she saw that his face was empty. For a moment, she searched it for regret; regret at kissing her; regret at giving her the opportunity to make this investment; regret at what he'd done all those years ago; regret at ever having reconnected with her. But there was nothing there. Absolutely zilch.

She downed her pint and said, 'Right, I have to go.'

'Just like that?'

'Just like that.'

21

Now

4.23 pm: Daylight fell on Shane's skin, dazzling him like a bright tunnel leading from this life to the next. Things were beginning to feel out of his control and that had always made him nervous – the fact that you *can't* control the things you can't control. Surely this day couldn't get any worse?

After bumming his first cigarette in ten years from a teenager outside the local Spar, Shane pushed on through the afternoon shoppers, dragging on the smoke as if his whole existence depended on it. *She ignored everything you'd said, and she betrayed you. She betrayed you in a way you couldn't have imagined possible…*

Flagging down a taxi, he sat in the back and tried to streamline his thoughts.

The way she spoke to you. The things she said. This was not a spur of the moment decision. Jenny's a ditherer. She's always needed time to make a serious decision. Therefore, she'd thought long and hard about it… and then went ahead and did it.

Opening his phone, Shane clicked on his wife's social media accounts. Her feeds were ticking along, but he knew that she often scheduled that stuff in advance. Jenny's Instagram account had been updated twice that day. The first was a picture of her hugging a nurse before a backdrop of flowers and cards. Shane wasn't in the shot and didn't know it had been taken. The second picture was a selfie taken in the lobby of the hospital – looking as if she was checking out of a five-star hotel. Beneath it, she had written:

First off, hubby is 100% fine. And now he's coming home! Secondly there's the small matter of #LaLucia – today is the opening of the incredible new store. I designed and outfitted the kitchenware department, so I'll be there. Lots of updates coming this week from the hottest #launch in town! #IrishInteriors #womanboss #DesignerKitchenWare #InteriorLiving

Sitting on top of the flood of comments congratulating Jenny on her first corporate gig, were the most recent ones that happened to condemn Jenny's blasé attitude in the wake of an 'incident' that had nearly killed her husband and *did* kill a young woman. No doubt there had been plenty of other similar comments earlier; but those would've quickly disappeared, deleted by Jenny on the go. She was a tenacious censor of her own streams.

Since the interior design magazines and supplements had started to run articles about her, Jenny was spending more and more time facing the glow of her social media platforms. Each paltry like was a titillating touch, every gushing comment a deep welcoming kiss and every private message from a consequential luminary, a shivering orgasm. Sometimes, it was as if Jenny's life had become one big boast.

On Saturday morning, a radio show had wanted to interview Shane from his hospital bed, but he had, of course, turned them down. Shane would never allow his life to become their movie of the week. Instead, they took Jenny for an interview about her 'hellish experience' and she'd managed to mostly talk about how her domestic assignments had inspired LaLucia's project manager to hire her – and, as usual, she came across as intimidatingly smart. Since then, a cluster of front-line, blue-chip architects had left emails wanting to set up meetings to nail her on as a style-ambassador for their projects.

Is Jenny the type of person who would gladly use her front row seat at Deirdre's extinction to advance her own career and get a hashtag by association? The fact was, Jenny's guilt at being a benefactor of Deirdre's death had already been smothered by the raw excitement of her career having a late flourish of supernova proportions.

There was a feeling in Shane's stomach. Disenchantment? Deirdre was one of the world's forgotten. She'd never had a chance. No expectations weighing. No great future awaiting. Soon, no one would know her name except the person who mowed the lawn near her headstone. She deserved better than this.

Shane thought of the subject of his investigative work-in-progress – Samantha: a YouTube beauty vlogger who, before she was murdered, had been making six figures from her bedroom in a Midlands backwater by getting half a million hits a week on her make-up tutorials, all of which were eagerly watched by a galaxy of young girls.

Am I finally seeing Jenny for what she is? Is my own book trying to tell me something? Is the dead Samantha very much like the alive Jenny? Samantha was a standard-issue influencer, who only wanted two things from life – to be liked and to be envied. Jenny, too, only wants two things from life – the Clareville house and her mother's recognition as to just why she was her father's favourite.

Shane exited the taxi directly outside the Speed of Light Building – a twenty-storey modern office block, with rows of square windows climbing to the sky like blank eyes staring down. It was home to several merchant banks, a stock brokerage, insurance firms and a few floors of independent offices, one of which belonged to Otto Lubber.

The revolving door spun him into the marble-floored lobby. Two- and three-seater sofas were sprinkled about, all occupied by people with mouths full of Bluetoothed urgency. The concierge, in a smart three-piece suit, stood still and silent behind his desk like a tailor's dummy.

Shane was stunned to realise that he didn't have a plan. Otto was on the top floor – Jenny had told him enough times. But how to access him? If he asked the concierge to phone up, he'd sacrifice the surprise factor.

Just then, the doors to an elevator slid open and a woman stepped out. Shane swung away from the desk and entered the lift, which was already occupied by three other businessmen arising from the underground car park.

He jabbed the highest number – 18. As the elevator dinged its floor-by-floor beat, Shane backed into the corner and kept his head down. *Just act like these guys. As Sun Tzu put it, 'To know your enemy, you must become your enemy.'* The three men got out on floor 15 and the lift continued its ascent.

As he stepped out onto the eighteenth floor, the doors of the elevator next to his slid shut. Trying to look as if he knew where he was going, Shane strolled down the corridor and noticed that, on this side of the building, people worked behind closed glass doors in offices that became progressively larger. At the end of the passageway, the space opened up into another lobby. There, behind a desk, was a young woman in her mid-twenties with a perfectly straight fringe and high ponytail – hair that one had to live up to. Clearly adept at multi-tasking, she issued instructions via a Bluetooth headset while editing a document on her laptop.

As Shane approached, he slowly turned his head to one side, as far as it would go, until his neck joints crackled and sent jolts of satisfying pain down his spine. The receptionist's tapping fingers slowed up. When Shane reached the desk, she raised her right hand to her ear.

'Yes,' she said.

'Otto,' he said.

Her head perked up like that of a dog who'd just heard its master's distant voice. 'You are?'

Ignoring the secretary as if she might want something from him and he was too busy, too important to indulge her, Shane checked his watch – 4.40 pm – before stepping around the desk and approaching the only door left on the floor. *As Sun Tzu said, 'It is the unemotional, calm, detached warrior who wins.'*

'Stop!' She rose from the chair. 'You can't go in there.'

Shane kept going, feeling that, finally, after all these years, a full stop was going to dot his relationship with Otto; that what was going to happen was an exorcism, banishing from his psyche, once and for all, that appalling moment from twenty-four years ago.

22

Twenty-Four Years Ago

With his eyes on a first-class honours degree, Shane, at nineteen, was sitting his first-year exams in business and arts. In the packed examination hall, life felt special, the future was electrifying, and he was about to make his life's first real mistake.

Shane looked up from the answer booklet and carefully peeled back the wrapper of his tissue packet. Pulling free the first tissue, it revealed the one beneath, which was scribbled on with black biro, outlining in tiny bullet points the tricky third question that he'd just completed unaided. Shane smirked down on the unused cheat notes. For the past two hours he'd been 'in the zone'; his head a clinically efficient reference library of everything he'd studied. Dotted around the exam hall, his colleagues and peers were still frantically writing away, trying to get every iota of information down from the overstuffed compendium of their brains.

'Ten minutes. Ten minutes to finish up,' the lanky, bespectacled invigilator announced.

With the final exam in the can and the prospect of another night with Jenny only hours away, Shane sat back in the plastic chair and enjoyed a long, deep yawn.

A hand landed on his shoulder and a smooth voice whispered, 'It's over for you, Shane.'

Black spots floated across his vision. All the while, soft noise seeped into Shane's well of dark, cold despair as around him a low, frantic, Morse-like communication occurred between nibs and paper. Pages turned and students murmured madly to themselves as they scribbled.

The invigilator squinted through thick, round glasses; his tall gangly body bent almost painfully over the small desk. He whispered, 'What were you thinking? You know this stuff. You're an excellent student.'

At the bottom of the last page of the answer booklet, Shane watched the marbled red barrel of an Aurora Fuoco fountain pen scribble **VOID AT THIS POINT**; the scratching of the nib the sound of his life collapsing. Shane looked up into the face of the invigilator, who was also his Economics lecturer. He was only eight years older than Shane but, being dressed in a pinstripe suit, white shirt and blue tie, seemed to be from an entirely different era. That Easter Island face had a natural authority, and, for a moment, Shane mistook its look of disbelief for pity. The name badge pinned over the chest of his jacket read: **Otto Lubber, Invigilator**.

Otto whispered, 'Shane, you shall remain seated here. After I've collected the booklets, I'll be back for you. Then we'll go to the dean's office.' The voice was almost friendly, as if Otto was not the man who was about to annihilate Shane's future. He picked up the tissue packet and dropped it into his pocket.

Shane tried to think of some way out. Life couldn't falter like that, surely? It wasn't even like facing a firing squad, where there would be an end, a very final full stop fired through his skull. This way, there was only an eternity of disgrace and infamy.

As Shane remained in his seat, stuck in his clotted silence, memories came at him like bee stings. He remembered the huge obligation he owed his parents for putting him through this first year at college. As the others exited the hall to their bright prospects, their sparkling chatter sounded like radio static. His own worthless future had already begun; a long path to a long old age without respect and an end that would be welcome because it would be the end.

About twenty feet away, Jenny smiled and waved at him to join her. Shane just shook his head and gestured for her to go on. For a moment they gazed at each other with blank interest before Jenny walked away, chatting to another of the many handsome young men that orbited her throughout any given day.

During his brief journey to the dean's office, for the first step of his inevitable expulsion, Shane, hands in pockets, walked with head bowed like a snared thieving slave. Next to him Otto offered Shane advice his own father had given him. 'The rule of life is that you're either always on the way up or always on the way down; the trick is making sure that you're always on the way up.'

As the door to the dean's office approached, the bright sunlight shone through the corridor window and fell on Shane like a mallet.

23

Now

4.41 pm: 'Where do you think you're going?' the secretary shouted.

As Shane opened the door, Otto's office finally revealed itself to him, like the sight of land after being lost for weeks at sea. It was a spacious, somewhat vintage, wood-panelled suite; the sort of place where the very wealthy might go to buy a yacht. *Welcome to the one per cent.* There was a huge desk with a green banker's lamp. Despite the fact that Otto didn't drink, there was a drinks cabinet with a Waterford crystal whiskey decanter and a fully loaded rotary spirits dispenser. There were leather couches and a spectacular corner city view – you could actually see the weather in the next county. Finally, there was an ornate Asian cabinet with huge drawers – large enough to tidily store the plans for an office tower that would soon be going up to help those Russian, Chinese and American tycoons launder their money.

But there was no Otto. The suite was empty.

'Where is he?'

'He just left. You should've passed him. And now I'm getting security.'

Shane remembered the other elevator door closing as he'd stepped out onto the eighteenth floor. That must've been him. 'Believe me, he'd prefer it if you *didn't* get security.'

'I seriously doubt that,' she said.

Shane retraced his steps to the lifts. *I can still catch him on the road home.* Otto lived near the Speed of Light Building and often walked to work from his house by the bay. Stepping into the elevator, he watched the illuminated numbers decrease. Again, he thought of Sun Tzu: *'In Chinese text, the word "crisis" consists of two simple brush strokes. One represents danger. The other, opportunity.'*

The doors slid open, and Shane immediately saw him. He was sitting on a sofa against the wall; a location that gave him a panoramic view from the elevators to the exit.

It's actually him.

Black beard. Shaved head. Mid-thirties. Shades. White earbuds. The man who had been standing at the bottom of his driveway earlier that day. He was wearing the uniform of a world citizen – jeans, T-shirt, trainers – but worn by him it had an air of decadence, as though he was really a cowboy, shrouded in gritty history. Bunched up on the seat next to him was the black leather jacket.

It was as if the reappearance of that man was telling Shane something that he couldn't yet hear. Or see. Or decipher. *What game is being played out?* A very singular dark thought hardened, and the weed started to curl across his exhausted brain.

24

4.42 pm: Finishing a much-needed glass of wine and two slices of toast, Jenny went upstairs to redo her make-up. After all the drama and shouting and fighting, her smudged eyes looked like two lumps of coal on a snowman. She recalled what the bearded stranger had said – 'By nightfall today, I will fucking destroy you.'

It's a weird coincidence. But there's no magic spell being woven. Losing out on Otto's deal and then Joan's attempt to mention the unmentionable... they're all just unconnected elements in a particularly shitty day. They have to be, because that creep is not a seer. And how could he be influencing things? How could someone like him influence anything? Anyway, today can only get better – right?

The master en suite was effectively Shane's bathroom. The whole area smelled of clean man. There was a giant container of shampoo on the window shelf. The fact that Shane kept his toiletries outside the cabinet was a bachelor crease she'd failed to iron out over the last fifteen years; along with his refusal to replace the toilet roll if there was as much as a single final sheet left on it.

Looking into the mirror, she hurriedly, but expertly, put her face on. It seemed impossible to think that in a year, someone else would be using these rooms; that someone else would be gazing into this glass.

The house is lost. Shane is too close to finding out the truth. Her father had maintained that the key to power was having the guts to choose wisely between two equally unpleasant options. *Let Shane get the money back and I'll find out what Mum is up to. Then I'll stop her. If I don't, then I'll lose the only thing that ever really counted – my husband.*

'There you go,' she muttered to the panoptic mirrors. Three layers of mascara; the first to darken, the second to condense and the last one for drama. She also applied a new lipstick, an unorthodox daytime choice – red. Jenny considered herself to have a thick skin – except with her mother. One could shine a torch through it, then. She needed these cosmetic shields.

Shane thought her mother had narcissistic personality disorder. He'd printed out and given Jenny NPD-related information from the internet, and Vera certainly did tick most of the boxes on the identifying questionnaire: eighteen out of twenty, when only twelve positive answers were required to comfortably fit the diagnosis.

But Jenny refused to acknowledge the high probability that Shane was correct. Vera hadn't turned on her until she was eighteen. When Jenny thought of her life before that, she just remembered contentment, serenity, certainty that the best would always be available to her and that her future was gold-plated and guaranteed. So much so, that when Shane asked about her experiences growing up, she would feel obliged to trawl through childhood memories for instances that would satisfy him; scraps of suffering, that's what he wanted. The truth was – they barely existed.

Sure, she was hurt that Vera clearly favoured first Hugh and then Joan over her. But that also meant that she'd been able to do whatever she wanted. just as long as she caused no unnecessary drama that would force her mother to have to focus her attention away from herself and onto her youngest child. In fact, Jenny had liked Vera's spiky humour, her endless stream of gossip. Had they not been related, she'd still have liked her. If Vera was a fully blown narcissist, then all those years leading up to her eighteenth year had been based on nothing real.

Don't fuck with my happy memories. People only have so many of those.

Grabbing the car keys, she remembered that the Land Rover was a write-off and so left the house to walk to her mother's, which was just ten minutes away in St Catherine's Hill; an even more exclusive neighbourhood than Clareville.

As Jenny walked along the pavement, she played a message from Detective Murray. 'Sorry, missed your call earlier. I'm actually on my way down to Deirdre's burial. You learn more about a person from the forty-five minutes you spend at their funeral than the entire day you spend at their wedding. If you can tell your husband what I'm up to, I'd appreciate it. He seems to doubt my dedication. I'll try you again tomorrow. Cheers.'

Jenny disconnected and once more thought of the bearded stranger's threat. *Will tomorrow be too late?* There were just four hours till sundown.

As Jenny closed in on her mother's road, she proceeded along a sliding scale of house prices – expensive to exorbitant to prohibitive – as the terraced Georgians became detached Victorians which then became modern architect-designed homes, surrounded by landscaped gardens, which were indisputably the prized properties of the elite of Dublin's privileged class. These homes included treats such as cinema rooms, balcony Jacuzzis, indoor heated swimming pools – all of which had probably seemed like a good idea when the architect, the owners and the developer did all that coke together.

Stepping into a corner shop to buy a very specific packet of mints, the elderly man behind the counter said, 'Oh, hallo. You're one of the Donaldson girls.'

Instinctively, she beamed the way she'd been trained, and said, 'Yes. I'm Jennifer.'

'You're both so like your mother. Same eyes. Same faces. But you're blonde. Haven't seen your mother in a few days. Wonderful lady. So elegant and yet always has time and a quick word for everyone.'

'She'll be delighted to hear that.'

'She'll think I'm the right ladies' man now. And you two girls – you're a tribute to her. You both look so well and are *so* friendly. Anyway, tell Vera that Jim was asking for her.'

'Will do. Bye.'

Jenny left the shop, thinking of Hugh and of how he was never, ever, mentioned by anyone in passing.

She turned onto her childhood street; a road most taxi drivers didn't know existed. When people became aware of it, they seemed amazed that it was there – as if it only existed every second Wednesday. Jenny noticed how so little hurrying was going on. Time actually expanded here. It was like leaving the city and returning to a town she'd grown up in. Everything was connected in small towns. That was why interesting people wanted to leave them as soon as possible. Everything reminded them of the stupid shit they did, or the shit that was done to them.

As she walked towards her family home, the fresh chlorine bouquet of a nearby pool carried on the breeze. There were two vans parked before the first house – a three-storey, red-brick restored mansion. About six people were unloading a sound system and food, as caterers and the event manager waited for the marquee to be erected in the garden.

Jenny remembered her own birthday parties. They had always been lavish affairs with the best and the most of everything. Everyone wanted to come to them. Hugh and Joan had had big parties, too.

Up ahead, her family house loomed into view behind a six-foot-tall wall. It was certainly a happy looking home. There was a swing chair on the upper balcony and birds sang in the background. Keying in the security code – Vera's birthday – the pedestrian entry gate clicked open next to the huge, solid, 'fuck-off' car gates.

As Jenny strolled up the wide gravelled driveway, which split the field-sized landscaped sprawl of lawn, she couldn't help feeling that she was making a serious mistake by coming here. Since her father died, she must have been home no more than three times – all for family emergencies. The last time was two years ago, when Joan found Vera unconscious on the sofa after having a violently negative reaction to her flu vaccine. Each of those visits had been short, and all had ended in screaming matches between Jenny and Joan.

As the front door drew ever closer, she inhaled deeply. Jenny's anxiety was gruelling. Waiting, waiting, waiting for disaster. Yet disaster, by its very nature, was the one thing that you could not expect. Therefore, she must expect everything.

Jenny pressed the doorbell. Its *ding-dong* was soft and polite. *Be prepared – she gaslights. She lies. She denies. She knows that chronology is sanity.*

25

5.20 pm: Otto's shirt was air force blue, which clashed with his red tie. The colours soothed him, and he'd worn them because he had to put in an appearance at a reception given by an innovative Dutch bank. Otto liked to get his nose into the trough for first dibs.

Most of the suits there had been continental blow-ins, soaking up the Dublin-4-ness of D4. Those who had buttonholed him talked small and gestured big, because they knew exactly how important Otto was. If people on the outside of his social circle were not jealous of those on the inside, then he was hanging with the wrong people. Otto had listened magnanimously, while thinking, *if you and I were the same, then you wouldn't need to spend ten minutes sucking up to me. We would already know each other. We would probably have worked together.*

After twenty minutes, Otto exited the stilted atmosphere of the hotel lobby with the relief of walking out of a bad play. The bank's complimentary limo took him home.

His house was an architectural marvel. Situated on a quiet headland on Dublin Bay, near the city centre and surrounded by landscaped gardens, it was a five-bedroomed, two-storey, windowed concrete bunker. But inside, the colours were warm and the lighting and space, enticing. The stone walls were painted a Moroccan red hue and throughout the house the Egyptian antique lamps exuded poetry.

All of it was down to Jenny, who had decorated every room. Her expertise had been much appreciated, as the high end fine-art-and-décor market was like the Wild West, but politer. Jenny had explained that the value of all this stuff was simply what people paid for it – that nobody could say what the *real* value of a work of art was; that price was just symbolic. 'Like Bitcoin,' Jenny had elucidated, and immediately, Otto had finally understood.

She'd also installed a UX system – tech speak for user experience – that bypassed all the manual switches so that he could simply clap his hands or give a voice command for the lights and fun stuff to turn on and off. But Otto had never activated it, even though it had cost a fortune. He'd finally reached the age where all new technological advances were unwelcome.

Since leaving home, he'd never lived with a girlfriend or anyone else. Despite the affluence, space and luxuries, there were many signs of the bachelor life. Styrofoam shells crowned the overflowing kitchen bin, and the double sink was stacked with dirty cutlery – just two days since the cleaner had been in.

On the second floor, Otto entered his bedroom and closed the door behind him, gently, as if the noise would spill his secret thoughts out into the empty house. The bedroom had lots of impressive equipment: a fifty-inch smart TV, home cinema system and piles of history and economics books. Framed photographs adorned the side tables – family snaps.

Otto, the progeny of talented and wealthy parentage, was proud of his pedigree – but in a secretive way, because he realised that people prefer the underdog. The underdog makes them believe that *they* could've done better if *they* had just had the chance.

Another reason he kept historical nuggets from the 'my story' section of company portfolios, was that the Third Reich cast a lengthy shadow, almost a century long, over Otto's family. His father, Andreas Lubber, was an unspectacular millionaire bohemian playboy with a large stake in Jutland Petroleum Technologies. The company had been founded by Otto's great-grandfather, who'd made his fortune supplying the Third Reich with compressed propellant nitrogen for their Panzer columns. He had also killed Russians with his sniper rifle across the Red Steppes. 'Not enough,' he'd always said.

An only child, Otto was born to parents intent on raising him a perfect little factualist. Au pairs had nursed him through his formative years in Austria and, when he was eight, they moved into a superb maisonette in the *Île de la Cité* in Paris. Besides the race riots and their accompanying Parisian car barbecues, his most vivid memory was hiding outside the kitchen, watching his father fuck a stunning student from the Sorbonne over the kitchen table, her jeans lowered to her knees. On the opposite side of the table, Otto's beautiful mother inhaled a Lucky Strike and blew a cloud of smoke into the student's groaning face. After his father collapsed onto the girl's back, little Otto tiptoed back to his bedroom which faced the gloomy winter sky behind Notre Dame. From that moment, his favourite fact about the world was that, out there somewhere, it was always summer for someone.

Otto was then educated across the US, as his parents hopscotched about American cities on their great adventure. He made no friends, since when he was not being home-schooled by tutors, he was passing through different classrooms; he was a quiet teenager who seemed to spend his whole adolescence as a sleepwalker that his parents were unable to shake awake. By fourteen, he was on a pack of cigarettes a day – just for something to do.

At seventeen, he entered the Erasmus University of Rotterdam to study economics: a degree, according to his father, which would ensure he would never be pigeonholed. After his masters, he opted out of academia for three years, instead cutting his teeth on the board of Jutland Petroleum Technologies and deeply impressing his uncles – who had assumed he would be as frivolous as his father. Then, on his mother's recommendation, Otto once more took up the mantle of the scholar to begin his PhD, with the intention of killing three more years at university – this time in Dublin. Part of his remit was to supervise undergraduate theses and give the odd class.

But after just one year, a shocking event occurred that made him abandon Ireland for a mews house in London's Camden Town. There, he hid out from his family, ashamed of the terrible thing that had happened in Dublin, ashamed of abandoning his PhD, ashamed of how he had amounted to nothing much.

Otto, alone in London, spent hours every day weeping, convinced that the world had used him badly. He would look from his window across Camden Lock towards the packed market, acutely aware that he'd never had any close friends, a real love affair or true ambitions. His life had simply amounted to one cocktail party after another, stints in a few universities and an almost ruinous end to his PhD attempt – one that had almost destroyed his life and someone else's. Sitting in his room by the canal, Otto had understood just how lonely a human being can make itself, and he wondered how he'd ended up living such an existence. But the answer was too large, too tangled to clarify.

One day, as Otto watched the barges cruise by, the post arrived behind him with a thud. Otto had always had great faith in the power of letters to transform his existence and, true to form, his father had somehow found him. Without referencing his disappearance, or seeking an explanation, or even hinting at his breakdown, Andreas Lubber asked Otto to steer the UK wing of the clan's new investment firm, one that was intended to create and manage commercial property bonds for pension funds and banks. The package enclosed a detailed business plan that his uncles had put together.

After reading the letter, Otto looked up to the London sky and once again considered himself to be an integrated part of a whole. For, suddenly, Otto had a plan. He would turn down the position. In fact, he would tell his father to go fuck himself. Instead, Otto would use his uncles' business plan, which was really just a portfolio of hungry international connections, to set up the same venture, but in Dublin, and just for himself – which would be easy, as he reckoned Dublin to be just a more manageable London. His family would be initially shocked, but that would pass and be replaced with admiration. For what were the Lubbers, if not ruthless pioneers afraid of no arrows?

5.25 pm: Standing tall and priestly by his bedroom window, Otto gazed down to his garden. The sun was just low enough to spray everything pink. He poured himself a glass of water. Twenty-four years ago, things had got out of hand, and since then he had been teetotal and Class A-free. It wasn't for his health. He didn't work out. He didn't knock back supplements. He didn't watch what he ate. He smoked cigars four or five times a week. And Otto slept with actresses and models.

Like Russian dolls, each new girlfriend seemed to be younger, slimmer and prettier than the last, and they all fucked him like they owed him money. Before, that was why he believed he was happy. However, gradually over the last year he'd come to realise that he wasn't in fact happy – he was just making do. The source of this realisation was Jenny. *She's still young-ish. I'm middle-aged. She's still beautiful. I'm past my peak. It's a match made in heaven.* Her currently intermittent presence in his life was something that he'd suddenly wanted to make constant, and permanent.

Is Shane truly happy? Women can fake an orgasm, but men can fake an entire relationship. *I mean, who exactly is Shane?* Shane was one of those men that could feel justified in viewing all of the pretty Clareville housewives walking by as potential sexual partners. Yes, he was also smart. Not educated smart – obviously. He had no degree, but he was the type of guy who understood the laws of physics without being able to name a single theory.

He remembered when Shane had firmly entered his life. Otto the invigilator had spent that morning fetching paper for undergraduates like some type of servant. But then the day got interesting, as he watched a student remove a tissue from a packet and gaze down upon the notes beneath. It was like watching a car wreck happen in slow motion, for this wasn't any student – this was one of *his* students. This was, in fact, Otto's *best* student.

The exam was almost over, and Otto didn't actually want Shane's future in his hands. He just wanted to go home and nap before heading out to the end-of-year party at Krystal. He was due to join a few young lecturers and the odd sixty-something anti-establishmentarian. They liked to turn up at these things to sniff out the type of ripe, blithe undergraduate flotsam that stood out with their over-analysed feelings and condemnatory sentiments towards everything, but were a bit damaged and fucked well. Shane was now a potential spanner in the works. *Ignore him. Just walk on.* But his ancestral sense of rigid, systematic order kicked in and his hand landed on Shane's shoulder.

After collecting the booklets, Otto looked Shane in the eye. He'd always struck Otto as a happy young man. It wasn't too improbable. Happy people existed, too. 'I have no choice, Shane,' he whispered, like they were having a conversation in a church.

Shane sighed as if having just seen his future. 'I know.'

Sitting on the side of his super-king mahogany sleigh bed, he wondered how Shane had become a writer of repute. Otto did have doubts about how good the books were. True crime – surely that's just turning newspaper articles into a compendium of adjectives? Earlier, when he'd called into Clareville, Otto had noticed the shelving behind Shane's desk. Between antique bookends were copies of his books, each one in a different language – Chinese, French, German and so on. Languages that no one in his house spoke and the English versions Shane had presumably read as he had written them. *The vainglorious prick.*

People who were expelled from university were not supposed to turn out like Shane – especially if they'd also failed to come from a significant family. It was not so much that Shane thought that the rules of life didn't apply to him. It was more that he'd identified that one of his life's great pleasures was bending them. He was the guy who had decided to go to university, not because of any passion to learn, but to avoid the ongoing humiliation of factory-line and shelf-stacking gigs. Shane, the young man who cheated and was expelled, came from a shithole where growing up was like living in a vast open prison; where becoming a manager in Spar was seen as the top of the totem pole; where young men who made it to twenty without doing a spell inside were seen as good catches. His parents were of a particular Irish generation that believed God had sent JFK to restore Catholicism and would've been over the moon if he'd become a civil servant.

Otto also knew that there was a shadowy tone to Shane that made him attractive to a certain type of woman – the type of woman that Jenny was. Shane certainly preferred to take the dark view of life, and he was often right. He had no illusions as to what people were capable of. Otto supposed that Shane's habit of suspicion came from an insight into his own character. After all, there's a reason why Christ was a humanitarian and not a creative.

Otto did not like how close Jenny and Shane were, but he did admire it. What he'd told Shane earlier, about how happy they were, he'd meant it. True, Shane and Jenny never acted like each was a half of a whole. She didn't sit on his knees. He didn't fawn over her. They didn't hold hands all day long. But Shane would occasionally touch her shoulder. It was an affectionate gesture – not intimate – just enough to remind Otto that he was an outsider. Then there would always come a point where he would have no idea what they were talking about. Even though they wouldn't be speaking in code or whispering, it would sound private and therefore like something he would be very interested in. But he wouldn't get their jokes and he couldn't share their history. In the dense compact of their marriage, they were each other's alibi.

5.28 pm: Something moved outside the window. Otto stood from the side of the bed and winced as his knees crunched like tyres on gravel. It was a crow, crossing the ledge. Then, something below caused it to glance downwards. Cawing with alarm, it jumped off the sill and fluttered off to the trees.

Taking out his phone, Otto opened the app that hooked up to

the security cameras. His home and the gardens surrounding it were fitted with a state-of-the-art alarm system, comprising laser-activated lights, cameras and microphones. He opened the feed of the front gate, but it was blank. He tried the one scanning the driveway. That too was blank. Finally, he tried the front door and was not surprised to be also greeted by a vacant screen.

What if somebody is out there? He tapped a reminder into his phone to call the security firm in the morning and have it fixed. *Don't be stupid, Otto – you're in a great house, in a great area, in a great city.* However, high finance had shown him, time and time again, that civilisation was just a thin veneer. Underneath it, was humans' default mode – savagery, greed, lust.

26

5.29 pm: The door opened.

'Ah, Jennifer,' Vera said, and smiled as if she always smiled at the mere mention of her daughter's name. She was looking good – vital and happy. Jenny's mother was one of those old ladies who went out power walking at 10.00 am in an elegant tracksuit and white runners, as if the main street was a racetrack, as if life was so good that she wanted it to last forever.

'Hi, Mum,' Jenny said, and held out the packet of mints.

'Oh lovely, my favourites. Yum!'

Jenny did like to see Vera's face happy: her big brown eyes, the laughter lines, the elegant perm, the bold pout of her lips, the sharpness of her thoughts visibly conducting the rise and fall of her deeply furrowed brow.

'Is Joan here?' Joan lived a quick drive from Vera.

'She's at the church. She helps clean it every Monday.' Vera then continued as if Jenny and Joan were close. 'Joan has so much going on in her life with the separation, the children finishing college and… well, she's got such a big heart. Always looking after others. Joan is too kind for her own good. She's always had an over-developed conscience. Now, look at this.'

Vera held out her mobile with a photograph on it, taken from some website. Joan continually sent her pictures of funny things during the day, as if she was a dog bringing back sticks to its master. 'I don't understand it.'

Vera wasn't good with any humour that was more complicated than someone tripping over or unknowingly walking into clear glass. There was something lacking in her brain that made her imagination almost totally void. Even though she watched a lot of TV, it was a strict diet of current affairs, chat and reality shows. Anything with actors was avoided.

Jenny glanced at the screen. It was a visual pun of a street weirdo standing beneath a funny street sign. Instead of wasting time trying to explain it, she said, 'Me neither.'

Vera ushered her daughter deeper into the hallway. On the side table was a tall vase supporting a huge bunch of sunflowers, their stems stiff and muscular, the soft petals stretching and strong. Jenny listened to the silence. Even though only her mother remained, the house had always been big enough for so many people to reside there and yet simultaneously live separate lives. On one of Shane's first visits, he'd told her that while he knew lots of separated parents, Jenny's were the first he'd come across that lived in separate bedrooms. He'd said, 'It's a good job you have so many of them.'

Jenny looked up the staircase to where her bedroom was, in the back wing. She pictured her Polaroids on the wall, the long mirror, the pile of cute teddies, her favourite books on her dressing table. Then she thought of the bedroom next to hers – Hugh's.

'So, tell me pet, is everything all right?'

Calmly Jenny told her usual lie. 'Everything's fine.'

'Good. I'm glad to hear it. We've been worried.'

The visage of her sister drifted across her brain. The only thing Joan had ever been worried about, concerning Jenny, was that she just might *not* fail.

Vera said, 'It's so good to see that you're not shook up. Many people who have gone through what you did… well, it leaves them marked, you know?'

Jenny felt a splash of gratitude soak her very being. 'So, Mum, you sent me a weird text this morning and then sent Joan around—'

'Go on into the living room. I'll just get my tea from the kitchen.' Vera would never answer questions that she didn't want to answer – there was always something to put in the oven, a call she had to make or a kettle to click on.

Hands in pockets, Jenny entered the sprawling living room. The huge window framed a spread of the outside road, as if it were a work of art; giving the impression that Vera owned what could not be possessed, making private that which was, in fact, very public. In the distance a man was walking the pavement and Jenny couldn't help from squinting to see if he had a beard and a shaved head.

Her father's armchair was still in the corner. Vera obviously wanted it to stay there, otherwise Joan would have it by now. Jenny pictured Lorcan on it, reading the paper or taking a call. In his hand would be a tumbler of the finest gold whiskey, swilling about. Lorcan's gait had always said, 'Average stuff? Why bother with it? Shouldn't you go through life experiencing only the supreme prose, the finest food, the best whiskey?'

Jenny had been too young to understand her parents' marriage.

She'd just thought that they never much liked each other. After all, they rarely fought in her presence. Instead, crucial conversations were routed through Hugh and her sister. Vera might say to one of them in the kitchen, 'Go and ask your father if he's away next weekend.'

It wasn't until her adolescence that she gained an insight, absorbed from her friends, that the stiff formality shrouding her parents' relationship was unusual. Other people's parents laughed and joked with each other; sometimes they even kissed, on the mouth. It had been strange just to see someone's mother arc her body affectionately towards her husband.

The problem for Lorcan was that he would be made to suffer for *not* pulling his children into his marital strife, preferring to disappear into his work instead. Conversely, Vera told Hugh and Joan everything, and they sympathised deeply with the one-sided narrative they were continually exposed to. With their father away so much, and Vera more a close friend and leader than a mother, they never doubted who the flawed partner in their parents' marriage was.

When Jenny had lived here, the atmosphere was entirely determined by her mother. If Vera had been out drinking lunch with a friend, it would be convivial and gossipy. If Vera had opened a bottle in the kitchen, it would be bitchy and scandalous. But if Jenny's father was present, Vera would be sober and a frosty atmosphere would be endured until Lorcan retired to his wing of the house, alone.

Jenny looked to the door, but there was still no sign of Vera. The clock on the wall read 5.35 pm. It was getting on. The day was disappearing.

By just standing in this room, the past was swamping her. Jenny smiled at the old sofa. She was glad it was still there. It was the same one on which she'd made out with Shane countless times in her eighteenth year. Afterwards, he'd liked to pull the cushions off to prospect for coins. People didn't lose money in his house.

There were new paintings on the walls. All of her father's Connemara landscapes were gone – no doubt hanging in Joan's penthouse. They had been replaced over the years by religious works – 'The Last Supper', 'Christ Taken in the Garden', 'Christ Revealing His Wounds' and a selection of colourful renderings of The Cross minus the suffering Christ, to add vibrancy to the room. Vera had always espoused the power of prayer; even intimating that by kneeling before sleep, she may have saved lives. But while these paintings removed any doubt as to Vera's religious certitude; what they really said was that this lady had wealth. Her mother may have believed that every day she metaphorically bathed in the colour of the Holy Lamb's blood, but Jenny suspected that even Vera would admit that the real cleanser of souls was money.

While Jenny lived here, she'd pretended to go to a Mass once a week, but had really only attended those where she'd be expected to sit with the rest of the family. Her father, too, had only attended the major ceremonies – Christmas, Easter, funerals and weddings. One afternoon, Lorcan, well-oiled from a business lunch, had muttered, 'Who knows anything, Jen? If Jesus was the intellectual they say he was, then if he'd lived to be fifty, he'd probably have seen religion as just a youthful folly.'

At that moment, the ends of religion seeped out of her. It was like forgetting a language she'd only spoken as a child.

Finally, Vera appeared at the door holding two cups of tea. 'It was a girl? I saw her picture. The papers didn't show it, but Joan found it online in one of those internet news things. She was very pretty. Everyone thinks so.'

'Everyone' was Joan.

Vera continued. 'She must have had a terrible time of it in life to do that. I mean, obviously she wasn't evil like the men you see on the news who do things like that – they'd scare the pips out of an apple by just looking at it.'

'Evil,' Jenny repeated; that most overused and weakened word in the twenty-first century. Like 'awesome', 'evil' had lost its meaning. 'Just because she was pretty doesn't mean that—'

'I don't want to know the ins and outs of her. It's enough to know that you're fine.'

'It wasn't me who was smashed up in the car. It was Shane.' She waited to see how Vera would manage to, once again, avoid direct mention of her husband. For Jenny, it was like being a spinster when talking to her mother. When she and Shane had returned from the Caribbean it was, 'How was *your* trip?', 'Did *you* enjoy the weather?', 'Are *you* jet-lagged?'

Vera said, 'Yes, well, as I said – it's all fine now. Which is a relief.'

'Mum, you do know that my husband almost died, right?'

'*Almost.*'

Jenny stared at this elegant old lady with cheekbones one could cut your thumb on.

Vera said, 'But he didn't, Jennifer. He's fine. You've always had your marriage on a pedestal. I mean of course I would never encourage either of my daughters to be a bad wife. But with you and Sh—… well, Jennifer, you're now one of those women who has to ponder which of your friends you can impose yourself upon at Christmas. See, a marriage without children is surely just another type of ordinary, not very special, relationship. Isn't that so?' She raised threaded brows above big brown eyes. '*That's* what makes a marriage special – children.'

Jenny muttered, 'It didn't make Joan's very special.'

Only Vera's lipsticked mouth revealed her displeasure – lips pulled together like a little red fist. She had never liked her youngest rudely pointing out and parading about things the rest of the family were currently sweeping under the rug.

Offering a smile that announced the topic was about to be changed, Vera gestured to the cups still in her hands. She said, 'Oh, your camomile tea is getting cold.' Back-kicking the door closed, she crossed the living room and handed Jenny the cup. Her own tea was English and black – Vera didn't waste calories on milk and sugar. 'Well, Jennifer, as you know, I've been trying desperately to get in touch.' Vera did not at all sound desperate.

'One text, Mum. That's all I got.'

'I've been waiting all day for you to get back but at least I got to clean out the oven.'

Jenny pictured Vera reaching deep into the dark cavern, scrubbing. 'I was at the launch.'

Vera shrugged. 'Ah yes, *the* launch. You always loved the idea of big glamorous occasions. From the moment you could shop you were packing your wardrobe with "maybe someday" clothes.' Her gaze drifted to the window, and she looked out to the distance. As if to herself, Vera muttered, 'I always appreciated your confidence, but beauty is sometimes ugly when it's too self-aware.' Turning back to Jenny, she stated, 'The problem with looking younger than you are, is that one day you suddenly won't.' Vera seemed to enjoy that pinch of sourness, as if she wanted her daughter to realise that soon she would no longer be desirable; that she'd be off-putting to men in some way. 'I noticed, from the pictures Joan showed me on her phone, that your husband didn't go to LaLucia's today.'

'Mum, last night he slept in a hospital. It was even on the news. You know this.'

'I notice he's never in any pictures of you at work on the internet-a-majig, either.'

'*Either*?' Her mother had a knack at keeping Jenny off-balance and constantly questioning herself. 'It's *my* work and *my* career. I don't photobomb his author pics.'

Vera looked amused. 'Like the rest of the world, he's just a spectator. Be careful, Jennifer. There's only room for one star in every relationship.'

'I thought you'd be… at least *pleased* about the launch.'

'You know, your father said that launches and openings were just a useful invention to justify daytime drinking.'

'It wasn't "daytime drinking", Mum. It was, like, the pinnacle of my career so far. It was really important.'

'Pinnacle of your career,' Vera paraphrased grandly. 'It's a *job*, Jennifer. There are lots of them out there.'

'But this can open up so many doors for me. If certain companies notice—'

Vera shook her head. The movement was firm, full of adult certainty. She wasn't communicating that she disagreed with Jenny. It just meant that she didn't want the conversation to run off in a tangent that she had no interest in. 'I had to send Joan to you when I heard nothing back.'

'Mum, I really wish you hadn't. I don't need any more—'

'Jennifer, your first word was "more". I remember you saying that on your father's lap. Right there in his chair. Tickles and food or whatever. More, more, more. Your first word.'

'You've told me many times.'

'Lorcan thought it attested to your adorability, but the others adopted it as evidence of your ingrained greediness.' She paused to let that soak in. 'Oh look – now you're in a mood.'

'No, I'm not,' she replied, cringing at the sulky sound of her own voice.

'But I don't blame you. We were just saying this morning – Joan and I...' She paused as if to purposely give Jenny time to conjure up the frankly repulsive image of her older sister sitting in her mother's kitchen for the first of their twice-daily meet-ups to bitch about neighbours, friends, Jenny. 'We were just saying,' she continued, 'that you've had it so tough this year and it's only June.'

That sounded like a threat.

Jenny steeled herself for whatever was coming.

Vera took out a neatly folded note from the breast pocket of her blouse. Opening it out, she held it up and nodded with satisfaction. 'Right, there are some things I need to discuss.'

Incredulously, Jenny said, 'You wrote them out?'

'Jennifer, you know I'm a person of lists. If I could, I would have my entire life columned on a single sheet of A4.'

'Will we sit?'

'No. We're fine, aren't we? Now, when I sent you the solicitor's letter, I hoped you would take it in the manner intended. Like, I didn't want to blindside you. I mean, I am not trying to upset you or cause you difficulties. I trust you understand that?'

Jenny swallowed. When her mother or sister had to say that they were *not* doing something, it usually meant that they were.

Vera said, 'You never acknowledged that letter my solicitor sent you.' Then she craned her head, as if peering into her daughter's life.

Jenny didn't like being alone with her in this room. 'The room' was where Stalin killed you. 'I did. When we were last out for lunch, you asked if I'd got the letter and I said yes.'

'But you never *asked* me about it.'

'Why would I? There was nothing mysterious or confusing about the instruction it contained. Unless, it *didn't* mean, "Get out of the house in twelve months"?'

'Don't be silly.'

'It didn't mean that?'

'Of course it did, but—'

'But *what*? You're throwing me out of a house that Dad promised me. It's mine. It's mine in every way except the one way that counts in this world – on paper. But you know it should be mine.' Jenny felt surprisingly formidable, finally getting to speak to her mother like that. It had come naturally, when usually every moment in Vera's presence was like a tricky chess game. 'Dad bought Clareville years ago as an investment and he told me it would be mine when I got back from Canada. You know this. And you are taking it away from me.'

Vera raised her eyes dismissively and gestured to the window. 'This street is full of families. Neighbours are how you designate a child's future. They go to the same schools. They become their friends. If your neighbours are fine, your children will be fine. Clareville is wasted on you. You'll be happier in an apartment or wherever childless middle-aged couples go to live. I wouldn't know.'

Jenny was stunned at her mother's gall. It was as if Vera expected praise for making her realise that this was all for her own good; that she was actually doing Jenny a favour.

'Now, you've had a good run in the house. How many years have I rented it to you?'

'Eight.'

'Yes, eight. Expensive to run but built to last. They have grace, those old Victorians. Today, they'd make houses out of Styrofoam if they could get away with it. But I presumed you would have questions. Questions to keep yourself informed.' Vera spoke with casual conviction; a woman who didn't expect to be doubted. 'And I am the person who can inform.'

Jenny inhaled, seeking courage, and then spoke softly: 'Mum… you'll only tell me whatever version of the truth suits yourself and suits Joan. In that order.'

Vera's lips straightened. They were lined from decades of smoking a pack a day, which at seventy-five had had zero effect on her health. Likewise, the bottle of vodka that still needed replacing every three days. 'No. You have my word…'

Jenny smiled at that. The word of a trained liar. If you couldn't tell the truth by your seventh decade, you were never going to. On a purely superficial level, Vera probably believed what she was saying; the best liars believe their own deceits. Jenny had always regretted reaching the age when she discovered that people could lie to themselves as well as to others.

'It doesn't actually matter, Mum. I'm not here to talk about that. I'm here because of what Joan said to me, in front of Shane, in Clareville today. What the hell was she—'

'It's all connected.'

Jenny placed her teacup onto the side table. Something was certainly amiss. She could feel it. It filled the room around them, crackling and sizzling and calling out to be noticed.

'What is connected?'

'The Clareville house and what Joan was talking to you about… that business twenty-five years ago. *That's* what is connected.'

Jenny looked as if a memory had suddenly returned that was so vivid, it was a haunting. *We remember what we can't forget.*

'I just think, Jennifer, that there are wheels and cogs churning all around you… that you're not aware of… that just might be secretly working *for* you… and you'll see the results of it sooner than you think.'

'Mum, I don't understand.'

'I've something to tell you,' Vera said with a hint of glee.

She's going to tell me something that she knows will upset me.

'Twenty-five years ago. It's the anniversary and recently I was thinking…' Vera's eyes narrowed, and Jenny stared into them. They both soaked up the silence. There was an echo in their lives of a sworn vow to never broach the subject. 'But first, have you told him?'

'Shane?'

'Yes. *Shane.*' His name was long and drawn out on her mother's tongue – a special treat she'd allowed herself. 'And don't even think about telling me it's none of my business. It is. I'm your mother. And I was there. Do you understand the point I'm making, Jennifer?'

'Yes. And fine – I told him.'

Vera nodded slowly. But it actually meant that she didn't believe her. Jenny had learned the subtle signs from a young age. 'Where's your dad?' meant Mum was in a good mood. 'Where's your father?' meant she was in foul form. Jenny knew that when her mother stared while nodding thoughtfully, it was a forerunner to shutting down the entire conversation, and taking the course of action she'd intended to take, regardless of any petitions to the contrary.

Jenny said, 'OK. Of course I *haven't* told him.'

'Jesus,' Vera snapped – and by her taking the Lord's name in vain, Jenny knew that she meant business. 'It's twenty-five years since it happened. If you're not going to tell your husband now… then I'd ask myself *why?*'

'I know why.' For Jenny, talking to her mother was like talking to the police, or worse. It was like being on the stand, fighting for your freedom, when you know you're guilty of something but only the prosecution knows what for; and so, there is no alternative but to wait to see the direction the questioning will take. 'Look, Mum, what do you want from me? Why can't you all just leave me alone?'

'Things like that don't simply go away. You can't outrun your past, Jennifer.'

'Why are you doing this? And what has it got to do with taking Clareville off me? But fine, if you still want to punish me for what happened when I was just eighteen years old, then give it to Joan or one of her girls.'

Vera looked genuinely puzzled. 'I'm not giving the house to Joan or any of my grandchildren.'

'Huh? Then who? You don't need the money and obviously it's not for Hugh and—'

'Of course it's not for Hugh. Don't be such a… a bitch.'

'You know I didn't mean … Sorry. But just tell me, Mum. What's going on?'

There's a split second before Vera chooses her response. Blink and you'd miss it. But Jenny didn't and she doesn't. Whatever Vera was planning to do with the house, it made Vera uneasy – and Vera was never uneasy.

Just as her mother was about to speak, the living room door opened, and Jenny's stomach took an alpine plunge.

27

5.54 pm: Having put the failed security cameras out of his mind, Otto's lean angular face stared at the TV, changing station each time his thoughts switched theme. The flickering screen created the illusion of activity, allowing him to sit still in his edgy state. He was thinking too fast, as if he had two brains, passing ideas from one to the other and back again.

So what if Shane is an accomplished writer? Most arty types weren't smart enough to make money. The few that were – the kind that ended up hiring him – didn't really make art; they created wealth under the guise of art. Such as his favourite painting that hung above his bed that portrayed a map of the world in matte colours that had cost Otto fifty thousand euros at auction. He craned his neck and looked up to the painting. *I have what I want.*

Even as the words drifted across his brain, he knew they weren't true. If he had what he wanted, he'd have a Rothko over the bed. But he wasn't at that level – yet. *I'm full of shit.* He actually hated Rothko. *I don't know what I want. I have millions and I'm going to make millions more and I haven't got around to spending the millions I made years ago.*

He'd always felt that he could paint a Rothko in five minutes; though he knew that to even think such a sentence was utterly forbidden. *Jenny could've sorted my life out. I could've loved her.*

His thoughts always swung back to Jenny. From the day she had re-entered his life, the calendar pages had flown off the wall. The world spun on, and she'd remained entrenched in the front of his brain. Now, they were done. All it had taken was for the stakes to be raised –and he'd raised them by trying to kiss her.

After he'd abruptly left the university and moved to London, Otto assumed he'd never see her again. Then, after eight years, she'd texted him. He was making waves in the Dublin business scene, and she was a burgeoning interior designer who was wondering if any of Otto's clients might like to see her portfolio. Considering his unspoken debt to her, they met up and he was delighted to see that she hadn't changed much since he'd been her lecturer. Back then she'd been fresh-faced, golden tanned; in another age she could have been the poster child of the Hitler Youth. Eight years on she had been much the same: still blonde, but now buttery blonde. The passing years had given her face angles that she'd been missing, and which her intelligence deserved. Time had framed her jaw and lengthened her neck.

It had not been difficult to set her up as a consultant. She had the right attitude from the start – bringing all the formality of her parents' life of wealth and influence to her own, post-wealth, life. Her late father's name was still respected, and Otto bore witness to Jenny rolling that old business establishment grenade of the Donaldson name into many boardrooms.

Fixing his pillow and checking the time – 5.56 pm – Otto considered going out to empty his head at the cinema. The dark auditorium was the equivalent to a garage or shed: a place to relax alone without the problematic condition of finding himself alone with himself. Then, afterwards, he would pick up some greasy chips and take the long way home, his favourite drive, that detoured through the heart of Clareville. Otto would look into those fine Victorian homes, because most of them left their blinds open to let the expensive lamps and ceiling lights illuminate the type of life that he hadn't experienced since living with his parents.

As his car crawled down Jenny's street, he'd tune in the classic rock station that played hits he hadn't heard in decades; songs that, when he'd first heard them, he assumed would be with him forever. While eating chips, he'd watch Jenny in her natural habitat so that he could convince himself that it was her *un*natural habitat. He wanted her to be the person she used to be when he taught her. Then he could be the man he had once been – the one that he liked.

It was a week since he'd last taken that drive. Parking opposite Jenny's, the car stinking of salt and vinegar, he turned off the headlights, so the SUV's interior was no longer illuminated. He then stared over at the half-pulled blinds that revealed Shane sunk in his beanbag, slowly killing the evening with a hardback.

For Otto, that bright window was like a movie screen playing an alternative reality, one where he'd stayed in Dublin twenty-five years ago, finished his PhD, married Jenny and she'd stayed with him forever.

So, this is what I could've been.

With 'Careless Whisper' oozing from the car speakers, he experienced a thrilling intimacy knowing that Jenny was somewhere in there, only twenty feet away, having no idea who was outside her door.

He'd finally made his move today. The kiss. What had he expected? He had expected her to kiss him back, and within his kiss she would've received the message that she'd been institutionalised by marriage;

that she'd been labouring under a form of Stockholm syndrome; that he was here to save her; that adultery was not the worst crime in the world. Not by a long shot.

But he had misjudged, and it was his job never to misjudge. That's love – it corrupts. Distorts. Warps. Desire and ruination were essentially bound together. They were absolute and unchangeable, a consequence and its cause.

It was obvious now, that once this investment was put to rest, he and Jenny would drift apart forever. He'd overstepped a critical line. What could he offer her in the future, anyway? He was getting old while a girl like Jenny belonged to the nationality of the young, regardless of her actual age.

It was a sign of waning, the need to spend time with younger people. Maybe he'd just wanted to tell her how he felt; that he suddenly found himself lacking in hope; the blood and meat of the young. *I am now Jenny's antidote to desire. She'd rather throw back a jar of strychnine and spend hours writhing on the floor in spasms of agony while her internal organs give up one by one than sleep with you, Otto.*

Otto liked to ponder her circumstances; as if something was at stake for him, too, in how her life unravelled. Jenny was obsessed with owning that house she lived in; as if her name on the title would make her someone, the way her neighbours were all somebodies. He'd tried to ease that obsession by suggesting she downsize or at least try another neighbourhood where all her spoils from the investment wouldn't be swallowed up in one go. People think that if you owned a beautiful house in a great area, then you were rich. But the fact was, that for most of those people, they were only rich if they sold that house. He told her, 'You're white, educated, pretty and speak English. That means, if your dream dies, you get another.' But it had been to no avail.

From downstairs came a knock on the front door – loud and solid.

Why didn't they ring the bell? *Hold on – how did they get through the electric gates without buzzing me?*

Another loud knock.

How afraid should he be?

Otto's unease momentarily raised his glasses a few centimetres off his nose and his eyes stared with pupils like manholes. Another thump sounded, and he suddenly realised that what he was hearing were not knocks, but kicks.

The door was being booted in.

He stood, and like a cat trying to calm itself with the sound of its own purrs, muttered, 'Don't worry – everything's going to be alright.'

He didn't believe for a minute that everything was going to be alright.

The front door swung open, the frame hitting the side table next to it. Heavy footsteps pounded on the wooden floor. Boots. How many were there? His heart smashed against his ribcage. The footsteps moved up the staircase and onto the landing, then past the first bedroom and the second, towards the master bedroom, towards Otto; louder, more forceful, marching along until directly outside his door. For a second Otto thought about diving beneath the bed. He wondered if he'd ever had a more cowardly thought.

Then he remembered his gun.

He owned a pistol. A small Glock. When working in an advisory capacity for a pharmaceutical multinational, they'd assigned him a bodyguard, someone highly trained in lethal mayhem, due to the death threats the executives had been getting after their briefly trialled product was firmly associated with causing neurological damage in the many children who had used it. Otto had bought the Glock from his bodyguard who had told him, 'This is for when you come across someone like me, when I'm not around. You'll be fine if the target is twenty-five feet from you or closer. If they're further away, then let them come to you and kill them or, if they're running, let them run and call the police.'

There was no time to call the police.

Otto wanted to run across the bedroom, but his legs only walked, his sagging untucked shirt hanging from him in awkward pain. It was like his body was on strike, refusing to function at anywhere near its potential. He made it across the room and jammed his fist into the drawer. There it was. The cold metal. The rough handle grip.

Behind him, the bedroom door swung open.

'Fuck you!' Otto said. He'd wanted it to be thunderous and defiant. Instead, it was quiet, inexact, like something from a badly tuned radio. Otto felt drenched in freezing water. His skin goose-bumped, his spine straightened almost painfully, and his fists balled but seemed to weigh too much. His entire being had never felt so unprepared, so unworthy of a challenge.

A muscular, bearded man strode into the room, a cut-throat razor held above his head, ready to slash down. His head was shaved, and he wore a thin leather jacket. Otto raised the pistol from the drawer, but the man was already on him. He gripped Otto by the neck with such force that his knees buckled from having oxygen and blood supply instantly denied. The pistol fell back into the drawer.

For the first time in his life, Otto made his 'Even Money Can't Save Me Now' face. With the blade to Otto's throat, the man's enormous hand clutched the back of his neck and wrenched him across the room. Otto's knees hit the floor, but he forced the pain to remain inside.

The man said, 'To kill an animal – any animal – you have to take it by surprise.'

Otto hooked a foot between the vertical ribs of a radiator, but the man simply bent over him like he might bend over a *thing*, and with a fist clenched in his hair, half-pulled, half-slid Otto across the varnished floor.

The man said, 'You have to seize it and then penetrate it. With a knife. Or a spear.'

It was daunting to be reduced to a piece of cargo. The pain from Otto's scalp poured into his sensory realm, hurting his head from the inside out.

'Doing it with a bullet just turns death into play with a remote-controlled toy. Where's the fun?' He had a bored, patient expression. His shaved head and beard made his deeper emotions impenetrable.

Keeling over, Otto saw his own face in the smooth polished floor. It was like diving into his reflection. At fifty-three, he'd already lived long enough to be present at the burial of his own reputation.

How would posterity judge him? Good? Bad? No, worse. It wouldn't even bother.

28

5.58 pm: 'Oh, it's Joan,' Vera said, as if the scene had not taken an even more unpleasant turn. 'You're supposed to be cleaning the church. You promised.'

Jenny snorted at the mere idea of the value of her sister's promises. In their family it was a good idea to make a promise. But it was usually not good practice to keep one.

Joan said, 'It was… closed.'

'Ah,' Vera said. The unquestioning way she sided with ignorance over truth, simply because it was easier, was infuriating. She'd always appreciated Joan's skill for reshaping life's events to make them 'suitable'. Similarly, Vera did not appreciate Jenny's disparagement of this skill by pointing out that it was actually called 'lying'.

With Hugh originally anointed as the golden child, Joan had spent the first half of her life in the wings of their mother's life: discreet, patient and loyal. Jealous and protective. Jenny had never been close to her sister. The most vivid childhood memory Jenny had of them together was of Joan standing over her bed when she'd been very sick with glandular fever, saying, 'Christ, you're such a black cloud,

Jennifer.' Joan had married an unspectacular man who had quickly learned that when he pleased his mother-in-law – by lavishing attention on her – he would be rewarded: a holiday paid for in June, school fees taken care of in September, a nice new watch at Christmas. It had worked for him until Vera realised that her own life would be even more wonderful without him in it. Jenny remembered that when Joan married, there had been a sadness about her – an obvious reluctance to leave the family home, to leave Mum behind.

Jenny had not spoken to Joan much since she'd been eighteen. In the meantime, Joan had cheerfully soaked up the excess wealth that came their way from Jenny's slice of the family pie. In the last few years, she'd usually only come across her sister at things like a cousin's wedding or an uncle's funeral. Jenny still had to make an appearance at the 'big' functions, if only for an hour or so – just enough to give Vera capacity to project the family as totally normal to the outside world. It was easier to turn up rather than face the barrage of pressuring calls from her mother. At these events, Joan had completely ignored her and kept her distance but unless they were watching closely, no one would've noticed.

Staring at Jenny from across the living room, Joan pressed her Ray-Bans tighter to her face and stepped forward. 'How can you show your face here, after the way you treated me?'

'This one,' Jenny said, gesturing grandly to the walls and roof, 'is not yours – yet. I'll come here whenever I please.'

'You murdered your child. You killed it. Because you're so, so, *so*, selfish.'

Had she *really* just said that? No, she couldn't possibly have. Yet she had.

Joan continued. 'Surely you realise that you can't keep running away from this. Did you think it would all be forgotten when you first ran away from home to—'

'When you're over eighteen, Joan, "Running away from home" generally means "moving out".'

'You'll never escape what you did to your child; to our father; to all of us.'

For one futile moment Jenny waited for her mother to intervene. But of course, that didn't happen. Joan was Vera's favourite and, therefore, with Joan, even the most objectionable was always tolerable. That had always been the case in Jenny's family.

'Jesus Christ, Joan, can't you just for once shut your mouth and mind your own business? Can't you just leave it? Can't you just leave me *the fuck* alone?'

'You think that's even possible after what you did? The world may have changed in many ways over the last twenty-five years, Jennifer; but some things are sacred and will never be acceptable and, as far as I'm aware, Hallmark aren't making cards for abortions yet. What sickens me is that all of this is just because you couldn't keep your legs together, you tramp.'

'Wow… so, you're slut-shaming now?'

'Slut-shaming? Well, that *is* what happens when sluts get shamed, isn't it?'

Vera snapped, 'Joan, stop that now.' It was a conversation-ender.

Joan removed her shades and glared at her mother; mouth open as if she'd just been slapped. But the inescapable fact was that she *had* stopped, and now stood there like a blinking cursor awaiting direction.

Vera continued to glare at Joan, and Jenny watched them both. Speaking the truth was usually against the rules. Speaking the truth usually got you punished. Therefore, it was a pivotal moment in their family history – three Donaldsons in a room, getting ready to undress their lies.

After a few seconds, Joan and Vera refocused their attention on Jenny and Jenny experienced an old – yet familiar – sensation: the absolute nausea of feeling her mother's and sister's eyes bore into her as they over-analysed every flicker on her expression, every word that came out of her mouth.

There had always been something unpleasant about the way Vera and Joan conducted themselves. When a teenager, Jenny would sit in this room and turn the TV up to drown out the sound of her mother and Joan laughing in the kitchen – no doubt at someone else's expense. All day, they would gossip away like bitchy soap opera vamps. One of Vera's favourite sayings was that the nice thing about gossip was that it doesn't really matter whether or not it is true.

Jenny said, 'Mum, tell her to get out and leave us alone.'

'No.'

'*No*?'

'I can't control what my daughters say and do. And I won't be made to choose between my daughters, either.'

'I think you already have.'

'I don't know what you're talking about.' Vera spoke slowly, which was a giveaway flagging her insincerity. Her regional accent came to the fore too, stomping all over her usual melodic southside Dublin enunciation. It showed that she was trying too hard. 'Jennifer, you're acting like a baby. Are you trying to get even with Joan or something? Is that it? Is that why you've decided that you're being picked on? Are you jealous, Jennifer? Is that it? There is nothing to be jealous about. We can all be together in one room, surely?'

Vera smiled sweetly. That was the indignity of what her mother inflicted; her *modus operandi* was to deliver a loaded sentence that communicated so much bile and hate and then, seconds later, to wash her hands of it, so that however she may have changed that person's life, she remained unchanged herself.

Jenny said, 'After what she just said to me. In front of you. In *your* house?' Even as Jenny spoke, she knew it was pointless to challenge her mother. What did she expect? Sympathy? Vera loathed pity. She would rather flay another person alive than pity them.

'As I said, I can't control what my daughters say or do.'

Calmly, Joan said, 'I have never understood the meaning of "off your meds" until this very moment. See, Mom? That's what she was like earlier. I told you. That's what she's like every time we have words.'

We have words. For most people, words were the nails that hammered down reality. But not for her mother and Joan. Already everything Jenny had said – or would say – had been dampened down with a harmless catch-all cliché. That was Jenny's family. Avoid the truth, avoid the harsh realities and blame anything else – even God or nature. But never blame nurture, because that would mean it could be Vera's fault – and Vera was *never* wrong.

Jenny said, 'Mum, I just can't take this anymore. I have Shane and… he's always been there for me. So please, leave me alone.'

Her mother's eyes widened a little. She was judging her, weighing up her daughter's mood, analysing the tone of her voice, seeing how seriously she should take the directive. Vera approached; fists balled by her side. There was a barely audible intake of air, as if she wasn't going to give away anything that she didn't have to, not even her breath. Especially not her breath.

With a voice that had the authority of an artillery battery, she said,

'You were just damaged goods selling fancy goods – and that fool was buying. *That's* who your husband is. And that – *pet* – is who you are.'

Her hardness was chilling. Yet Jenny was not totally surprised. Vera's behaviour was actually quite predictable. Usually, she was all sweetness and light until something eventually snapped and then Jenny was made to pay for all the things that Vera had not been honest about.

Jenny's eyes watered. She hated the way her mother could be mean and cold and right all at once.

No. She's doing it again. That's not how things are. You are better than this.

Jenny reminded herself that she had regretted every return visit she'd made to her childhood home, and each time had admonished herself for ever daring to think that it would be different.

Jenny crossed the living room, her expression neutral, pretending that her thoughts were already elsewhere though they were really sifting through the depths of her guilt from which she could find no way of liberating herself. She felt weighed down, as if moving in zero gravity, like she contained all the anxiety that her mother and Joan were not showing.

Vera said, 'Where are you going? I just said what needed to be said.'

As always.

'I am so sorry if the truth hurt you,' she called out in a sincere, high-pitched tone that mocked the very thing it strove to be.

Jenny turned the handle of the door.

'No. Don't go. Wait!' Vera sounded urgent. Genuinely urgent. And yet… Vera never sounded urgent.

Something was off. Jenny sensed her mother's repressed anxiety like sonar.

What's coming? A splinter of the future leaked into the present.

Jenny soaked up Vera's alert face, which was now reddening with the blood that still had a reason to circulate, even if the body it pumped through had aged more rapidly than she wanted.

Vera said, 'You don't understand what's happening. You have no idea what's going on. I never had the chance to—'

'And you never will.'

Jenny's face blanked over as if her past was an overgrown graveyard she never visited anymore. Stepping out into the hall, she opened the front door and slammed it behind her.

She walked slowly along the driveway, her full-of-thinking head down.

Someone was behind her.

She glanced back. Joan. Ten feet. Five feet. It would take about twenty seconds to reach the front gates. Once there, Joan would leave her alone. No matter how extreme things got, the world must only ever see the family smile.

Joan was beside her now. Jenny kept her eyes on the gates. How long would it take her to walk those twenty-five metres? A few short seconds or half a lifetime?

At her uncle's funeral a year ago, she'd listened to Joan make an emotional speech about an extended family holiday they'd all gone on to Egypt. 'Those weeks in Egypt,' Joan said, 'were the happiest times for all of us Donaldsons.' That had made Jenny resentful because she could hardly remember Egypt, except that it was quite boring and dusty. It had made her realise that she had absolutely nothing left in common with Joan – they didn't even share the same memories.

Joan kept pace, arms folded, her head turned towards her sister's, smirking. 'You are an idiot,' she said. 'Hear me? You are a *fucking* idiot.'

'Go away.'

Joan did not go away. Instead, she mimicked Jenny in a high-pitched squeal – '*Go away. Go away. Go away*. Jesus, you are a child.'

Jenny kept walking. Joan careered into her, shouldering her.

'What the…?' Jenny said – not slowing, but feeling a lump in her throat as she still had a child's impulse to cry when wrong was done to her by her big sister. 'Do not touch me. Ever.'

'*Don't touch me. Don't touch me*,' Joan caricatured, while making sure her shoulder continued to force down against her quarry.

At the gate, Jenny faced her middle-aged tormentor. 'Know something, Joan? Just for once, I want us to relate to each other without Mum coming between us.'

'*What*?'

'No pretending. No script. Just ourselves. Is that possible? Do you think so?'

Joan smirked. 'You torched your family. You burnt it like every other bridge you've ever crossed. And just so you know, so there can be never ever any doubt about it, let me reiterate – I *haaaaate* you. In fact, it makes me so happy that you're being thrown out of Clareville. Not because I want it. I don't. But simply because I don't want you to have it.'

Jenny soaked up the enraged face, shades raised onto her head, eyes like her own but wide with frustrated fury. It was a visage that said, suffering does not make you a nice person. In fact, it makes you a bad one.

Suddenly, just for a moment, Jenny felt as if she should help Joan. That it wasn't too late for her sister to turn her life around – not too late for her to actually *have* a life. It must be awful to be Joan. People always abandoned her in the end. Maybe she expected it to happen and therefore always made it happen.

But whatever was wrong with Joan, Jenny hadn't caused it and she couldn't cure it. *So, fuck her.*

'Enjoy your revenge, Joan – I hope it soothes your envy.'

Jenny looked away as if Joan wasn't even worth loathing and let the gate swing closed behind her. As she walked away, Jenny touched her forehead as a headache suddenly bubbled up from her core. It was as if she'd been walking away from Joan her whole life, trying to escape the biological imperative that they would spar, that they would thwart and provoke.

When did it all go to hell? When Dad died? No, before that. When I went away for my abortion? No, before that, too. When Hugh went to London? Yes, that's when it all went to hell.

29

Twenty-Four Years Ago

Before Joan, Hugh had been Vera's golden child. Vera had groomed him from the day he was born to think that he was magnificent – even though he'd never wanted to 'be' anything, except on Halloween. Of course, she'd smothered him in the blanket of her own neurosis. From the moment he was old enough to go out by himself, Vera had found herself obsessing about his safety. She'd needed to know where he was twenty-four-seven. When she gave him a time to be home, he *had* to make it. If he didn't, then he wasn't allowed out the next day.

When Hugh was only average at school, Vera explained to him that his talents were still hidden and would emerge at college. To be fair, he eventually got the grades for the best university in Dublin, with grinds, grinds and more grinds. But that was Hugh – always better on paper. However, once exposed to a university life where having an ordinary, mid-level IQ was akin to being mentally retarded, the reality of being ordinary had crushed him.

Most children gradually learn that their parents are unreliable from two big, universal lies: Santa Claus and sex. But Vera had a third lie. She lied to Hugh about his greatness.

By his early twenties, the only times Jenny saw Hugh was when he'd come home drunk from their father's firm. He wasn't rowdy or loud. Hugh was turning into the kind of harmless functioning alcoholic that perhaps fumbles with their door keys when getting in every night. He would sit in the kitchen and actually try to talk to her. However, Hugh didn't really understand the ebb and flow of conversation, and so instead he pontificated.

Over these odd kitchen meetings, out it all came – how he hated gay people; how he blamed the poverty of immigrants on innate weakness and most of all, how he hated slutty women. Jenny was only sixteen when these chats began, but by the time she was seventeen she realised that every word he'd said to her while drunk had been repulsive; that her brother was, in fact, a monster disguised by a mask of blandness.

Hugh was drinking in his twenties because he had realised that, under it all, he had become an equal opportunist disappointment – to his rugby mates, to his work colleagues, to the girlfriends who made fleeting appearances to be judged by Vera. Hugh's technique was to forge a bond, create a sense of expectation and then, ultimately, totally fail to deliver. When he was justly criticised, he reacted with the same insolence that he used to face every obstacle in his mollycoddled life. He would walk away, as if nothing had ever happened.

Back then, Shane had said to Jenny, 'Hugh is the type of lucky, over-privileged wanker who was able to choose exactly what they wanted to be the moment they hit twelve – and yet he's still doing nothing with his life.' Lorcan, too, noticed his son's lack of progress. Hugh had been given everything Lorcan himself had never received – a loving household, security, access to money and a top education.

And so, despite Vera's protestations, Lorcan forced Hugh to move to London, where he was shoehorned into the boardroom of the UK wing of the company.

Hugh did not flourish in London. From the moment he arrived, he began to rot from the inside, eaten up by the bitterness of being mediocre. One of his problems was that Hugh only ever trusted people who wanted things from him, and in London no one wanted anything from him. For the first time in his life, he was truly alone.

Twelve weeks after his arrival, Hugh's cleaner found him hanging from the hook on his bedroom door, having failed at the one true duty of all living things – endurance. Hugh's eyes, which had once been full of confidence and choice, had ended up – at twenty-three – bulging from their sockets, dimmed. His death mask communicated his final realisation – that there was not always a way out of the darkness; that most people fall, eventually, without a net.

Typically, he left no note.

His death had been a surprise to Jenny. But not a shock. You had to care for it to be a shock. Hugh had no longer been her brother in any sense besides blood. She did feel sorry for him, though. How horrible it must have been to die like that, toes stretched down, a carpet centimetres out of reach that would take his weight, just for a moment, and let the rope slacken to allow air down his throat. As he struggled, the tighter the rope would have pulled.

Jenny reckoned she knew why he'd done it. It was the stark realisation that his father had always wanted a son – just not *him* for a son.

The family travelled to London when his body was discovered. Jenny's parents couldn't bring themselves to visit his apartment, but Joan and Jenny did. They found a mini shrine by his bedside comprising a framed picture of his mother, the gold miraculous medal she'd gifted him for his twenty-first and a box holding at least a dozen handwritten letters from Vera, each one nine or ten pages long. Flicking through them, it was evident that they were meandering missives declaring how much she missed Hugh and that she thought of him every minute of the day. Jenny had been stunned at the depth and focus of her mother's adoration. Vera had never spoken to *her* in the tone of those letters. Postcards were all she'd ever got.

After the funeral, Vera retreated for two months to a private 'institution' to recover. When she emerged, Vera examined the two remaining daughters on the family shelf, snatched down Joan and anointed her the new golden child – as if there had ever been a choice.

After her brother's death, Jenny returned to college and her great romance with Shane. But by the end of that first year, everything had changed utterly. She was pregnant. Jenny couldn't tell Shane. He would want the baby, he would be happy, he would stick by her, he would do all the right things – which, for Jenny and her vision of the future, happened to be all the wrong things. She certainly couldn't tell her parents. They would insist that she give up the rest of her life to mind it. As for Joan – her reaction would be just an intense bitch-fest over her immorality. For her sister, sex was a flame that belonged in a sacred fire grate, because if it got out of control it would burn the house down.

The day before her flight to London for the abortion, her mother and Joan were waiting in the living room. They knew. Joan had read the scribbled notes on her desk. Joan had dialled the number underlined in black ink. Joan had figured it all out and told Vera.

In the living room there was shouting and insults – all from Joan. Vera had simply cried before finally saying, 'If you kill your child, you are finished with this family. I will be finished with you. Your father will be finished with you. When he gets back to Dublin… I don't know what he'll do.'

By that stage, the eighteen-year-old Jenny felt so entombed, so fretful, that her dismissal from the family seemed a godsend. Locking herself in her room, she wrote two letters. The first, to Shane, was posted that day. The second was to her mother, warning that if she or Joan told Shane about her pregnancy, then she would ensure that the whole world knew of this messy business – the whole world being Vera's church congregation, Vera's deeply conservative relatives and Vera's prissy social circle. The next day, she flew to London to terminate her pregnancy and somehow begin a new life.

After going to London to have her abortion, Jenny moved to Canada. Over the next year, no one told her that her father's bad back hadn't healed after an operation. Or that his prostate hadn't decalcified after taking all the meds. Or that his gut and thyroid were mortally worse despite constant monitoring.

With Jenny exiled from Ireland, Lorcan and everyone who knew him resigned themselves to the fact that he would have an unfinished life. He suffered a massive heart attack a year into her stay in Toronto. Joan informed Jenny via a perfunctory message left on her condo's answering machine. He was still alive, but in a critical condition.

Jenny flew home and, not knowing which hospital he was in, and with no one answering her messages, went straight to the family home. Her mother brought her in, welcoming and pleasant, her lack of make-up and dark eyes the only signs of the forty-eight hours of crisis she'd endured.

In the living room, they both faced Lorcan's empty chair as if he was still in it. Vera said, 'Your father isn't with us anymore,' making it sound like he was simply elsewhere and, therefore, might soon be coming back. After telling Jenny that she'd missed his passing by five hours, Vera calmly said, 'I suppose, since you did what you did, he'd been rotting from within for quite a while. But a heart attack had the honours in the end.'

'I'm sorry, Mum.'

'It's not enough. But you can ask the Monsignor at the funeral about forgiveness. He's a man. One expects less from them.'

Jenny cried while her mother sat opposite in her father's chair. When she finally stopped, Vera said, 'Of course, it's totally understandable that you won't be travelling to the funeral in the family limousine with the rest of us. That's OK,' as if it was Jenny, rather than Joan, who had decreed that fact. 'But I insist that you sit in the front pew with me and your sister. Is that understood, Jennifer?'

Jenny agreed and felt that perhaps with this momentous occurrence – the death of a parent –her father's end could somehow magic a new beginning for them all. How wrong she was. Her father's death, instead, signified the moment that her family's world, once and for all, fell out of love with love, when they all stopped even pretending to care.

Jenny hoped that Shane would *not* be at the funeral. How could she face him after abandoning him, with no explanation but a brief letter, telling him that she was dropping out to travel? But when he didn't show up, his absence was a new, acute wound.

After the burial, Jenny returned to Toronto. For months, she cried a lot without realising that she was doing it. It was like having a scratch on her face that would bleed with no warning. It was her body expelling grief without her knowledge. Her whole body stung with it. It wrecked her appetite, her menstrual cycle, her sleep, her skin.

After a few more months in Toronto, Jenny had had enough and moved back to Dublin. Short of funds, lacking qualifications, having no family support and with her old friends having moved on, Jenny found a job as a shop assistant selling first perfume and then cosmetics. By the time she was twenty-two she was also working weekends in bars. When she was twenty-five, she was managing a shop during the day and, on Thursdays, Fridays and Saturdays, worked as a greeter in a members-only nightclub. From there, Jenny would post pictures to her blog of herself with movie and rock stars. A Dublin tabloid or an Irish women's magazine would often purchase the photos for their social pages. She did this not simply for the attention, or to supplement her income, but also because Joan would inevitably show the pictures to her mother, and her mother would feel excluded, jealous and resentful – all those things that a normal mother was never meant to feel. There was drama and excitement around famous people. It would also have the effect of luring Vera into keeping in touch.

It had all been exhausting as Jenny was also, on her free evenings, studying for a degree in interior design because, in the future, she fully intended to justify her position as her father's favourite. And she knew exactly why she had been Lorcan's preferred child. It was because, unlike his only son and his eldest daughter, Jenny had never been reality challenged. She'd always understood that life was simply a game of snakes and ladders. It consisted of unjust advantages and catastrophic falls. And as with any game that depended on pure luck, the only way to be absolutely sure of winning, was to cheat.

30

Now

6.25 pm: Otto seemed totally relaxed, settled and still like a rock at the bottom of a pond. The top few buttons of his shirt had been ripped free and his body was stretched to such a degree that his chest muscles looked like the exoskeleton of an insect. Blood was smeared beneath his nose, while his lips drooped – making him appear harmless and badger-faced. He had pissed himself. The lap lake spread.

His bearded persecutor towered above, staring down, half bored, half interested, as if he was gazing into a colourful fish tank. He had eyes that had seen everything; everything that humans can do to each other to elicit pleasure and pain. The eyes were deep brown and seemed to flicker as they processed thoughts and emotions. Otto felt as if he could read them. Dismiss, disdain, dismay – all the 'dis' words.

The man finally spoke, his voice resonant and husky. 'You don't know why, do you?'

Otto concentrated, and wondered what he'd done to deserve this. It was almost as if he recognised something in the bearded face of his oppressor, and felt that he *should* know exactly why he deserved this – but the answer was just out of reach.

Otto thought of his favourite summer, the happiest time in his life. He was twelve and on holiday with his parents in Holland. Otto remembered his favourite cycle, down country pathways that were shortcuts between Berkhout and Avenhorn and then a flat empty road all the way to North Beemster where he had a secret meadow, where sheep would stare at him like members of a firing squad while he lay beneath the slow twirling paddle blades of a Bosman windmill.

The man said, 'You want to know who I am and why I'm here.' He picked up Otto's phone from the bedside table.

Otto was sobbing. At what exactly, he didn't know. Otto wished that he had the strength to roll over and crawl beneath the table, like a dying cat shunning daylight in preparation for perpetual darkness. He tried with all his might to focus on the reddening sky outside his window. Only those who loved him would help him now – and no one loved him.

The man rubbed his beard and said, 'I thought you'd know by now. But it's too late. That's disappointing.'

Otto closed his eyes. Life was very easy to give up on. It was strange how much fuss he'd made about it for fifty-three years. Soon, someone will knock on the front door. Then the banging will begin, when it doesn't open. Then the shouting. And then – finally – the screaming.

31

6.30 pm: As Jenny left her childhood road, she sank into a depression so deep it was tranquilising. A corpse-pale light had already begun to seep into the air as the sun disappeared behind the city buildings. The day's end was approaching.

Across the street, the low wall demarcated the lush green of the small city park behind it. Shane and Jenny had spent many afternoons there. In winter, it would be speckled with people the world didn't want: the elderly, the unemployed, the sick, anyone who didn't make money. But now, in the full glory of summer, the lovers had all returned and Jenny scanned the men in case one of them had a beard and shaved head.

As Jenny approached Clareville, thoughts were gnawing at her; the types of thoughts she'd managed to banish from her conscience for decades. Shane would've been a great father. He would have been the best of fathers.

She'd taken that away from him.

What was it she'd said to Otto, earlier that day? 'Do you think I ever gave one moment's thought as to whether I was right for Shane? Of course not. He was right for me. The end.'

It's OK. It's OK. It's OK. She could handle this. When facing the loss of everything, she realised that the only real thing that mattered was Shane. She couldn't – mustn't – lose him. It wasn't over yet. Fine, she was losing the house. But there were positives, too. She no longer needed to have any ties with her toxic family. She could finally cut them off. Totally. Forever. Just like Shane had always wanted. Just like she should've done twenty-four years ago, when they tried to stop her abortion. With her family conclusively out of her life, her secret would remain safe. Therefore, Shane would never know, and he would not leave her, and they would live happily ever after. *Yes, it's all good.*

Yet, no matter how hard she tried to spin them, things just wouldn't sit right for her. She looked up beyond the rooftops. Like a current, the rouge of evening spilled across the sky, and she thought of the bearded man's promise: '*By sunset today, I will have destroyed everything you hold precious. I'm taking all that's good in your life and I'm wrecking it.*' For the first time in her life, Jenny felt the icy reality that everything might *not* be alright in the end.

'Who the hell are you?' she muttered. 'And what do you want from me?'

As if somebody had just flicked on a light switch, Venus appeared low on the western skyline. Jenny slowed as she approached the gate to her house. How wonderful it would be to return to Clareville, open the front door and hear nothing but the tap-tap-tapping of Shane's fingers on the keyboard as he continued hammering words onto the page like vermin flattened to country roads.

Would anything be normal again?

Opening the gate, she gazed up at the house's façade. *What is Mum doing with Clareville? She doesn't need the money. And if she was giving it to Joan or her children, then she would've told me. Mum doesn't do delayed gratification.*

Jenny entered the hall and froze. Shane was sitting on the bottom step of the stairs.

'You're back,' he said, rising.

'Yes. Did you see Otto? Is it sorted?'

'No and no. He wasn't there. But I've called and left messages.'

'Good.'

There was a measured silence and then Shane said, 'Good?'

'Good that you're sorting it.' Fearing that silence would smother them again, Jenny blustered, 'I'm sorry. Really sorry. About everything you said earlier… you're right.' She tried to ignore the wretched truth that, like most confessions, hers was blatantly self-serving.

Shane opened the study door and gestured for her to enter. 'Where were you?'

'Mum's.'

He followed her inside. 'Oh God. Why?'

'Just wanted to make it clear that no matter how urgent the message, Mum was to put her faith in phones or pop in herself, and not send Joan around. It went fine. No drama.'

Shane looked at the wine stains on his bookcase. 'Joan is pathetic.'

Jenny thought of her sister's penthouse apartment, the holidays with her kids, even the groceries – all paid for by Vera. 'Joan's not as pathetic as people think.'

'Let's not get carried away here.'

Just like that, the sun came out on her face again. She laughed and it was as fake as his smile. But it felt like the ice was melting.

He asked, 'Are you happy?'

Yes. No. Yes. No. She hated how vulnerable that question made her feel. 'I am.'

'But do *I* make you happy?'

Her eyes widened. 'Yes. Of course.'

'It's just that you seem… off. Like, I know you've stuff on your mind like the money and getting kicked out of the house soon but… something else. Was the launch OK?'

'It was fine. Good, even. It's nothing. Just tired. It's been a crazy day. And I hate us fighting. Shane, I know you're angry with me. I understand that. But—'

'I'm not angry. Forget it.' He took out his phone. 'Hold on – a message.' Shane looked at her. She couldn't read his expression. He said, 'It's Otto. *Finally*, he texts back.' Then, reluctantly, he read out the message:

Shane, come to my house now. I'll sort it all out in person. Don't call me. Won't be answering. Long story. But it'll make sense when you're here. Text me when you're on your way.

32

6.44 pm: Jenny said, 'That's all a bit secret agent-ty. Even for Otto.'

'The nerve of that guy. After everything that's happened… after everything that *is* happening… then coming into my home earlier today, all smiles and giving me flowers, all the while lying to my face… I'd use a blowtorch on him, and my pulse wouldn't change.'

Jenny's eyes widened. 'That's kind of extreme.'

He stage-whispered, 'That's because you're sensitive.'

'Shane, what we were talking about before Otto's text… You do forgive me? Like, properly? You, really, *really*, properly and truly, forgive me?'

'Yes. Of course I do.'

Jenny smiled and colour popped across her cheeks because she could see that Shane was telling the truth. 'Thank you.'

6.45 pm: He'd lied. Shane wasn't sure he could ever forgive her. *Can we really recover from these lies? Is it too late? Are we now too old?*

But he certainly didn't want to leave Jenny. Nietzsche had said that each man is entitled to as much truth as he can bear. Did he really need to know everything about his wife? Maybe Shane wasn't seeking the truth. Maybe he was just seeking his own limits for tolerating it. So, while Shane would never forgive her, he could *pretend* to forget. That was what you did when you managed to get from life what you'd really wanted, and intended to keep it.

Thus, instead of once again confronting his wife about her deception, what Shane really wanted to do was to tell Jenny everything about the creepy texts that he was receiving from someone who seemed to know where he was and what he was doing. He wanted to tell her that he thought the texts had come from the bearded guy hanging around outside their house earlier – a guy whom he also suspected of being the second burglar that no one but he believed existed. He especially wanted to tell her about seeing the same guy in the lobby of Otto's building that afternoon.

Shane had watched as the man plugged in his white earphones, put his rolled-up leather jacket under his arm and walked towards the exit. As Shane followed him across the concourse, he hadn't known what he was going to do. Approach him and say... what? 'I saw you walking through Clareville earlier'? The man disappeared into the revolving exit but, on the other side, there had been no sign of him on the pavement. Instead, a taxi had pulled out and executed a U-turn before speeding off towards Dublin Bay.

However, Shane knew that telling Jenny all of that would just make things worse. All it would achieve would be to worry her. Then she'd make public his fear. She'd say in the daylight the type of things that should only be thought of late at night. Shane believed that if you have something to hide, then hide it.

He felt the outline of the phone in his pocket – a phone loaded with menacing texts. It was like the weight of a lie. *I'm not dishonest. I'm just withholding.*

Anyway, maybe it was all just nothing, wrong numbers or some other perfectly reasonable explanation. Perhaps Shane was being paranoid. *You're a writer. Doubt is your life. Another day, another doubt.* All that had happened was that the man who had walked past his house that morning and looked in, had also been in the lobby of Otto's building. Maybe he worked there. Maybe he was a courier. It is not *that* big a coincidence.

Jenny scanned the study, clocking the wine stains on the floor and the dark patterned blemishes running down Shane's foreign editions.

'Sorry about the mess,' she muttered.

'It's OK, we'll just call the landlord.'

Jenny half snorted, half laughed. 'Stop it. I'm in a perilous state of mind. Making me laugh could push me over the edge and I'll never come back.' She then ran her hand through the thickness of his mane, playing with its texture. 'Look at your hair, with its speckles of grey. Surprised Joan didn't turn it white.'

Shane had to fight the instinct to recoil. *Would Jenny turn into her mother? Was she already like Vera? Was she a covert, furtive narcissist, keeping the traits secret?* Heredity was a patient spider, spinning in the shadows, often unknown even to its host. But no, Jenny could never be accused of being cruel. She was kind, non-judgemental and humane. While with Vera… even Joan would agree that her deity was an unpredictable and demanding idol, capable of hurling thunderbolts when blue skies were needed. You never oppose such a divinity; you offer everything without question.

Jenny flopped down into the two-seater. Her toes pointed inwards, and it looked as if it meant something disheartening about her. Shane perched on the armrest, admiring her smooth shoulders and clavicle. Though he'd never thought Jenny was perfect. He knew her flaws. Jenny hated confessions. She liked to be right all the time, especially when she was wrong. Again, it was her family. She'd grown up in a house where her mother ensured that everyone had to battle each other for her affections and assistance. Because of this, the law within Jenny's family was, everything, no matter how big or small, was on a need-to-know basis. So it wasn't that Jenny liked to hide things. It was just that Jenny felt that some things were better off as lonely facts.

Shane moved from the side of the sofa and crouched before his wife. His hands rested on her thighs. He felt a sudden wave of regret for her. Today's launch should have been one of the highlights of Jenny's year. But the odds were fairly high that it had ended up being one of the worst days of her life.

'You know I didn't want to hurt you, right?'

He wanted to say more. To explain. To make her realise that they would be better off without the house because it demanded too much of them. It always had. He needed her to understand that when the gods want to punish us, they grant our wishes. But before he could put it into words, Jenny spoke.

'You're a good man. And you did the right thing. I tried to do the wrong thing.'

'I'm over it. Don't worry.' *Or rather, I'm beyond it now.*

Shane had pretended to forgive Jenny before. He'd pretended to forgive her for leaving him when he was eighteen.

33

Seventeen Years Ago

In the days that followed Shane's expulsion from university, Jenny opened a distance between them, claiming that she was unwell after the exams and needed time alone. She insisted it had nothing to do with his cheating and that soon they would figure out a plan to neutralise this great shame. But at the end of the week, Shane received a handwritten letter from Jenny, telling him that she had left college and had gone away, travelling for a year, and that they – as a couple – were finished.

Shane called into her house but Vera, with a strangely subdued fury, told him, 'Jennifer is abroad and doesn't want people to know where – especially you, young man. Now, I'm not getting involved in any ridiculous lovers' tiff. So… I'm sure you understand the tricky corner I've been painted into.' With that, the door closed.

For the rest of the summer, Shane wandered through his house, ignoring his parents, disinterested in books, passing from his bedroom to the living room to the kitchen. He'd find himself standing at the upstairs window, facing the night, waiting for morning.

Over the next year, Shane worked on building sites with a roofing firm. With mainstream social media still more of an idea than a reality, the only information he could glean was whenever he came across one of her friends. All they could ever tell him was that the last they had heard, she was living in Toronto.

After almost a year on the building sites, Shane studied nights to get a TEFL certificate and, just before Lorcan died, moved to eastern Europe and later Dubai and Malaysia to teach English. Life had to go on; which it did, with several girlfriends – there was Hannah, a student in Poland; Yaz, a cellist in Dubai; and Moon, the Israeli trust-funded dropout in Penang. As the years flipped by, he assumed that Jenny had continued to travel, married someone talented and ended up doing something like owning a little shop in a beautiful warm city, selling urns to fascinating people, while a nanny looked after her spectacular children.

Then, eight years after being expelled from college, Shane returned to Dublin. Meeting up with friends, they ended up in a club that was infamous for having about ten people outside at any one time, all being denied entrance. It was the type of place you *told* people you went to.

There, he saw her: a striking twenty-five-year-old in elegant hostess regalia, holding a tray of four champagne flutes behind the velvet ropes of the VIP area. She moved among the crowd with a wistful, sedative vibe; as if she were drifting and dozing in the quicksand, like an alligator in a swamp, plotting the next drama to inflict upon the world.

Shane slipped away from his friends and ordered bottle service from a table. As she approached, he checked her out. Jenny, nipples blunt and protuberant beneath her black blouse, looked like a slinky bank teller in a dusky silk skirt that stopped just above her knees.

Wielding her beauty like an AK-47, she presented the bottle to him. Her brown eyes reminded Shane of the Shiraz and he stared into them, already hard. He immediately wanted to consume her, to take her inside of him, to eat her like the Eucharist. He wanted to protect her, to be – without her ever knowing it – her reward for falling back to earth, for abandoning her absurd idea of leaving him, for once again becoming *his* desire.

'Well,' she whispered, sounding calm but her face electrified.

'Well, well, well,' he murmured and hoped it sounded funny and not sleazy. 'Lightning strikes twice.'

Jenny looked rather sad. 'But it doesn't really, does it? Lightning *never* strikes twice.'

'Actually, it does. Some have been hit three times. There's a metal compound in blood that certain people have too much of. So, let's call it *déjà vu*.'

'It would depend on what you're about to do to me.' She laughed wickedly.

He'd always liked her laugh. It made him want to fuck every other man out of her. He couldn't even blink. She'd blossomed into an even greater beauty; the kind that age would never diminish. He could picture those angles calcifying into stone.

She said, 'Hey, you're making me self-conscious.'

'I was just thinking how little you've changed all these years.'

'Nah, Shane, I need to lay off the Pringles.' She patted her tummy, acknowledging that she had gone up a size while also showing that she didn't care. 'So, why are you here?'

'I'm back from teaching English abroad. I'm taking time out. Believe it or not, I'm about to publish a book. Investigative journalism if you please. On-the-ground gonzo-type thing, about a big news story I was part of in India. But hold on – why are *you* here?'

'I'm at work. This is what I do now. Well, one of the things.'

'But your family. And… again – your family?'

'Oh, you know the drill: rich girl manages to make a struggle out of being privileged.'

'Yeah, well I'm here to rescue you.'

'I need rescuing?'

'Someone took you away from me. Stole you away. Because there's no way on this earth that you would've left me – *us* – of your own free will. I'm here to take you back.'

'Shane… when I left at the end of college… when I wrote you that note… it was cruel and terrible. But I wasn't well. College… home life… to be honest, I think I had a breakdown. And it went on for years. That's the most I've ever said about it. Because I can't even explain it to myself. I just needed to go. I needed to go until I came back. And I've been back five years. Working in a shop during the day. Here three nights. Studying the other evenings. What's left of my family doesn't speak to me. See, I left them too. And like you, they were pissed about it. But unlike you, they don't want to talk to me. Basically, everything's been shit for about eight *looooong* years. Everything's been shit… without you.'

'Why didn't you get in touch?'

'Anytime I met someone who knew anything about you and your whereabouts, the anecdote always included some mention of your latest girlfriend. So, you were happy. Great.'

'There weren't that many. None were serious. I mean, Yaz was sort of—'

'Shane, the fact is that hearing about your girlfriends only meant that you'd forgotten about me. I wasn't gonna hurt myself by getting in touch, even though I deserved to be hurt.'

'I would've left them immediately.'

'Why didn't you… I mean, why didn't you get in touch?'

'I tried to.' His voice rose a little, as he felt the injustice of being labelled a deserter when he'd actually fought to the bitter end. Sipping wine to compose himself, he explained. 'I tried at the start, but you weren't answering. Then, I was on the other side of the planet most of the time… and, well you know there were others. I had to face up to the fact that you were done with me and if I was to have any hope of moving on… of finding happiness… then, I needed to stop looking for you. In other words, I decided, eventually, that I didn't *want* to know about you. So, I stopped asking. I stopped looking. I mean, are you online now or anything like that?'

'Yes! I'm a blogger. For this shit.' Jenny nodded over at the VIP enclosure where he vaguely recognised a touring rapper and her clique, their faces bright with ecstasy-wonder as they lay about the sofas, trying to prove that they didn't notice all those people outside the ropes noticing them. 'Ten thousand followers, if you're counting. And I am.'

'Jesus. I had no idea.'

'Well, it's nothing really. I take a selfie with whatever celebs are here – they all agree because they love being famous. It means that they exist. I stick 'em up and wait for my loyal editors to buy them from me. And then companies give me stuff – clothes and tech – and if I like them, I plug them. Though, they're free, so I always like them. That's it. But I've plans. I'm getting a degree in interior design and… well, you'll never guess who's helping me set up my business?'

'Who?'

She paused. 'Actually, I'll tell you later.'

'There's going to be a later?'

'Shane, I feel as if I was just driving by and out of the corner of my eye I saw you and thought, *Oh my God, that's Shane Smith*, and then here we are, me giving you a lift and you making small talk about how I haven't changed – but I have – and me pretending not to be flattered – but I am – and then you say "thanks" for the lift and I say "bye".'

'We're never dull, so that's *not* how it's going to happen.' Shane leaned across the table. 'So, tell me, how *is it* going to happen?'

'You're going to tell me that you're single and free and no one in the last eight years came close to what we had. And I'm going to tell you the same. Then I'm going to get my coat and leave early. And we're going to go back to my flat. And you're going to make me come. And then you're going to make me come again. Then you can come. And then we'll fall asleep, and I'll have the best night's rest I've had in eight years, and in the morning you'll still be there, and I won't be afraid. The fact is, I like to daydream and, in my daydreams, my fantasies – well, you've always been in them.'

'I never forgot you, Jen, even when I tried. Not for one day. I always had hope. And when all is lost but hope – then, suddenly, all is saved.'

For eight years Shane had tried to convince himself that 'love' was a short word because it was a meaningless word – a rubbish word. But then he ended up finding Jenny in a swanky nightclub, and there were suddenly no other words.

34

Now

6.47 pm: It had been seventeen years since Shane had found her serving celebrities in that nightclub; seventeen years they'd been back together. Seventeen years a supposed team. As he crouched before her on the floor of his study, Jenny sat forward on the sofa, placed her hand on the back of his head and pulled his face to hers.

'Jesus,' Shane said in mock surprise. 'Are you trying to flirt with me?'

Their mouths locked. A moment later, Jenny pulled back.

'Wait,' she said.

'What?'

'Do you need me?'

'I need to fuck you. So… yeah?'

Her face clouded. 'Lovely.'

'What? That's the highest compliment I could pay anyone. What do you expect from me – some chick bullshit about emotions and feelings?'

She suddenly laughed, demonstrating how she still had the ability to switch from gravity to joy with just the twitch of her lips. Jenny's mirth set Shane off, and he felt like a teenager who had just been dared to lock himself in a closet with a girl. They slipped off the sofa onto the floor where Jenny straddled him, one leg pulled free of her trousers. He wrapped his hands around her and tested the elasticity of her underwear's waistband as Jenny's fingers slipped between the buttons of his shirt to touch the smooth-stone hardness of his ribs. Her thighs were soft and warm, and Shane experienced the buzz of knowing that you're only midway through an excellent movie and there was much more to come. Pulling up his shirt, she kissed his stomach, following a gun-powder trail of dark hair leading down.

Shane whispered, 'Here? On the floor. With the curtains open? You sure?'

She unbuttoned her blouse and took it off. 'Do I look like I don't know what I'm doing?'

Flipping her over, so that she lay under him, Jenny was presented to Shane as if she were a platter of food; diminutive pale breasts with shell-pink prominent nipples, the perfect little crease between buttocks and thighs. He reclaimed her by exploring her, measuring her, sampling her. They kissed and Shane wanted to be eighteen again. Or twenty-six, when they'd reunited and married. Or just to sense how he'd felt up to three days ago, before the crash. It was like he was next to a wormhole where his youth, his mistakes and his triumphs all glistered before him, just out of reach. It was as if Jenny could be the vessel to bring him back to the time when he believed that he was the man most likely to change the entire fucking world.

Jenny whispered, 'C'mon, let's do it.'

She had always called sex 'doing it'. When they were young, it sounded a little repressed. But ever since they'd married, he liked it a lot. Now he wanted to fuck her to death. He wanted his cock to touch her heart. He wanted to fuck her, fuck her, fuck her forever. And when he came, he nearly had a whiteout from the surge of pleasure.

7.25 pm: Shane lay on the ground, panting, recognising a sacred truth that only men of a certain age can receive from an unblushing woman; that life is of the flesh and if there was nothing more to it than that, then sometimes it was enough; enough to make it worthwhile to get up in the morning and struggle on and on and on.

'You OK?' Jenny asked, standing above him, fixing her hair.

'If God comes to me on my deathbed and says, where would you like to go back to – I would say, this moment.'

'It would be perfect if this peace and calm could last forever.'

'It will,' Shane said. *No. It won't.*

Shane knew that there would never be harmony as long as Vera and Joan were entangled in their lives. The problem with Jenny's family was that their personalities had never evolved. They were the exact same people they had been ten, seventeen, twenty-five years ago. Marriage, having children, separation/widowhood, the death of a brother/son – none of these things changed them. They basically lived their lives as if on a train that goes round and round on circular tracks… and from that train, they occasionally flung cluster bombs into the quiet, peaceful living rooms of those whose lives they touched. Yet, they themselves were never marked by the indignities they caused. Instead, they had the delicious dramas that their cluster bombs created, to gleefully scrutinise in Vera's kitchen over vodka and wine.

Jenny helped Shane pull up his trousers and then she fixed his collar. It was a thing of hers – to always dress him after daytime sex. But for the first time it made him feel old, as if he needed a helping hand, as if from here on in, life would be a worsening struggle.

She said, 'Oh yeah, Otto – what you gonna do?'

Shane muttered, 'Forgot about him.'

'Look, whatever Otto is, he isn't a bullshit artist. He doesn't play games. He said it'll make sense when he sees you so… it'll make sense.'

'Well, I want this sorted. So… I better go.'

35

7.40 pm: In the kitchen, Jenny poured two glasses of wine and buttered a cracker. With hands full of Shiraz, her laptop tucked under her arm, and a buttered cracker between her teeth, she turned the lights off with her nose. Climbing the stairs, she heard the spraying water. Shane was taking a shower before heading out to Otto; his lingering was probably a power-play.

She opened the en suite's door, swallowed the rest of the cracker and called out, 'Your wine's on the sink. Decided on a title yet?'

'Major feels for *Bad People from Good Homes*.'

'I like it.'

'My phone's out there. Will you text Otto? Pretend you're me. Tell him I've left and am on my way. Precisely that. Cold and impersonal. And be sure to spell his name with a small o, please.'

'Sure.' Shutting the door, she kicked off her shoes, sat on the side of the bed and, gulping a mouthful of Shiraz, texted Otto on Shane's phone. The restored antique brass iron bed was the only piece of valuable furniture in the house that had not been owned by her father. All her jewels, letters and 'things' were stored here in the bedroom.

It was her private vault. This was where she read, relaxed into a face mask and had sex.

Opening the laptop, Jenny groaned; there were so many clients to get back to. The bottom corner of the screen said it was already 7.45 pm. Focusing on the most important email, she began typing at bunny rabbit speed, but changed her mind and flopped back onto the bed, her head falling onto the pillow. Looking at the ceiling, she wondered how many chins she had, how much her roots were showing, how dark her under eyes looked, because none of it mattered. She'd just been fucked. Jenny took her sex life seriously. It was important, like an ongoing rating system for her marriage.

Screwing on the floor, it had been reminiscent of life in her flat. She thought of the night she'd brought Shane back from the club when they'd reunited. They'd still been so young. It hadn't mattered that the paint on the walls had been like a skin disease, that the stench of stale tobacco remained from the previous inhabitants, or that the windows were layered with grime – they had made it the most consecrated sanctuary in the world.

Stretching on the bed, Jenny relaxed for the first time that day. It felt so good to be putting it all behind her. It was over now. Her family was out of her life. The secret of her abortion would disappear back into the past with them. The price to pay was this house. It was worth it. It had to be. But she still deeply regretted losing the opportunity of Otto's investment. She imagined a brick of hundred-euro bills. She imagined five, six, ten of them. *Stop it. No regrets. You've got off easy.* Looking across to the free-standing mirror, it was like seeing someone else. Not younger. But someone more awake.

Her phone rang.

The odds were high that it was a client or, since the launch and her media exposure over the weekend, a potentially big contract. Or could it be Vera? Taking the phone out of her trouser pocket, she looked at the screen. **Unknown**.

Don't answer.

She answered.

'Hi, Jenny.'

'Erm, hi? Who's this?'

A deep cloudy voice said, 'Three is the magic number, Jenny. We see it all the time out there in our culture, in our society. You know, instinctively, it's important. It equates to some form of truth in our subconscious. It's divine. Jesus rose on the third day. The Holy Trinity. Third time lucky. For you, Jenny, it's three strikes and you're out.'

Jenny whispered, 'Oh, no…' as the bearded stranger's face filled her brain.

'Strike one was when we met this morning. I trust I ruined your big day? The photograph I've just sent you is strike two. Your husband should enjoy it, too. After I send it to him, you can kiss your marriage goodbye. Strike three – the big one – will come by nightfall.'

'What photograph? What are you on about? How did you get my number?'

'Remember what I told you; by the time the sun is gone… let's call it 9.00 pm – as in ninety minutes from now – I will have destroyed *everything* you hold precious. I'm taking all that's good in your life and I'm wrecking it.'

'Fuck you,' Jenny hissed into the narrow slice of plastic and metal in her fist. 'Fuck you to hell, you fucking arsehole. It must feel good to play with someone, right? Because it only takes people, what? a few seconds to realise that you're one of those losers who were always fucked around with when growing up and are out for revenge ever since.'

'Finished?'

'So, I'm the scapegoat? I'm the convenient one. You think I'm rich, so therefore I can't possibly be innocent, and you can therefore randomly try and destroy my life without guilt.'

'Randomly?' He laughed. 'You still have no idea.'

'You want to make me pay for all those people who squashed you again and again in life because we're all interchangeable. Right?'

'Stop thinking, Jenny. You can't work this. You can't figure a way out. Nothing will make it better. There's nothing you can give me or do for me that'll make me go away. I'm like your mother. I'm like your sister. Vera. Joan. See – I know everything.'

His laughter ricocheted down the line like machine-gun fire. The sound was triumphant. It was the last laugh. He hung up.

The sound of water hissing from the en suite stopped. She opened the photograph that he had texted. Immediately, the colour drained from her vision as her eyes widened like a woman who had just woken from her worst nightmare to realise that it was all true after all.

The picture. That picture. She remembered it being taken.

As she stared down to what had been revealed, she actually stopped breathing. It was as if the harder she looked the more likely the image would disintegrate into something innocuous. The picture was of her world falling apart. How nice it would be to have religion. How she could do with her family's high of believing what you cannot explain, knowing without understanding; without even having to *try* and understand. Jenny could then promise Him something in return for making the picture disappear – because her family's god never stopped bargaining, making deals. But for Jenny, there was no god. This picture proved it.

Jenny put the phone back in her pocket. It was over. Her marriage. Her future. She had not thought it was possible to feel worse than she had after leaving Vera's. Yet here she was. There were always lower circles in hell.

How did the bearded man get the picture? Something unbelievable began to suggest itself. The guy at the launch was not some sick stranger arbitrarily picking a woman to harass. *This is all part of a plan. That was all meant to happen. How else could he have known of the picture's existence? How and where did he find it? How would he have known its relevance? How could he know how dangerous it was? How could he know what it represents?*

Her stomach was so full of knots and tension, it felt like cramp. An even more frightening thought occurred; why was this happening today? She recalled her mother trying to tell her something. Could it all be connected? It was as if the bearded man was in everyone's shadow. Was it merely a coincidence that everything that could go wrong had gone wrong in the same twelve hours? *No. It's a funny old world – but not that funny.*

Jenny had never before been in such a perilous position. Everything was out of control because everything was being controlled by out-of-control people. Could her family really have something to do with all of this? *They're not the fucking mafia.* But she also knew that you can never be too paranoid with some people. You cannot think crazily enough.

For a moment she considered calling Detective Murray. Let Murray hunt the bearded man down. Have him arrested. Press charges. Sue the bastard biblically. Alas, getting the police messed up with this would mean getting the police messed up with everything else too. They would want to know about the photograph; what it meant; why she was so scared of it. Worst of all, it would ensure that Shane found out.

Jenny felt a great sadness about her relationship with Shane. She realised that these had been her golden years; that this had been as good as it was ever going to get. *The stakes have been plain for Shane and me; we prosper until I'm caught out, and then I lose everything.*

If her husband saw the photograph, it was all over. The truth of a person was in their scars. If a person feared abandonment, then they had probably been once abandoned. Her father had abandoned her by dying. He had left her alone in the world with her narcissistic mother and her sister. *I'm like Mum. I'm going to lose every significant male figure in my life.*

Jenny spun off the bed, grabbed Shane's phone, put it on silent and jammed it under the mattress. Lying back across the bed, she watched as he emerged from the en suite.

'Jenny… is there anything else? Like… you've told me everything, right?'

'Of course. I'm just glad to be home. With you. There's nothing else.'

Even as she spoke, she was aware that her lies now had an expiration date. Today. Tonight. Any minute now. It wasn't fair. How could some nobody just decide to ruin everything; to take Shane from her; to destroy her future? Shane and she – they belonged together like two clasped hands.

Shane smiled and quickly put on boxers, black jeans and black T-shirt.

Jenny, acting disinterested, tapped the odd key on her laptop, her face blued by the screen. Lazily, she said, 'Your jacket is downstairs in the kitchen.'

'Cool,' he muttered and left the room.

She breathed slowly and waited. A minute later his feet pounded on the stairs. Surging into the bedroom, he said, 'My phone – where is it?'

'Your phone?'

'Yeah. Come on, I'm late. You used it to text Otto. Remember?'

'Yeah. Of course. You took it just now, before going downstairs. I saw you. You just snapped it up. Are you mad? Check your pockets.' It was a skill inherited by all the Donaldsons – the ability to effortlessly gaslight.

'Fuck. It's not in my pockets. Call it, will you?'

Jenny took out her phone. 'Sure.' She dialled his number and said, 'It's calling.' Beneath her ass, was a very slight and silent vibration from under the mattress.

He stood still, ear almost comically cocked. But there was no sound.

She said, 'Must be on silent downstairs somewhere. Just go without it. You'll survive.'

'Right,' he muttered, taking one last scoot around the bedroom, lifting papers, kicking clothes. 'I'll take a taxi. Should be less than an hour.' He kissed her on the cheek. 'See ya.'

Watching Shane leave, Jenny had an unaccountable feeling that she'd never see him again. It was so urgent, so powerful, that she had to bite her lip to stop from calling out for him to stop, to not go, to stay with her. But she needed Shane out of the house. She needed to remove the picture from his phone. She needed to make her plans.

The front door closed.

Jenny rolled over, curled up, jammed her face and mouth into the pillow to mute her scream. All she could do was delete the picture from his phone *if* it arrived while he was at Otto's. Even then, the bearded man would just send it again and again, until he knew for certain that Shane had seen it. *What else can I do?*

The doorbell sounded.

Jenny climbed off the bed, checked herself in the mirror and went downstairs. Opening the door, she saw who it was and thought, *how much reality can I stand?*

'May I come in?' her mother asked.

When Vera spoke softly, when she gazed at her, Jenny remembered what it was like when she believed that her mother was like all other mothers – fair, protective and supportive. She remembered how secure life had been. Whatever the problem was, Mum could fix it.

Jenny leaned against the door. 'I wasn't expecting you.'

'I can call in to my daughter, can't I?'

'You can. But you never do.'

'I was out walking… taking some me time,' Vera said, as if her time wasn't 100% me time. 'And I decided to pop in and visit.'

'Mum, I really don't care for your drama games. I have my own concerns.'

'Which are…?'

'None of your business. Look, I assume there were no comebacks from earlier?'

'No comebacks? Now isn't that a holy terror of a phrase.' Vera's voice wasn't as clear and forceful as usual. Jenny squinted against the fading backlight of dusk sky. Vera was crying. That scared her. Her mother wasn't the crying type.

Jenny softened her voice. 'What's wrong, Mum? Why are you really here?'

'I know everything,' Vera said.

The moment Jenny heard those words, she told herself that they *had* to be untrue. Surely no one could know everything about *this*?

36

7.53 pm: Settling into the back of the taxi for the short journey out to the coast road, it occurred to Shane that, so far, he had been assuming Otto would simply hand back the money. But what if he couldn't? What if it was too late? What if he refused to? He needed to be prepared. *Remember the words of Sun Tsu – 'Victorious warriors win first and then go to war.'*

What did he know about Otto? He had broken Jenny into the interior design business. He did her accounts. He advised her. But why was he so eager to help her? Why was he always available? Most importantly, why did he feel the need to try and make Jenny an overnight fortune? There was nothing in it for him unless she was sleeping with him – and she definitely wasn't doing that. It was as if Otto owed her for something. It was like he was deeply in her debt.

Or maybe my opinion of Otto is coloured by what happened in that exam hall. The worst part of that twenty-four-year-old memory was not the being caught but afterwards – the conversation they had while walking to the dean's office.

Shane said, 'I never looked at the notes. I got zero sleep last night, panicked this morning and just brought them in. Totally forgot about them till the end of the exam.'

'That doesn't get taken into account, I'm afraid.'

'But it *should* be taken into account.'

Otto did not appreciate Shane's tone. 'Fine, I'm now taking it into account.'

'And?'

'*And* you cheated.' Otto stared at Shane as if judging the depth and width of his deception. 'This time, you were caught. What about previous exams? What about the other students' results when compared to yours? What does any of it mean if *your* cheating is tolerated?' Otto stopped walking and held up Shane's exam script and packet of tissues. 'What were you thinking? Shane, you were worth first-class honours. It was a pleasure teaching you. But alas, we must remember Feste's warning; *Cucullus non facit monachum*.'

Shane muttered, 'Yeah. I don't know what that means.'

'"The hood does not make the monk".'

Otto's condemnation had lingered about Shane for the next eight years. When he achieved anything – such as securing his TEFL certificate while working as a roofer – he felt sheepish, as if he had somehow hustled rather than earned it. When he had travelled to teach English, amassing glowing references wherever he went, the memory of Otto's blunt appraisal left him feeling like an impostor. Then he wrote his first book, and *that* changed everything.

Having finished a spell of teaching in Dubai, Shane took two months out to backpack in India. Drifting along the Goa coast, he hooked up with a faded Australian soap star called Lance Molko, who had set up a commune based on a kibbutz he had once stayed in.

Shane had been there just a week when Lance stole money from his long-term disciples and fled to Las Vegas where, lodged in a penthouse suite above the main strip, he binged for forty-eight-hours on cocaine, call girls and lady-boys. Then, out of cash, he jumped from his balcony and fell thirty floors. Crashing through the glass dome of the hotel's function room, Lance splattered his guts, eyeballs and brains all over a major oil company's banquet table, causing a spectacular detonation of roast duck, caviar and human mulch. At that very moment, the Texan CEO had been toasting the future for a battery of photographers. Instead, they snapped the precise second when washed-up glamour collided with current ostentation as the ultra-privileged Texan gazed with dismay at a partly eviscerated soap-star-has-been.

The news story went viral and within forty-eight-hours Lance's suicide was hailed as a Christ-like sacrifice and his became *the* face on activist T-shirts, symbolising indignation at eco-destruction and 'the 1%'. However, Lance's sainthood was fleeting. Details emerged as to his thievery, his subsequent drugged-fuelled bisexual orgies and his complete obliviousness to the oil banquet thirty floors beneath him. Finally, it was revealed that his last – sobbed – words before jumping were, 'I was somebody. Even Kylie sucked my dick.'

Upon his return to Dublin, Shane rattled off his book in a bedsit paid for by the dole. His manuscript drew on the week he'd stayed in the kibbutz before offering a dramatic account of what *really* went down in Las Vegas. Shane wove a theme into the story concerning how, due to the then burgeoning internet, dropping out of the modern world was no longer possible unless one is clinically insane and can therefore drop out of reality itself.

While waiting for it to come into print, he met Jenny in the nightclub, and they became a couple again. For both of them, the publication of his book was as if he had won the Pulitzer. In reality, it was issued by a small Irish company that printed up a few thousand copies with a shoddy cover. However, it was well reviewed with a media splash of zeitgeist baiting inquisitiveness and soon the international rights were snapped up for five figures.

Shane had named it *Cheating;* officially because Lance Molko had cheated obscurity, cheated his disciples and finally cheated himself of his own principles. But Shane had really called it *Cheating* because, by publishing it, he had nullified his college expulsion and therefore duped his own destiny.

8.07 pm: After catching every red light on the way to Otto's, the taxi turned onto the coast road that ran for miles ahead, visible due to the rows of orange, yellow and white street lights – urban pointillism. Here, each magnificent sea-view house and garden occupied as much real estate as a block of twenty houses on the estate in which Shane had grown up. These properties were owned by people for whom there was no magic number where you just stop. For them, there would never be enough luxury goods to buy, security to beef up, club memberships to amass and art to hang. In their worlds, you just kept dealing, earning, accumulating.

The taxi pulled in and Shane took out a spool of bills to pay in cash. He always had a roll with him. It brought him back to when he'd worked on the roofs and, every Friday, he'd get a precious brown envelope. Cash reminded him of who he was.

The taxi U-turned, leaving him alone on a broad, tree-lined street that seemed to have no houses on it. But every so often, large gates were implanted into twelve-foot-high walls. One of those gates was a wrought iron monstrosity of heft and industrial design. It blocked the way into Otto's. There was a keypad to the left and Shane pressed the biggest button.

Rumbling like a powerful engine starting up, the huge gate then smoothly swung inwards with surprising grace. A wide curving driveway was revealed, illuminated by spotlights high up in the trees. Inevitably feeling dwarfed, Shane walked up the drive that had been laid for hulking SUVs. As the floodlit, architect-designed home grew closer, he could not help but be awed by its spread, by the clever flourishes, its perfection. The crunch of waves sounded from the back of the house and the Irish Sea seemed to be just another thing you could buy. It wasn't until this moment that he realised just how rich Otto was. He'd known of his exclusive address, but to see it all with his own eyes was something else.

Spots beamed down on the parking area from the edge of the flat roof, while inside, the windows and hallway contained an array of lamps and ceiling fittings all blazing bright. Shane couldn't help but think of his immensely frugal father, always running around turning off the lights and pulling out plugs.

Shane considered Jenny and her obsession with Clareville. *If you came from this world, who could blame you for doing anything to keep it.* But then he reminded himself that getting the Clareville house had always been a remote possibility, not only due to Vera's mistreatment of Jenny, but also because he would have been a beneficiary.

Vera detested him for many reasons but, ultimately, on behalf of her precious and lost son, Hugh.

A quarter of a century had passed since he decked Hugh in that inner-city pub. He now had conflicting feelings whenever he thought of it. Shane still felt pity for Hugh when he pictured the spectacle of his humiliation. He still wished it hadn't happened – or rather that it had never *had* to happen. But it had felt justified, and still did. How thoroughly deserved. How damn good; like something every man should experience at least once in his life.

After her son's death, Vera had rarely spoken to Shane again. The last time they'd exchanged a sentence of true importance was on the day of his wedding.

37

Seventeen Years Ago

They had decided to tie the knot just three months after getting back together. But despite their telling only friends that they were going to Edinburgh to sign the papers, Vera and Joan had miraculously appeared in the lobby of their three-star hotel on the morning of the wedding.

The desk girls sensed something significant about Vera – helped, no doubt, by Joan's relentless fussing. When Jenny and Shane appeared in the lobby and experienced the shock of Vera's presence, the staff almost ignored the bride-to-be, so intent were they on making sure that Vera had her coffee in the most comfortable sofa with the nicest street view. Shane then had to hear, again and again, how wonderful and lovely his future mother-in-law was.

Greeting Jenny, Vera and her youngest daughter mimed a kiss. At least, their cheeks brushed against each other. Barely exchanging pleasantries with Shane, Vera then explained where she was staying (a five-star hotel), that she was in Edinburgh for one night and that she would accompany them to the meal afterwards. All of this was done in the manner of one finally accepting a long-standing invitation, rather than that of a gate crasher. Throughout all of this, Joan remained to the side, like an interpreter for a foreign dignitary, while snapping pictures of Vera with Jenny and Vera with her new friends, the hotel staff. When Vera was ready to move, she would say, 'Joan,' as if to a dog; and Joan would perk up and follow.

Despite the jolt of Vera's appearance, Shane hoped that this would be the burying of the hatchet between mother and daughter. Perhaps their marriage had the magical power to heal this broken family. Even though Jenny whispered an urgent, 'I'm so, so, *so* sorry,' Shane detected in her a suppressed elation at her mother's unexpected presence. Could this be a sign that her mother still loved her; that a page had been turned?

At the registry office, Vera's charisma resulted in the registrar and his secretaries addressing their attention mostly to her, rather than to Jenny and Shane. When one of the office staff stepped forward as witness, Vera dismissed him with a wave and, uninvited, signed in his place. Of course, she also made it into every photograph, carefully curated by Joan.

Shane had booked a brasserie recommended by the hotel. It was a classy restaurant but not filled with particularly, visibly, classy people; a 'dress stylishly, but don't bother sporting your best attire' kind of place. Vera sat opposite him, looking at her new son-in-law, eyes wandering to the left, to the right, and above him. She was trying to take in as much of Shane as possible. Finally, she said, 'You are well, I hope?' She did not hope that, but Shane let it slide. Then she added, 'You look… all spruced up. A nice effort.' Her carefully delivered compliment made Shane feel belittled. He knew he was being put in his place.

At Vera's right hand sat Joan. When the waiter brought over the slabs of menu, she almost vanished behind hers, and Shane pretty much forgot about her. Joan was like wallpaper under the stairs – just *there*. It was something he'd learned to take for granted when he'd first gone out with Jenny – that if Vera was somewhere public, then Joan would be, too, as her plus one, her driver, her personal shopper.

At that stage, Shane's attitude towards Joan was of empathy. In public, both sisters were well-liked and admired. But only one of them needed alcohol to turn the shine on. Despite her love of parties, Joan had lived her life as if guaranteed another one someday; one where she could *then* be cool, free and have lots of sex. She had taken to religion and, like their mother and even Hugh, had always been very extrovert with her devotion. The family liked to pray in public, as if that made their prayers purer. So yes, Joan *was* devout – when sober. But when drinking, she would often trot out her mother's favourite saying: 'Commit one sin and you might as well commit a few more. One or ten – they earn the same sentence. Eternity.' While Joan was often the life of the party, outside big social events she kept the world at a polite distance, so that people never noticed that her public gaiety was based on nothing; a light coating of cheerfulness stretched over an empty void.

Jenny turned to Joan and said, 'I heard you and Ted have split.'

Shane suppressed an audible gulp. It had been Jenny's big news a week ago – Ted had finally left Joan, after giving her a chunk of his life and three daughters. Shane was amazed that Ted had lasted that long, considering his wife visited her mother twice a day and in between he had Vera popping around unannounced to take the best chair in the house for the chat shows that she and Joan loved so much. Vera even had her own key. Ted's daily life had been reduced to sleeping for five hours, going to work and then coming home at seven to his big house to face three daughters and a wife who had all come to hate him – thanks to Vera's unbending desire to have Joan and her family all to herself.

Joan looked at her mother and snapped, 'I thought we were sworn to secrecy.'

'Oh, come on, it's only Jennifer.'

Shane noted the 'only.'

Jenny said, 'Well, I'm genuinely sorry to hear that. I hope you and the kids are all fine.'

Joan had taken off her shades. It was just for a moment. She put them back on and said, 'Thank you. We're all fine.'

Jenny said, 'Well, now you're single, you're on the market again. Imagine the exciting possibilities. You can find someone new. A proper Mister Right. This can be a big adventure. Joan, picture this – starting again with someone lovely.'

'We may have separated, but Ted is still my husband. Are we ordering?' She refilled her glass, already demonstrating her inability to attend any dinner without drinking the weight of the main course in alcohol.

That was the last civil exchange Shane ever witnessed between the sisters. They would never bother even to pretend again. It had occurred to Shane, even then, that Jenny's first mistake was talking about relationships to the envious Joan at the precise moment when Jenny's marriage was beginning, and Joan's had just ended. Her second mistake was suggesting, in front of Vera, that Joan might, in the future, divide her attention between her mother and a new lover. Vera's displeasure was evident in a forced smile that looked more like a wound. Vera had, doubtlessly, played a role in fast-tracking Joan's separation. Jenny had told Shane that, when Ted suffered a health scare, her mother had told her that Joan would be better off if he died – though qualified with a 'may God forgive me'. But of course, what Vera had really meant was that *she* would be better off if Joan's husband died.

Shane spent the rest of the meal attempting to entertain his mother-in-law. Silence was always just one step away and it was a struggle to stop it from coming any closer. He tried to fill the distance between them with chat about their visit to Edinburgh Castle the previous day. 'Interesting,' Vera said, her muttered inanity a blatant sign that she had already tired of the topic and turned her head to gaze out the window to Princes Street, as if generously giving Shane a moment to soak up her noble profile.

Shane gamely persisted between long flatlines of silence. He tried to draw her in with news about his book deal. At first her expression never shifted from 'uninterested in the particulars'. But slowly Vera began to relax in his presence, feeling more at ease with Shane, now that she had identified his weakness – professional pride. With a warm smile, she said, 'That's nice. Making money from your hobby,' as though he was making model ships. 'I'm sure if it's well received, some doors will open for you.'

At the end of the long, long meal, Shane was pleasantly surprised when Vera accepted the leather envelope containing the bill for their wedding meal. Glancing at it, she passed it to Joan with a muttered aside. As usual, Joan sprung to life as if she was voice activated. She examined it for about a minute, making calculations, and muttered something back to her mother. Then, with a smile expertly calibrated to let you know how long was left in the conversation, Vera announced,

'It should be fifty-five pounds each, including tip,' and placed, precisely, one hundred and ten pounds into the leather envelope.

By the end of the meal, Shane was reassured that his suspicions about Vera were correct. She was the definitive narcissist – and a narcissist was *always* just a narcissist. She could not change. She would not change. When his mother-in-law looked at a person, including her own children, all she saw was what she could get out of them. It might be attention. Sometimes it was someone that she could manipulate and control. If she couldn't dominate the person, she'd try to make them fear her. By persistently doing all those things – controlling, dominating, using – she created all the drama that guaranteed her so much attention.

Shane knew that Vera would always resent him, because he would never let her deep enough into Jenny's life to mess it up with her type of crazy. Conversely, Vera would never let Jenny go, because that would be proof that Jenny didn't need her and that she had no power over her. Therefore, Shane knew that going forward, there would be only two ways to deal with Vera. He could cajole her, endure her manufactured emotional dramas and be a doormat. Or he could limit contact with her.

Shane had already made *his* decision.

Because of all of that, Shane reckoned that it was to Jenny's psychological benefit that her mother and sister had ostracised her since the age of eighteen. He'd always thought that it was amazing Jenny wasn't totally screwed up. He couldn't begin to imagine what Jenny would now be like if she'd been exposed to those people on a regular basis for her entire life. She'd probably be just like Joan.

However, it did dishearten Shane that for the next seventeen years, Jenny would continue to go for weekly morning coffees and walks with Vera, despite the fact that as Jenny gained her own identity and built a happy life, she zoomed more centrally into the crosshairs of Vera's scope. It was as if his wife was unaware that every minute in her mother's company was just more of her life that Vera sucked on, fed on, nourished her sickness with. But it would continue until Vera was in the earth.

38

Now

8.08 pm: Holding the front door, Jenny's eyes met her mother's and she asked, 'You know everything? What do you mean?'

Vera was inside almost before she had finished talking. Jenny was not entirely sure how she had done it. Vera had stepped forward as if there was room for her and her daughter's body had shrunk back and made it true.

Jenny corralled her into Shane's office. That was where the drink was.

'Where is Sha—' Vera closed her eyes for two long seconds. Then, 'Where is he?'

Jenny eyerolled. Even now, her mother would not allow herself to use Shane's name. Nothing would make Vera happier than if he had a quick sudden death from pancreatic cancer or a car crash. Though it would be perfect if he left Jenny. Not only would he be gone, but Vera would be able to laud her failed marriage over Jenny and say her favourite phrase over and over – 'I told you so' – even if she *hadn't* told her so.

Jenny said, 'Shane's out on some business.'

'Look at the state of this place. How does anything get done in this room? It's chaotic. Most messy people aren't geniuses, Jennifer. They're just messy.'

Even if there had not been wine stains on the floor and across the book spines, the room would still have been far too messy for her mother. Vera had a cleaner who came twice weekly. For her, everything had its place and she found it immensely annoying, that there were people in the world who actually went to bed at night without first zipping their house up.

Standing over Shane's desk, Vera placed a condemnatory finger on his leather-bound journal. It was his work diary which, without fail, he filled in last thing at night – like a kind of prayer. Jenny placed a hand on Vera's shoulder and edged her away from it. Picking out a bottle of Shiraz, she said, 'It's been a hell of a day... and it isn't over yet. Want one, then?'

'Of course,' her mother replied, offering her exaggeratedly fake smile that made the tendons stand out in her neck. 'Let's have a heart to heart – or rather, a liver to liver.'

Vera's eyes shone as Jenny unscrewed the bottle and she edged towards it, like a plant in a dark corner of the room reaching and stretching towards the sunlight. The bottle had never disappointed, never let her down. Vera's hand, wrinkled like an old apple, trembled when she lifted the glass; the journey from counter to mouth was a perilous one. The grey plague.

Jenny sipped hers and, sneaking a glance at her watch – 8.10 pm – asked, 'So, what's this about?'

'First, you and Joan. Sisters fight, Jennifer. Even the closest ones. I fought with mine, too. Just remember, that at the end of the day we are all family and, of course, that I love all my children equally.'

Jenny stared at the deepest furrow on her mother's forehead, as if that was where all her deceits were generated. Even when she was a child, she'd known that she was a distant third place to Hugh and Joan in their mother's affections. Vera didn't try to pretend otherwise. When Hugh was alive, Joan and Jenny had clearly been just luxury goods to her – dependable, rewarding things, to be taken out and played with a few times a month. But neither had minded being used by their mother. It had made them feel useful.

Vera took another sip and placed the glass onto the side table. 'I had told Joan to never bring up that London business, as who knows what will come creeping out if we overturn *that* stone? But today she did it anyway and I was not happy about it.'

Often, her mother did not have a two-way conversation. Sometimes she simply talked *at* people. She forced words into their mouths. She was a master at making people say what she wanted to hear, and Jenny said, 'OK.'

'But Joan has never forgiven you. Because of that, it's hard for me to… to keep her under control.'

'Forgiven me for what? Living my own life? Anyway, I would've thought throwing me out of the house would sate her thirst for revenge – for this year, at least.'

'Why do you insist on going on about that?'

'We're not going to talk about the house? Like, the fact that you're throwing me out barely registers anymore. As in, "we've already done that" earlier today. Another item ticked off your Monday, A4, to-do list.'

'Yes – we *have* done that. And I don't see how you think rocking the boat is going to help matters.'

'It's not rocking the boat, Mum. It's actually called *communication.*'

Vera's eyes glistened with a cruel intelligence that never ceased demanding the pleasure it needed to thrive. 'You want to have a conversation? Well then, let's have a conversation. Twenty-five years ago, you did the worst thing in the world. To your baby. To all of us. Yes, that and this house are connected. It'll make sense but you'll have to listen first.'

'Stop, Mum.' Jenny sounded like a child.

'You wanted the conversation, so you're getting it.'

'Not *this* conversation.'

Vera moved in even closer, which made it easy for her to momentarily grip Jenny's arm, proving that Vera wanted her youngest daughter's drama, any drama, all the drama. 'You're the one who returned to *our* lives. We didn't come searching for you. We were shocked you came to your father's funeral. If you hadn't turned up, we could have said you were too upset to attend. Instead, you flew home, and we had to sit with you at the top of the church. You made yourself a distraction when no one wanted a distraction.'

It was as if inside Vera's brain there was a fountain pen, its nib soaked in cruelty, always at her disposal. She lifted her glass, her hand shaking so much, the wine splashed and stained her upper lip. Swallowing, she added, 'I'm amazed Lorcan didn't climb out of the grave at his own funeral.'

Jenny was not amazed, because funerals were not for the dead but for those left behind. Lorcan's suffering was over. Hers had continued. 'Enough, Mum.'

'No, it's *not* enough,' Vera said, wiping away Jenny's protest with a wave of her hand. 'Not after what you did. But you know what? I forgave you.'

Vera's lips pursed as they always did when telling a brazen lie. *She never forgave me.*

Vera said, 'But, I suppose, Lorcan had it coming to him. Unlike Joan and Hugh, you're more him than me. He moulded you. Spoilt you. Children decay and wither when they're indulged in too much love. I've always seen Lorcan in your features. But I see none of his strength. Your father was strong. His problem was that, sometimes, he was even *too* strong. Lorcan shouldn't have fought me so hard. There was no reason for it. I wasn't his enemy.'

Jenny could tell that her mother wasn't enjoying this. She was from a family that found the idea of burdening people with intimate details of their lives to be unfathomable.

'I lost Hugh six months before you went to London to kill your baby. I was still mourning my son. Hugh should never have left me. Your brother was irreplaceable.' Vera still spoke about her son as if he was an object, a priceless object, but still an object. 'I wanted boys. Lots of boys. After Hugh, we tried and failed and failed. You girls are great. But in some ways, Hugh was an only child. That's why it hurt so much. There are no positive adjectives for an only child; "only" sounds deserted and pitiful. I've had four miscarriages. *Four*. They devastated me. Each and every one. My last miscarriage came after three months. That was the furthest I'd ever got. For a few weeks, I'd believed we were safe. It had been a glorious summer that year.'

Jenny was shocked. Her mother had never spoken to her like this before. It made her incredibly uncomfortable.

'Jennifer, we had a *real* marriage. And believe it or not, one without too many secrets. We might have had our differences. But when it mattered, we were a proper team. Our marriage was a union. We were two chambers in a diseased heart – but a union nonetheless.'

Jenny said, 'Back in your house, before Joan barged in… you were about to tell me something.'

'Yes. And here I am. Third time lucky.'

Jenny thought of the bearded man – *Three is the magic number.* She said, 'I don't know where this is going.' But a voice in her head advised – *What's not to get? God is telling you not to fuck with Mother.*

Vera said, 'I have done something that you will find unforgivable. But I thought long and hard about it and it's for the best. Jennifer, I have never before woken up, knowing with such certainty that I would remember this day for as long as I live.'

Jenny's stomach shrank in on itself. Her mother had cracked open the past and she could feel it leaking into her bloodstream. This was going to be worse than she ever could have thought.

Vera lowered her voice, as if there was a third person in the room trying to eavesdrop, and added, 'I know your secrets. I always have.'

Then, her mother told her everything.

39

8.10 pm: Considering that Shane was surprised there was no helicopter pad, the routine front door almost astounded him. Despite the fact that it was ajar, he looked for the doorbell. There was none. Rattling his knuckles on the frame, he waited and listened to the low electric hum from all the lights above and inside. After a few moments he pushed the door fully open.

Calling out Otto's name, his voice carried deep into the hallway and up the bending staircase. When there was no answer, he stepped inside. A stilled wooden ceiling fan hung over his head like a sleeping bat. He remembered Jenny buying that in an auction for Otto.

Shane walked deeper into the show-house hallway. The silence, the lights, the ghostliness, all made him uneasy.

Footsteps sounded.

He turned and, bemused, watched the bearded stranger exit the living room and enter the hall. Shane was too surprised to say anything. It was as if he was waiting for this break, this fissure in the accepted normality of things, to close over and heal.

When only feet separated them, Shane took in the shaved head, the dark brown eyes, the black facial hair and small scar on his forehead. He was over six-foot-tall but broad enough to be anything but gangly. Shane hoped that some of his muscular bulk was due to the thickness of his jacket; but the leather was not padded.

Shane said, 'Where's Otto?'

A deep opaque voice answered, 'No. The first question's mine.'

'I *said*, where is Otto?'

The man cracked his knuckles. 'Do you know who I am?'

Shane's heart was pounding like a fist pummelling him from the inside. 'You were on the laneway the night of the crash. You're the other one.'

He immediately regretted saying that. Like the victims he wrote about, he had just betrayed the law that stated, 'If you want your life complication-free, then don't be a witness'. Shane tried to correct the course with, 'I didn't see you on the lane, right? I don't see you now. So just go.'

'My name is Ultan. Do you know who I am?'

'What? No. Of course not.'

Ultan nodded, as if the answer was regrettable but inevitable.

Shane risked no sudden gestures. If there was one thing being a true-crime writer had taught him, it was that there was nothing more lethal than an anxious individual forced into a corner. 'If you've done something you shouldn't have… something you regret doing… then now is the time to just turn around, walk out that door and keep walking. Understand?'

Ultan's arm stretched out, fingers wide, aiming for Shane's throat. Shane jolted backwards and swung his fist. Ultan blocked it with a raised elbow and his knuckles hit bone. A shock of pain electrified Shane's arm.

A hand grabbed Shane by the neck and raised him onto his toes. Ultan marched forward, increasing speed and Shane's spine smashed into the wall next to the kitchen door. A painting of a windmill fell and hit the floor, its ornate frame breaking into four pieces. Ultan seized him by the hair and slammed the back of his head against the wall. There was a flash of red light inside Shane's skull. Slam. His ears were full of ringing noise. And again. Back against the plaster.

'Don't underestimate me,' Ultan calmly said. 'I'm a tough fucker. One thousand per cent tougher than you.'

Shane did not underestimate him. He appraised Ultan's bearded face and decided that almost every moment of his life had been painful. This was a person accustomed to trouble spots, civil wars, humans behaving badly. It was all visible, like a book's index; his history was in those rigid lines. If they had been mortared with dirt, they would belong to an old ploughman rather than someone who was in their thirties. No wonder he had grown a beard. His face was the real story. He was like a Francis Bacon portrait come to life.

Holding Shane against the wall with one hand, the other scratched his beard. 'Remember, I'm faster than you. I'm stronger than you. And I've fighting skills. If I'd wanted to kill you, I'd have simply cracked your skull open against the wall. Or maybe I'd have inserted my thumbs through your eyeballs and finger-fucked your brain.'

Shane coughed and it felt like a shock grenade going off inside his head. 'OK…'

Ultan released his grip on Shane's neck and withdrew the cut-throat razor from his jacket. With a curl of his wrist, it flicked open. 'And now, I'm armed. You'd do well to remember that people don't pass away from multiple slices – they die screaming from them.'

'I'll remember that.'

Passing the blade from hand to hand, he ordered, 'Calmly, walk upstairs.'

Shane approached the stairs and gripping the stainless-steel banister, began his ascent. Ultan followed about five steps behind. *Should I turn and kick out? Should I charge forward, find the bathroom, lock it and try to get out the window? Turn and kick. Run and hide. No. Just walk. He's a brick shithouse psychopath with a blade.*

At the top of the stairs, Ultan said, 'The first door. Open it and go inside.'

Shane turned the handle and asked, 'What did you do to Otto?'

A heavy hand pushed him into the door. It swung open, and Shane saw what Ultan had done to Otto.

40

8.13 pm: The door had opened, and light fell on his face. Otto had been in the dark too long and it took a few seconds for him to bear the brightness. Standing inside the door was Shane. Behind him, Ultan.

Otto, strapped to a chair with duct tape pinning his legs, chest and arms, observed Shane observing him. A gag muffled Otto but his eyes were all flashy-darty, full of hope, waiting for someone to help him because that was what people were meant to do – help each other.

A moment later the door closed and both Shane and Ultan were gone. Otto was alone again in the dark. He was past feeling shame for having wet himself; though the cold stuck to his groin – an unpleasant circle. He wished he could clutch his chest. *I'm going to have a heart attack*. He imagined a paper bag and tried to count between inhalations. It did not work. Otto was gasping as though he'd run up a staircase.

The door opened again, and the lights blazed. Ultan had returned, alone. Marching across the room, he pulled the gag from Otto's mouth and then, with both hands, simply shoved Otto in the chest. The chair, with Otto taped to it, fell backwards. He closed his eyes a second before his skull whacked against the floorboard. Squatting next to him, Ultan adjusted his low hung, baggy jeans, which seemed to have a tenderloin jammed into them.

'You and Jenny… does her husband know?'

'Know what?'

Gripping Otto by the hair, he lifted his head a few inches and dropped it back to the floor. His skull bounced on the wood, and it felt like being dropped into a bucket of madness.

'Yes! Yes! Shane knows about the money. It's all fine. He knows everything.'

'I don't give a fuck about money. I'm talking about you and her. Does he know?'

'*Me* and Jenny? There's nothing to know about. I'm her financial advisor. That's it.'

Once more, Ultan lifted Otto's head and dropped it. Again, it smashed onto the floor. 'I'm asking questions that I already know the answers to. So, I can tell when you're lying. Then, when I finally ask the real question, I'll know you're telling the truth. Get it?'

'Yes. I'll tell the truth. I promise.'

'Does Shane know about you and Jenny?'

Otto looked up into Ultan's eyes and realised that this was finally the moment when he was going to pay for what had happened twenty-four years ago. It wasn't fair. He had done all he could to make up for it. He was still trying to make amends. And if the future was not just about to run out, he would've never stopped trying.

41

Twenty-Four Years Ago

Otto sat in a corner of Dublin's Krystal nightclub, impressing his students by being so unimpressed. He was beginning to resent them. The students were supposed to be creative, interesting and lively enough to keep him feeling young and relevant. Instead, they inflicted him with the mental fatigue that comes from being surrounded for too long by people with lower intelligence. They seemed to be naively clueless to the fact that the new world, for which he was helping to train them, was one in which prestige, power and wealth would soon be the equivalent of popularity, size zero and perfect skin.

Jenny Donaldson, in a sleeveless white T-shirt, slipped in beside him. Even if her strong intelligence was not yet finely tuned, even though she lacked an implicit talent, it didn't matter – if Jenny had nothing to say at eighteen, she still had everything to say it with.

Unable to hide her awkwardness, she apprehensively ran her fingers through her bleached hair and said, 'Hi, Otto. I'll stop cramping your style in a minute but first, gonna give your favourite student a hint about the exams?'

'Interesting suggestion,' Otto replied, as if it was anything but interesting. He took his time observing Jenny before deciding that she was the type he was looking for. He liked them young but smart enough to recognise his power and influence. After a slow start to the year, Jenny had settled down and proved herself a surprisingly balanced, diligent undergraduate.

'Come on. Just a little-biddy, teeny-weeny hint.'

A power pause, then, 'I can't talk about that.'

'C'mon, Mister Lubber. You're not making it easy for me. You cut an intimidating figure. I mean it. You've got a certain… charisma.'

He smiled to show that he liked what he heard. 'If I told you, Jenny, it would be unethical.'

'No one has you down for being a moral humanist, Otto.'

Again, he smiled. Jenny had certainly flourished from a year in college. She would never have said something like that in freshers' week.

Suddenly Jenny fell forward, her face hurtling towards the table. Otto put a firm hand on her bare shoulder and jerked her up straight just before she collided with the hard surface.

'It's OK,' she said, letting him keep his hand there. 'Thanks. I'm fine. Just a bit dizzy. Too much… stuff. Need some water.'

Otto raised his palm like a traffic cop. 'Are you on something? You're wired and your eyes…' He leaned in and saw that her pupils were like sharpened pencil leads.

'Me? No. I'm fine. Sort of. Eamonn smuggled in a hip flask of vodka and soaked chillies mixed with cranberry juice.' Jenny wiped her clammy forehead, which was the most ungraceful thing he had ever seen her do. She tried to smile but the energy was draining from her, second by second. 'Otto, you make me say and do and think things that… confuse me.'

He took out a cigarette and, not allowed to light it, looked at it sadly. She wasn't drunk. She was high. Stoned girls were usually bad girls. Otto knew what women saw in him – the cynical intellectual, coldly Germanic, pomposity with a trace of the 'good' type of sleaze. It was time to ramp it up. 'Jenny, you're still young. Your duty is to experience. How could you go through college and not fuck a teacher?'

She slowly reddened, her face like a glass filling with wine. Otto enjoyed watching Jenny consider her reply. But she didn't say anything.

'Have you a boyfriend?'

Jenny's eyes narrowed. 'He's not coming tonight. Doesn't like the crowd. Neither do I. I'm here for exam tips.'

She was becoming even more desirable to him. Otto liked attached women. He was especially fond of fucking wives, and often wondered who their husbands hated more; the women who rejected them or the alpha males, like Otto, that they preferred?

Jenny whispered, 'I need air. I'm going… right now… outside.'

'So am I. I'm going back to my place. It's dangerous for me to even ask but… Coming?'

She nodded.

He helped Jenny to her feet and said, 'It's not every day a gal gets to go home with teacher.' Otto smiled, in case he'd taken her up wrong, and he could then pretend that he was joking like the funny, sweet guy he wasn't.

Outside Krystal, a taxi stopped. She followed Otto into the back seat as if he was a mesmeriser. Jenny's eyes were closed, though her lips mimed to the song on the radio. Otto stared at her profile, knowing that the Rubicon needing to be crossed was her age – eighteen. Perhaps too young, even for him? *But Jenny is a very hot girl. A very stoned girl. Super tits. I love girls in white sleeveless Ts.* He sniffed her. *No perfume. Organic. And she looks twenty-two. Easily.*

Otto had sucked hard on the nipple of paternal generosity. The studio apartment that his father paid for had a large skylight that glimpsed the Guinness storehouse down the road. A coffee table held a carefully written letter, to be posted to his grandfather. He owned a super-expensive stereo – the speakers alone cost a grand each – but the only CDs he owned were a few classical collections that had come free with the Sunday papers, and he didn't have an MP3 player. Otto basically didn't know what music was for. There was also a tropical fish tank aswarm with aquatic life drifting between cerise shells and reeds. Otto was specifically proud of Tipsy and Topsy, a pair of angel fish. On the floor was a wooden figurine, attired in traditional German dirndl dress, that his grandmother had made for his mother when she was little. Otto froze when Jenny accidentally kicked it out of the way before belly-flopping onto the bed.

Cutting out four lines of coke onto the cover of a hardback, Otto brought it over to the bed and placed them in front of her face like it was a bowl of milk and she a cat. Jenny hoovered three of them up, leaving just one for him.

'Easy with that. It's good stuff,' he admonished her.

Otto then knelt behind her on the bed and bunched up her skirt around her waist. His preference of conquest to cooperation, in all areas of his life, led him to say, 'We're going to do this my way, yes?'

'Your way – yes,' she muttered as he pulled her panties down to her knees.

'We're good here – yes?'

'Uh-huh.'

With Jenny on her hands and knees, Otto could see the weight of her breasts beneath the T-shirt. He liked that and dipped his finger into the snuff box of coke on the bedside locker. As Otto reached around and let Jenny snort from his hand, he offered as close to a grin as his neurotically frozen features would allow.

Otto muttered incoherently as he fucked Jenny; stoned free-associations, snippets of current fantasies. Jenny looked over her shoulder and Otto stared into what he considered were eyes glazed with lust and too many drugs. Had he fed Tipsy and Topsy? *Poor things lost in their quaint little ocean, forever searching for the food flakes that never came; much like man, earth and enlightenment.* Otto needed to focus and so gave her buttock a stinging slap.

Jenny smothered her grunts in the pillow as Otto picked up the jar labelled **Liquid Bliss** and popped its lid. Grabbing her hair, he jerked back her head. He was a demigod; the ransacked booty now impaled before him. Otto put the popper to his nose and inhaled as if about to dive to the seabed. The amyl nitrate vapours ripped into his lungs, his eyes bulged, and his cock contracted on the precipice of a dangerously intense orgasm. Aiming carefully, he again reached around and jammed the popper into Jenny's face. She cried out wildly and they both climaxed with such intensity that it felt like he was scorching an image of his penis onto the walls of her innards. Jenny's face buried into the pillow as she emitted what sounded like a snarl and Otto flopped down on top of her, muttering, 'Sweet, sweet, Jesus.'

For a few moments, they lay there, side by side, Otto clothed with his cock drooping out of his zipper; Jenny in her T-shirt, hiked-up skirt and panties still around her ankles. Then, he slowly climbed out of bed as if it was Sunday morning, rather than 10.00 pm on

Friday. Tipsy and Topsy hesitated in the reeds, perfect with strong dorsal fins and striking silver colours.

Otto inhaled the silence through his burning cigarette and in a blast of smoke said, 'They'll be wondering where you are. Maybe your boyfriend has turned up and he'll be suspicious. And if the dean or any other stick-in-the-mud finds out, then I'll be out of a job – or worse.' Otto realised that the drugs were making him paranoid. He also knew that the opposite of paranoia was not serenity. It was naivety. 'Now if you excuse me, I have to feed the fish.'

He liked spending time alone. If there was one thing he'd learned from his school days, it was how to be solitary. Then a wave of arctic pragmatism washed over his cosy self-satisfaction, and he reluctantly asked, 'Hey, Jenny, you OK?'

Thirty minutes later, Otto was pacing the emergency waiting room, never looking directly at anyone should they see the disease of terror in his eyes.

How could she OD in my apartment? What was I thinking bringing students home? If she dies, I'll fly out to mainland Europe tonight.

After being unable to wake Jenny, he had failed to detect a pulse. Grabbing a mirror, he had held it over her mouth and sure enough, it had misted. He called an ambulance, but they said they would be ten minutes. Instead, he had fixed her clothes, threw her over his shoulder and carried her to the lift like a rolled carpet. A taxi sped them to the hospital.

On the other side of the waiting room was a distraught family dreading the news on their father's condition after a heart attack. Otto wondered if he too was due a heart attack. The pounding in his chest was almost painful. There was a tap on his shoulder. He turned and was face to face with a uniformed police officer.

'Otto Lubber?' Without waiting for affirmation, the garda added, 'You OK?'

Otto wanted to be cool but instead he was so terrified, he was beyond contributing to his own survival. Instead, Otto swallowed air and felt a trapped nerve spasm in the corner of his lip. 'Maybe water. No. Actually, I'm fine.'

'Come with me, please.'

Otto found himself alone with the garda in a small white room with two chairs and an X-ray machine. He felt utterly defeated, as if all the disappointments of his lifetime had just come together in one final foregone conclusion. Lost in the horror of his situation, he held the garda's stare and tried to think of something to say but only came up with, 'Sorry.'

The garda smiled sympathetically and said, 'Nothing to be sorry about. Looks like you saved her. Some guy at Krystal has spiked his bottle with a tranquiliser and is passing it around. There's another few cases just called in. Jenny's given us a name. Eamonn, from her year.'

Otto knew Eamonn. He was just one of those slab-faced guys with no personality who seemed to take night classes in how to be as much like everyone else as possible. Those boys were always popular.

'We've sent a car down to pick him up. I tell you this, she's some girl you've got there. Head screwed on and real nice. A keeper. She's next door and I'm sure she wants to see you.'

Otto strode into Jenny's room. Beneath the blankets, she was pale but otherwise healthy-looking. Picking up her chart, he scanned it. 'You're absolutely fine. Thank God.' Sitting next to her, he removed a blonde strand stuck to her cheek. 'How much blow did you do before coming to my place?'

She brushed away his fingers. 'None. I've... I've never done it before.'

'*What?*'

'That was my first time. In your place.'

'But... But... I would never have given you drugs if I didn't think you took drugs. I thought you were really high. You were out of it.'

'That prick Eamonn – he spiked my drink with... some fucking tranquiliser. Didn't the police tell you?'

'Yes. But I still thought you did drugs. Jesus. Fuck. Jesus. Why did you take them? All three lines?' He thought of the extra bump he had given her while fucking, followed by the popper. All of that, on top of some rapey tranquilliser. 'Jesus. Fuck. Jesus.'

'Otto... I wasn't in control. I was messed up. I still am. If you'd put petrol in front of me and told me to drink it, I would have. Oh, Jesus...'

For a moment he covered his face with his hands. Through the cracks in his fingers he said, 'You're such a good girl. I was so close. This close.' Otto held up his almost touching thumb and forefinger. 'You could've taken revenge on, you know, *any* male – the way some girls do. But you didn't. Thank you.'

'I was... I had no control. I had no idea what I was doing, what you were doing. Anything. But we... Right? *That* actually happened? But I didn't want it to. I would never have. You better realise that. This isn't me changing my mind. I was drugged. I was poisoned.'

'Yes. Of course. I mean... we're both still trying to take it in. But we've taken way too many drugs, haven't we? Before you say anything more, I want you to know that I owe you big and the Lubber clan is one of entrepreneurs, academics and war heroes. We keep our word.

When the time comes Jenny – just ask. I owe you big. And I always pay my dues.'

'Otto, I never want to see you again.'

'You're tired. You've just had a nightmare.' Otto backed away to the door. 'Go to sleep, Jenny. You're safe now.'

42

Now

8.23 pm: Ultan rubbed his beard. 'I'm losing patience. Answer my question. Does Shane know about you and Jenny?'

Otto said, 'Of course Shane doesn't know. Why would he? It was… what? …twenty-four years ago. Me and Jenny. That night. It was just something that happened, something we've never spoken of again. I hardly knew her. She was just my student. It was messy. It was nothing. Why would she ever tell Shane? I mean… how the fuck do *you* know? Nobody knew. Nobody knows. It's not something either of us are proud of.'

Across Ultan's face, a new moon of anger revealed itself – cold, full and shining. 'And what about what she did afterwards?'

'I have no idea what you're talking about. What did she do?'

'Tell me.'

'I swear… I don't know what you're talking about. After that night, I didn't talk to Jenny again for years. I was her teacher. She sat the exams and that's it. She left college. Dropped out. Lots of kids that age do. And I moved to London and never taught again. The next time I saw her wasn't until she wanted my help. Years later. And, yes, I started up her business. I gave her clients. I gave her advice. I had to help her. I *wanted* to help her. Jesus. I'm telling you the truth. That's all I know. I'm not lying. Please… Please don't hurt me.'

'You haven't been with her since?'

'No. Jesus. Never.'

'I believe you. I believe everything you've just told me.'

'Thank God. Oh, thank you, God. You won't hurt me? You won't… do anything else?'

'None of this is your fault. That's clear.' With a grunt, Ultan see-sawed Otto and his chair back up into a normal position. 'You're totally innocent. I want you to know that it's been thought-provoking seeing who you are. It must never get boring to live in a world where a thousand euros is just a pair of shoes. It makes me… it makes me even more determined.'

'Determined?'

Ultan withdrew the cut-throat razor, opened it and ran his thumb across the blade. 'To finish this. To see it through.'

43

8.50 pm: In a guest room, Shane was seated with his back to the door, next to a single bed. Duct tape not so much tied as pasted him to the chair.

This must be about Dee, Ultan's girlfriend. So why get Otto involved? Was it just so Ultan could text from Otto's phone to get me to call around? Is that not too convoluted? It was hard not to be grimly paranoid. If this was about revenge, then what form might it take? Shane's pulse began to spike. *What if he's torturing Otto; doing him first; rationing us out?*

Uselessly, he tried to call out from behind the duct tape sealing his mouth. Barely a muffled grunt emerged. Anyway, even if he was able to shout for the next twelve hours, no one would hear him. Otto's house was about three hundred metres from a road that was an empty runway for the neighbourhood's SUVs and Porsches.

Behind him, the door opened. Shane turned his head as far as he could, but it wasn't enough. A hand landed on the back of his skull and fingers ripped the tape from his lips. Ultan spoke, his voice coming from behind as he towered above.

'I'm impressed, Shane. Not a sound. Total silence. Wish I could enjoy it.'

'What do you mean?'

'I mean, the white noise in my ears.'

'Shit, shit, shit,' Shane muttered. *He's insane. And now I'm going to die.*

'Tinnitus. I've had it since I was thirteen. It gets worse in times of stress, anxiety, anger. Sounds like air seeping from a tyre with a slow puncture. It's always there – the hiss of my life force gradually slipping away, second by second, day by day. If I ever experience silence again, it'll be too late. There'll be nothing of me left.'

Shane pictured Ultan's white earbuds. *Make a connection.* 'Does music make it better?'

'Henryk Górecki. Or trance. Usually trance.'

'Good. Is Otto OK? What've you done to him?'

'He turned out to be collateral damage. He's not the man I thought he was. He's… innocent. Though it wasn't a wasted trip. I managed to get you here.'

Shane wished he could see Ultan's face. 'I'm sorry about your girlfriend. But I had nothing to do with it. She rammed me. I didn't have time to get out of her way.'

'I was there. I know exactly what happened.'

'I wasn't intending to block her. That wasn't my intention.' He paused. *That was exactly my intention.* 'I was just intending to follow her. That's all. But she's dead now. Dee. That's her name, right? Is that not enough pain and suffering? I know you blame me but it's not my fault.'

'But I don't blame you. It was Dee's own fault.'

He doesn't blame me? 'Then why are you doing this?'

'And she wasn't my girlfriend. Stop presuming you know anything about me.'

'Who was she, then?'

Ultan impatiently sighed, deciding on whether or not to grant Shane an insight into one of the many mysteries afflicting him. 'Dee was a backpacker-dropout working in Bangkok bars for a few months, before popping over to Laos to top up her visa. That's where I met her.'

Shane pictured Ultan – another western weirdo hiding out in Thailand, spending his time wandering the feverish sweat of humanity that was downtown Bangkok; then bringing his obsessions to Ireland, choosing Clareville to ply his trade, it all going wrong and now here Shane was – tied to a chair, about to die.

'Man, Dee was crazy. She was just… Dee; mid-twenties and already coming to regret all that sun damage. Hippy type but not peace and love. She'd never even pretended to be a multi-ethnic-admiring, environmental-defending vegetarian, distressed by the injustices of the third world, like most of them do. Did you know, she had a photographic memory and never told anyone? I'd watched her filling in one of those tourist forms in Suvarnabhumi Airport after barely glancing at my passport. And when I checked it, it was correct. All those numbers and letters. All those dates. So, she was going home, and I came here with her because she knew Dublin. She knew Clareville and she told me she had a car. But she didn't have one. She stole it. I wasn't happy about that.'

Again, Shane tried to turn his head to face Ultan. Again, he failed. 'She was a thief. And so were you. You came to rob us. You broke in.'

'Not me. I just wanted to see where Jenny lived.'

'Why?'

Ignoring the question, he said: 'After parking out front and taking in Jenny's home, Dee drove me round the back to see if there were better views. And then she gets out this balaclava. There she was, putting it on. She must've been planning it all along. She gets out of the car, pulls up your garage and in she goes. She crossed your decking, not even creeping – like she was walking into a bar. Checking the back door, it just opened. I called her back, but she said she wanted a computer. Maybe a nice TV. She reckoned that if you left the door unlocked then there was probably cash all over the house. She said a certain type of rich don't believe that bad things can happen to them… until they do.'

'You didn't go in?'

'No. I was just watching. I was there to look inside from the outside. I had other plans.'

Why was Ultan still behind him? Why wouldn't he face him?

'I was just back in the car when Dee jumped in, real panicky, out of breath, balaclava still on and she sped down the laneway to a dead end. Getting more freaked, she turned the car and stepped on it. The laneway was just a dark blur. I started to tell her to turn the lights on and then *BAM*. I had my belt on. I turned to Dee, and she wasn't there. You know the rest.'

Shane remembered the cars meeting, and the sound of metal ripping that was like screaming. 'But if you don't blame me for Dee's death, then why send me crazy texts and—'

'They weren't crazy,' Ultan snapped. 'I tried to warn you about Otto. I did warn you. I wanted to help you. I've no beef with you, Shane.'

'Warn me about what? What are you talking about? You sent me fucking flowers this morning with a threatening note. You weren't trying to help me.'

Ultan started laughing. 'Oh man… really? The flowers weren't for you. They were for Jenny. I didn't even know you were home till you opened the door and took them inside.'

'They were for *Jenny*? Why would you threaten Jenny? Jenny never hurt anyone.'

'Really, Shane? Still? Even after the picture I sent you?'

'What picture? And why won't you fucking face me?'

'I'm late, Shane. No time. But it's all in the picture. It'll be clear when you see it. It's on your phone. I do feel bad for what I've done to you. All this hate, man. All this black energy from me – it burns you – when everything is aimed solely at your wife. Now hush, Shane.'

Ultan reached around and placed a strip of duct tape over his lips. 'You're here for a reason. I need Jenny alone. Just me and her. Finally.'

44

9.05 pm: Jenny placed a hand on the drinks cabinet, otherwise she was sure that she would crumple to the ground like clothes falling off a hanger. The time spent lying on her bed before Vera called would have been the worst in her life – if it hadn't been exceeded by the thirty minutes that had passed since her mother's arrival.

'Jennifer,' Vera said, her wide eyes examining her daughter's face as if it was a damaged artefact. 'It's going to be fine. I promise you. Don't be so—'

Jenny vomited. Red wine and buttered cracker. It spilled to the wooden floor and splashed over her shoes.

Vera covered her mouth with shocked hands. 'Oh my God.'

Everything was worse than Jenny could have imagined. No – 'worse' didn't do it. 'Worse' implied that there was still hope. *This* was in another stratosphere. Her life was simply over. Everything good in it was gone. Jenny never would have thought her mother was capable of doing such a thing. Fine, Vera was difficult. She was a liar and conniving. Self-centred and totally self-serving. But what she had done… it was beyond comprehension.

Jenny asked, 'How? *How could you do such a thing?*'

Vera slammed a fist into her palm and held both against her chest. 'Because I love you, Jennifer. It's for the best. I know it. I know it in here, so help me God.'

Despite the grandeur of her actions, she no longer looked so sure anymore. Vera's eyes were wide. There seemed to be genuine regret in them. Or at least an absence of the certainty they'd contained when she had told Jenny what she'd done.

'Go, Mum,' Jenny muttered. 'Please. Just go.'

Vera left the room. She opened the front door, closed it and Jenny watched through dazed eyes as her mother hurried out to the road aligned by trees that were still as monuments. Collapsing onto her husband's beanbag, she closed her eyes and listened to her heartbeat.

'Oh God, oh God, oh God,' she moaned into the soft material.

Her phone vibrated. Was it Shane? No. It couldn't be. His mobile was upstairs under the mattress. She glanced at it.

YOUR TIME IS UP.

'I know,' she muttered. But she typed nothing. When it was over, it was over.

The phone dinged again:

IT'S TIME FOR STRIKE THREE.

Jenny sat up. *No. I won't be threatened. Not now. Not ever. Not by him.* She typed:

I'm phoning the police. I'm calling them now.

She faced the window and waited for his reply.

From behind, a voice said, 'It's too late. I'm already here.'

45

9.15 pm: Twenty minutes before, Shane, duct taped to the chair, had listened through the darkness to the car starting outside. The engine had revved. Wheels had spun. Gravel had been thrown. Then it had gone, speeding down the driveway. Destination Clareville.

Jesus. Jesus. Jesus. Shane now continued to struggle against the tape, but it would not loosen. Every part of his body that could move flexed itself – fingers, toes, eyelids, stomach, chest. Finally, there was traction. The chair shifted. He increased the intensity. The chair shifted again – millimetres. Then centimetres. Enough to build momentum, almost like perpetual motion. Soon the chair was rocking.

With a final effort, the chair and Shane fell backwards, like timber falling. As the back of Shane's head collided with the floor, there was a splintering sound and the spine of the chair popped free. He pitched forward – enough to raise the weakened chair inches and bang it repeatedly on the floor. The tape loosened around his chest to give him just enough freedom to work an arm loose. Within minutes, Shane was on his feet and free. He reached for his phone, but it wasn't there. It was back in Clareville. With Jenny. With Ultan.

Shane entered the master bedroom, where Otto was still taped to a chair with moistness expanding around his thighs, like he was a woman miscarrying in a late trimester. As he ripped the tape from Otto's lips, the Austrian gasped for air, like a man emerging from the sea. 'Thank God, Shane. Thank God.'

'You OK?'

'Yes. Yes, I think so.'

'Where's your phone?'

'I don't know… I… he…'

'*Where*? Tell me.'

He nodded at the dressing table. 'He left it there.'

Shane snapped up Otto's mobile and dialled Jenny. It went to voicemail. He talked quickly: 'Jenny, something's happened. You need to get out of the house. Then call the police. Jenny, call me back. No. Don't. There's no time. Jesus. If you get this, just get out.'

As he struggled to free Otto, Shane told him, 'Call the police. Send them to Clareville. I've no time. Keys. Where's your car keys?'

'Wait. What? He's already taken my Porsche.'

'You've an SUV. Give me the keys.'

Otto was growing paler. Breathing more heavily. He pleaded, 'Don't go. Please… he could be still here. What if he just wants us to think he's gone? If you leave, he'll kill me. Or… or… you leave and that fucking psycho kills *you* in Clareville. Whatever way you look at it, if you go and I stay… then one of us is making a terrible mistake.'

For Shane, Otto's face represented the visage of a spineless prick that had some kind of empty dangling sack where his balls should be. Then, Shane felt bad. Before tonight Otto had probably never been punched in his life, let alone experienced anything like the trauma he'd just – barely – lived through. He looked a different man without his glasses. It was as if they were the key to him. Without them, he missed handsomeness by inches – his nose too sharp, eyes too beady, hair too thin.

'Otto, he's gone to get Jenny.'

'He's a nutcase, Shane. As strong as a fox.'

Shane, pulling the rest of the tape from the Austrian's body, said, 'It's ox, Otto. Ox. Now get me the keys.'

Otto staggered to his feet, wincing as his wet trousers stretched tight against his thighs. 'Yes. Ox. Whatever. He's a psychopath. Oh, look at the state of me. I'm so sorry, Shane.'

'Don't worry. It's understandable. Otto, I need those keys!'

Otto hurried to the dresser and threw them across to Shane. 'You're really going back?' He sounded incredulous. Then, clearly dreading the answer, asked, 'Want me to come?'

'No. I told you what to do. Call the police. Now.'

'Wait. Take this.' Opening the dresser, Otto withdrew the pistol and smiled, a hint of his old self returning. 'He's stronger than all us marines combined, huh? You'll need it.'

46

9.25 pm: Jenny was kneeling on the beanbag cushion, facing the window. Despite the city lights, the young night sky contained a visible star cluster that seemed like a weeping wound.

When had she started crying? Her tears sprang from a sudden remorse that if she was about to die, then she would never get to tell Shane that life with him had been a great adventure. He had kept surprising her and giving her reasons to get up in the morning. She didn't regret a minute of it. Then it occurred, that after he saw the photo on his phone, Shane *would* regret ever having met her.

She asked, 'How did you get in?'

'Same as last time. You'd think you would've learned. Or maybe you were expecting me? You now know who I am, right?'

'Yes.'

'So why did you throw me away? You owe me that, Mother.'

In London, the morning of her appointment at the clinic, her father had knocked on Jenny's hotel room door. He'd hired a private detective to find her, which had not been hard since she'd travelled under her own name.

Lorcan begged Jenny not to go through with it. He could not stand by as another family member was lost. But a tearful Jenny remained adamant. She was *not* having this baby. Before London, she had tried punching herself in the stomach. She had even sat in the bath drinking gin before passing out. But the baby had clung on to her insides like a parasite.

Lorcan offered her the deal – she could go to Toronto and put the baby up for adoption. He would take care of the accommodation and expenses. Within the firm, one of the Canadian board members was an evangelical, deeply involved in an American-financed zealous wing of the Catholic Church that steered pregnant women from abortion clinics to an unfussy adoption. If Jenny agreed to this, Lorcan would sign over to her his investment property in Clareville.

They flew out to Toronto and Lorcan oversaw Jenny settling into a downtown condominium and meeting his contact from the firm's board. Lorcan agreed that Vera must never know. She would consider giving up the child to be almost as bad as the abortion, and would forever hound Jenny as to the whereabouts of her grandchild. Especially if it was a boy.

When Lorcan returned to Dublin, Vera and Joan were appalled that Jenny had completed the abortion and was now living in Canada. They were doubly dismayed when Lorcan explained that he had *not* severed relations with Jenny; that she would be returning to Ireland within a year and since she was no longer welcome in the family home, he was giving her Clareville. In response, Joan refused to speak to him; a silent treatment that had barely begun to thaw before his sudden death a year later. She'd never forgiven Jenny for the guilt of that, either.

9.26 pm: Jenny stood and faced her son. The most amazing transformation had occurred. His beard was gone, revealing pale, soft skin and acne scars across his cheeks that made his face look like a rifle range. But without his beard, he was no longer a man in his thirties. He was clearly mid-twenties.

Again, she noticed the tattoos behind the V of his shirt spreading up to his neck. She assumed his entire torso was covered in them. Usually, Jenny was interested in men with tattoos. It often meant that they understood a few essential things about themselves; things that would never change. Carefully, she soaked up his eyes. They were hers. Then there was his now exposed chin that had been covered by bristles – it belonged to *his* father.

'You're not Shane's,' she stated. 'You're Otto's.'

He went to scratch his beard and was surprised to find it not there. 'You never knew?'

'I always knew. Shane and I were way too careful. It couldn't have been him. But that one time with… Otto doesn't know I had a baby, either.'

'He's a wealthy man. Surprised you didn't marry him instead of Shane.'

'I love Shane. If I were to have a child, it would've been with him.'

'You *did* have a child, Mother.'

'Stop calling me that.'

'You gave birth to me. Me – Ultan. That makes you a mother. It makes you *my* mother.'

She thought of Vera's lies, her game playing, her endless

manipulations. Jenny said, 'Giving birth doesn't make you a mother, any more than buying an easel makes you Picasso.'

'You tell yourself that. I hope it makes you feel better. But I'm your son. Like, haven't you a memory of pushing me out of your—'

She spun around. 'Don't you dare!'

Jenny remembered every moment of her pregnancy. It was like trying to carry a pint of lager around for nine months without spilling a drop. Shipwrecked in Canada, she'd never felt like a mother-to-be. Even after four months, the only thing she had to show for the pregnancy were sore breasts and an all-consuming desire to eat carbs.

She remembered the doctor squirting gel onto her stomach and then sliding a probe over it. Within seconds, Jenny saw the fluttering grey image on the screen. Her baby. The doctor flicked a switch and the room filled with a loud pulsating sound: the baby's heartbeat. Jenny listened, while looking at the strange seahorse-like image in the picture – and felt nothing.

Everything about the pregnancy was terrible. Eating constantly was the only way she could fill her days. The relentless poking and prodding by the examining medics, seemed almost as intimate as her sex life. During the final stages, the late prenatal ache between her legs was so intense that for weeks it had felt like the baby was about to drop out at any second.

When she arrived at the Toronto maternity hospital, a nurse told her, 'Don't worry, at your age delivery is straightforward.' But nothing was straightforward in that labour ward, where women with swollen bellies cried out all day in pain and fear, while stressed partners paced about muttering to themselves.

When the contractions increased in speed, she was rolled into the delivery room. There, the child arrived quickly, and she had felt little more than a heavy, deep stretching before it had suddenly materialised, slippery and shining in her own body's juices. Just like that, Ultan was dumped squawking and mewling into the world, a moist, ugly ball of toxic raw purple that had torn open the drapes of his mother's vagina. As they took him away to clear his airways, Jenny had not even asked whether it was a boy or girl.

When they brought it back, the baby was grey, gluey and angry with her. Clearly, he hated the world already. He smelt strange – sweet, unfamiliar and other-worldly. He terrified her. As the baby nestled into her shoulder, she had waited for that moment of bonding that would lead inevitably to heartbreak as it was denied. But all she thought was, *I'm too young for this. I never wanted it. I should be out there, living my life.*

In the days that followed, Jenny felt like a hideous creature, bleeding heavily and passing clots as big as mandarins. She had so much milk for the baby that she leaked whenever she bent over, while her flabby stomach was like a bag of glue that refused to hold its shape. It would take her months to get her figure back.

9.28 pm: 'I have to say, my grandmother is an incredible lady… just incredible.'

Jenny snapped, 'You don't know anything about her.'

'I know she found me. I know she welcomed me. I know she wishes I'd been in her life. And I knew that she could give me you.'

47

9.29 pm: Shane bleeped the SUV unlocked. Opening the door, two moths rushed inside like looters. *She could be dead.* Ultan was a dangerous stalker, obsessed with his wife. Ultan was armed. Ultan was insane. Ultan wanted to punish Jenny for being Jenny.

In the SUV, Shane jammed the nuzzle of the gun into his palm, feeling the 0 press hard on his skin, as if to contain its potential violence. He placed it on the passenger seat which was covered with a sheet of old chip paper, translucent with grease. Jabbing the key at the ignition, his shaking hand struggled to insert it. He needed a cigarette. Jenny would kill him if she knew he'd had one earlier. Yet, the idea of Jenny alive and angry with him in the morning was comforting.

The engine coughed and started. Accelerating down the driveway, he wondered whether he should just ram the gates, but they began to open of their own accord. Shane stepped on it and raced towards the city. Along the quiet empty street, the headlight beams illuminated the trees in a white glow, like a ghost flying through the branches. Despite the crisis, and much to his own self-loathing, he couldn't help but notice the quality of the car. The difference between his own wrecked ten-year-old Land Rover and Otto's glistening SUV was like the difference between his rowing boat and a fucking aircraft carrier.

Within minutes, Shane pulled out into the bay-front traffic and the car vibrated over the ruts of the weathered road. Clareville was only ten minutes away – less if the streets weren't busy. A white Lexus GX with the bumper sticker, **Jesus Would Have Driven a 4X4**, cruised at leisurely speed between two lanes. Shane repeatedly punched the horn until the Lexus moved over, the driver giving him the finger.

The closer he came to Clareville, the heavier the traffic became. While slowly passing a McDonalds full of inner-city kids queueing for their type 2 diabetes, his hand rebounded from the stick to the gun and back again. Further along the street a homeless guy faced the wall, aiming his yellow urine rope, pleased to be shocking a gang of passing tourists. A fox, its coat the colour of a traffic cone, ran before his car and into an alleyway.

The only thing Shane could do was watch it all and drive. He hit a speed bump and the car kangarooed. Jerking forward, he instinctively checked for his phone again – to call the police, to call Jenny – but of course it was not there.

Jenny needed him and *he* was not there. His wife – she was assured of the power of her intellect, and she was right. She was confident in her indestructibility, and she was wrong.

48

9.39 pm: Ultan said, 'I don't like this room. People can see in far too easily from the road. Let's go to the kitchen, Mother.'

As if she was an old woman, his hand pressed on the small of Jenny's back as he steered her out into the hallway. She opened the kitchen door and walked to the island.

'Can I sit?'

'It's your house.'

'So, I can leave?'

'No.'

She sat. He remained standing, towering over her.

'Where are you from?' Jenny asked, even though her mother had already told her.

'From inside you. But I live in Bangkok.'

'Bangkok? Why?'

'Either because I'm dumb or full of self-loathing. Which do you think?'

'What do you do there?' Jenny's mother had not told her this.

'I'm a travel guide. An exclusive one.'

'What's an "exclusive" travel guide?' Jenny sounded both surprised and disappointed. 'You drive the transfer from the airport to the six-star?'

'At first, I just worked for the Chatrium Hotel as a trainer, but I had nothing to do until late in the afternoon when some tourists trickled in. Throughout the rest of the day, a few mid-ranking police officials would tog out to hang with "whitey" and show off their wealth. To escape the boredom, I branched out to provide expertise for outdoorsy scientists – help them collect data while delivering trekking adventure know-how in hiking, biking and climbing. Then, one day, I'm in my room overlooking the royal park and the phone rings and it's a little old Irish lady saying that she's my grandmother and that it broke her heart that she didn't even know that I'd existed, but that she'd always wished I did.'

Jenny bitterly laughed. 'It's her dead son that she wishes existed. It's all the sons she didn't have that she wishes existed. It's not *you*.'

Less than an hour ago, Vera had told her that, as Lorcan grew weaker, he had divulged the truth about what happened in London and Toronto. Lorcan had said that there would always be hope of Jenny and her son reuniting. If that was to occur, then the only chance that Vera would have to be a part of that family would be if she kept some type of relationship with Jenny. Lorcan had made Vera promise to never tell Joan about the adoption, as she would use it against Jenny and ensure that she never came back to the family.

Vera had said to Jenny, 'Lorcan was right. Joan is too emotional. She sometimes doesn't think clearly. You see, Jennifer, I too know what's right. And I know how to do this. I know how to get my grandson into this family. But Joan would try and sabotage my efforts. I mean, it's *your* son. She would never accept him when she doesn't even accept you.'

It had been her mother's project – a twenty-five-year-long mission. *That* was why Vera had kept Jenny hanging by a thread; why Vera had let her rent Clareville with the vague hope that she might leave it to her. She had not just wanted Jenny around so she could incrementally punish her. She had actually wanted something tangible – Jenny's son. She was like a spider, unwearyingly waiting, year after year, for the prey to finally reveal itself.

Jenny had asked her, 'Is that why you never gave Shane a chance?'

'I've never made a secret of my views on what marriage is. It's children, Jennifer. He never gave you any. I know it's an old-fashioned adage, but he never *did his duty*. Someone else did it for him. You told your father who it was. A man called Otto.'

'Mum, you have no idea what happened.'

'I know he was your teacher. What were you thinking, Jennifer? But God works in mysterious ways. And through your… your sex sin, a beautiful life arrived. My grandson. That teacher gave you something that your husband was too selfish to give you. That's why, as you say, I never gave Shane a chance. Why should I?'

Jenny's eyes had watered. All she could think of was how much Shane had wanted a child and how it was *she* who had denied him. She asked, 'So, how did my son find you?'

'*I* found *him*, but of course. Year after year and no sign of you looking for my grandson. But I prayed, every night, that you'd be secretly arranging contact with him. And that you'd finally come to me and say, "Mumma, there's someone I want you to meet."'

It was incredible. Vera had managed to make even this all about herself.

Her mother continued: 'Over the last few years, our friends have started to die – like dominoes. Great men in your father's firm, long retired; they're all dropping like flies. Their wives, too.' She sounded sad, but her expression was triumphant – Vera survives, so Vera wins. 'One of them, Frank Bastick, from Canada, sent me a letter. His prostate was taking him. But he wrote charmingly about the times he'd had with Lorcan. He mentioned you and your adoption. Very casually. Very briefly. How far Lorcan went to protect your unborn baby. Frank assumed I knew. Or perhaps, he'd forgotten that he wasn't supposed to tell me. Or maybe it was a miracle – God's way of letting me know that my grandson was ready to come home.'

Vera didn't merely become involved in things. She took ownership of them.

'I called Frank, but he was very weak. His wife was so helpful though, and said they were still major benefactors of the organisation that had taken you under its wing. She made calls for me. She had her people access files. This wasn't any straightforward legal adoption. Yours had been done between the lines, so to speak, because your father had to bend the rules. You weren't Canadian so there were channels you had to skip. There were corridors you had to be quickly hurried down. My God, the things that man did for you.'

Without asking, Vera refilled her glass. 'Anyhow, Frank's wife had access to your son's name, and she was able to trace all the places he'd lived while in Canada until he was eighteen. She was able to contact his last address and received the news that he was now living in Thailand. She even had a number for me to try. I called, but of course he was no longer living there. However, they had another number and I tried that and so on – I was quite the Miss Marple – and eventually I called a number and my grandson picked up.'

Vera explained that, for a while, she'd called her grandson once a week to offer him abbreviated news from her life. 'I told him that I don't use the computer-email thing. Sure, why should I? Anyone who wants to contact me that way, does so through Joan. And, as you know, Joan also takes care of my standard correspondence, picking out the relevant ones for me to scan through. So, letters were also out of the question. Couldn't have Joan knowing what I was up to. But thank God, he was always there when I called or would get back very promptly. They were wonderful calls – his passion, hearing the proof that he cares so much about what I think and what I believe and how I… how I… I don't want to say "judge him", but that too.'

Jenny stared at her mother, aghast at how she was so pleased with herself, so utterly enthralled with her own efficacious sleuthing; at how the impact of her gross interference in another person's life did not even register in her thought processes. But all of that was nothing compared with what Vera was about to tell her.

9.42 pm: Ultan said, 'Just a week ago, I got a letter delivered to the hotel. From Grandmother. She wanted me to come "home", as she kept calling Ireland. To meet her. Before it was too late. She'd also included a small but precious gift. A photograph of Mommy.'

'So *that's* how you got it,' Jenny muttered. She didn't need to look at her phone to see it again. It was imprinted on her brain – a colour shot of an eighteen-year-old Jenny in her final trimester, all swollen like a tick; bulbous pale stomach, protruding belly button, white bikini top, black tracksuit bottoms. She was unsmiling, leaning against a brick wall outside the hospital. A nurse had taken it, as she had made no friends in Toronto. She remembered posting it to her father a few days before giving birth.

Ultan continued. 'The timing was almost mystical. Because I'd been thinking for a while… that my life wasn't washed away by misfortune. Instead, it was destroyed by a person. And suddenly, that photograph made me realise that this person must have a name and address. So, I got a plane to Dublin, just like Grandmother wanted me to. Now, the thing about new cities is that you have to try and learn how to trust strangers, and it never dawns on a lot of people that this might not be a good idea. That's why I went with Dee, who was going home too. I had her take me here. So I could look at *this*.' He gestured grandly to the kitchen, to the house. 'To look in your windows. To see what you took away from me. To see the value of what getting rid of me was worth to you. And *this*… this house and everything in it, is what you swapped me for. This house and all its pleasures is what you reckon I was worth.'

'So you think I denied you money? Listen to me – from basically the day you were conceived, I've had nothing. There was nothing to give you. Absolutely zilch.'

'Fuck you. This is about my entire fucking life. This is about the shit I've lived through. *Not* fucking money.'

'I left you in good hands.'

'Good hands? I was adopted by religious fanatics who home-schooled me till I was twelve. No wonder I went off the rails when I got to high school. The more difficult I found life, the more distant they became. It was as if they thought mild depression or anxiety were types of airborne diseases. Like swine flu or TB. I needed to place garbage bags on the windows because I had a sleeping problem. I needed white noise because I had an ear problem. I needed booze because I had an anxiety problem. I needed money because I had a living problem. When I was arrested a few times and thrown out of school, my adopted parents couldn't handle me anymore. They said they were scared of me.'

'Scared of you?' *How scared should I be?* Jenny noticed the switchblade sticking out of his trouser pocket.

'I *never* touched them. They were just delusional morons with no concept of reality.'

'I'm sorry. I didn't know.'

'Oh, that was nothing. I was fostered out to a family hundreds of miles north of Winnipeg where I learned to never underestimate the cold. Up there, you watch the environment disappear; you watch the earth disappear; you watch the ice dissolve like great big aspirins. Up there, I took the measure of my own insignificance and I survived. But that family; they were tough, harsh. They didn't take no shit from a troubled teen. They made me pray three times a day. Hardcore prayer. There were also little prayers to say before every snack and drink of water. These people were even bigger lunatics than my adoptive parents. Their favourite word was "no", and their motto was "What use is a parent who cannot prohibit?"'

'I am so sorry.' Jenny was suddenly amazed at the realisation that she had never thought that her son could have been lost in that labyrinth of horrific crimes committed by the Catholic hierarchy and its institutions. The scandals in the Church had merely confirmed to her that people with absurd beliefs could commit atrocities easily.

'I wasn't the only one they looked after. That lovely evangelical cult you gave me up to, they just kept feeding them other kids. And we all ran away. To get drugs. To sell ourselves at truck stops. But we always came back because there was nowhere to run to up there.'

'You've got to believe me – if I'd known… If I'd had any idea, then I would've—'

'That wasn't my last foster home. I had a whole raft of them when I was sixteen and seventeen. Two were OK. One was just plain old violent. Another was pervy. The last one like a prison camp. I almost starved there. And I learned that those people with the least to be grateful to God for, are those who thank Him the most. But when I turned eighteen, I was gone. I was free. I was going to sign up to the Canadian armed forces… 'cos, when you've been told for your whole life that you're shit at everything, it's not hard to miss when you can finally do something really, *really* well. But first I took a trip to Thailand… and once there, I never left the place until now.'

'But… you're not the only child who was put up for adoption. And most turn out OK.' She closed her eyes, embarrassed at how mealy sounding her point was.

Ultan flicked open another button on his shirt, exposing his chest, which was just more ink and no skin – Thai writing, old gods, guns and knives. 'Do I look OK? Do you think I was voted *most likely to succeed*?'

'You've made your point.'

'My *point*? Is that what all of this is to you? Someone making a point? Do you think that I'm a problem that will either be quickly solved or even better – just disappear? Like what happened to Dee?

When was the last time you thought of her? You watched her die only three days ago. I bet the memory is fading already. Sinking into the cushions of your life. But I'll never forget. She was only here because of me. She was just doing me a favour… but like anything that touches you—'

'Fine. You want revenge and I deserve it. For your childhood. For Dee. For everything. But you've sent the picture to my husband and ruined my life. Just like I accidentally ruined yours. So, please leave.'

Ultan laughed. 'You think I came here to *talk*? To have a catch-up?'

'What did you come here for?'

'I've come to give myself something God never can – justice.'

'What are you going to do?'

'I told you already. By sundown, I'm going to destroy everything that means anything to you. Look outside – your sun has set.'

'You've wrecked my marriage. What else is there?'

'Online, Mother, like most people, you're very disappointing. Your Instagram. Your Facebook. Your blog. You think you're unique. But then along comes social media to show the rest of us that you're all the same – going to the same beaches and countries, eating the same food, listening to the same music, walking the same galleries, reading the same books. Living in the same types of houses. See, I know exactly what you love the most. It's what you traded me for. Grandmother told me too. This. Clareville. Your house.' He walked around to the other side of the island and picked up a two-litre, green plastic canister. Staring at her, he gave it a shake. Inside, the petrol sloshed about.

'What are you doing?'

'I'm going to burn it all down. Especially the furniture. That was Grandfather's, right? You cherish that stuff so much. It's all you have of him. It's all that's left of who you were.'

'Wait...' Jenny was picturing it already – flames bursting out from the windows, sparks from her father's furniture spiralling upwards like dancing fireflies. For a second, the memory of her mother's final revelation smashed through her brain.

'Vera hasn't told you, has she? Her plans for the house. What she's doing with it.'

Vera had stood in Shane's study, wine glass in hand, enthusiastically explaining to Jenny that, 'Ultan is of the age where he should be at least settling down and thinking about having children. Oh, Jennifer, how I'd love a *great* grandson – a clear line from my son to grandchild to the next generation, and all within my lifetime. It's what any mother wants. My plan is for Ultan to first settle into Ireland and create a bond with you. See, I'm really doing it for *you*, pet. For what is best for us all.'

As usual, Vera had carefully picked the elements of her past and her present that were true and combined them effortlessly with utter fiction. Jenny's mother lived in a world where everything must always go her way. Her life and the lives of everyone in it must be exactly as she wanted them to be.

Vera expounded: 'At first, I imagined putting him into Hugh's room. Alas, I quickly realised that *that* is never going to happen. Every day since Hugh left me, I enter it and open the blinds that I still close every night. And I breathe in, deeply. There are molecules of Hugh's life floating around in there, you see, and I just want to swim in them. I couldn't have anyone else in there. So, the only alternative is... well, I think you can guess.'

* * *

9.46 pm: Jenny said, 'This house isn't mine. It's Mum's. I just rent it. And she's throwing me out. Know why?' Across from her, Ultan unscrewed the lid of the canister. 'She's throwing me out because she's giving it to you.'

Ultan's eyes narrowed. He was interested once more.

'That's her big plan. That's her *coup de grâce*. That's what she brought you back for. You – the soon to be stand-in son. She sees you living here, with her portrait on the walls. She sees you marrying and breeding and keeping her lineage alive. She sees you telling her great grandkids about how incredible she was and then, after you're gone, *they'll* inherit the house, and her awesomeness will live forever. So yeah – burn the fucking place down. Do what you want with it. It's yours, my dear son. All of it. Take it. It's cursed.'

He placed the canister lid on the island counter. Ultan was breathing heavily. He licked his upper lip. 'Back then, you could say and do whatever you liked, because you were you.'

'What does *that* mean?'

'It *means*, you could get away with anything because of who you were, because you came from money. You were white. You had great teeth. You went to uni. The list of luck and privilege was endless. And you gave me away because I was going to wreck the life-long party.'

'But it was wrecked anyway. My family disowned me. I lost my inheritance. I lost my family home. I'm about to lose this house. I'm about to lose my husband. So, tell me – just how did my wonderful life continue by giving you up?'

'Fuck you.' Ultan raised the canister, scanning the far wall for a spot to drench.

'I was eighteen,' she said sharply. 'What were you like at eighteen? Huh? I couldn't look after myself, never mind a baby. I never even wanted to have sex with Otto. Your grandmother never told you that – did she? Of course she didn't, because she doesn't know.'

'Did he—'

'No. It wasn't like that. I was drugged, but not by him. He didn't know. And he was on drugs himself. It was messy. And it shouldn't have happened. I didn't know how to deal with the whole situation. As I keep saying, I was *eighteen*. If I'd had that baby then, I—'

'*That* baby?'

'You. OK? *You*. If I'd had *you* and kept *you* then I'd have had to lie to Shane – tell him that you were his, and then watch for the rest of all our lives as Shane lived out my lie. No. I wasn't doing that. I'd have had more babies because I couldn't have Shane bringing you up, believing you were his and not actually giving him any of his own.'

Again, Ultan looked at the wall. Again, he looked back to Jenny.

She said, 'And that was only if Shane stuck with me. He was eighteen too, remember. If he didn't stay with me to bring you up, then by having you I would've been stranded at home forever. And believe me, I needed to get out of that bloody house. You have no idea what it was like. All I knew is that there was a sickness in my family home.'

'A sickness?'

'My mother. Nothing like your awful upbringing. But it was psychological. With my teenage years running out I was coming to see who – or what – Mum really was. Then there was my sister, too. The toxicity. The lies. The bitching. And I'd be expected to bring up a child in that atmosphere, with Mum down my throat, trying to replace Hugh with you. God, no – I couldn't do that. I *wouldn't* do that. Not when there were apparently hundreds of loving parents queueing up to give you the life you deserved. *That's* what I believed.'

Ultan rounded the island, canister by his side. 'You were originally going to abort me.'

Jenny looked away. *I can't believe Mum told him that.* It was something she never revisited because the thoughts that were behind the original decision were thoughts that only occurred in the dark; for the specific reason that they could stay there.

She said, 'Even though I was eighteen, I didn't take that decision lightly. How could I when I was well aware that I was losing my family and all that came with it? Jesus, I was seven years younger than you are now and look at you…' She reached out and, for a second, touched his cheek. 'You're still so young. I had to deal with being pregnant by myself and I'm not saying I did the correct thing but… you're right – being privileged gave me the power to do things that an eighteen-year-old shouldn't have been able to do… to make decisions about their future with naïve certainty. Unfortunately, I was too young to realise that there were – that there *are* – consequences to all my actions.'

Ultan's head lowered a little, eyes blinking in thought.

Softening her voice, Jenny said, 'The fact is, I'm glad you're back. I don't care if you believe me or not. But I'm glad that I've been able to tell you the truth.' Again, she reached out and touched his cheek, but this time allowed her hand to remain a little longer. 'If the only thing that makes you happy is to burn this house down… then do it. You have my blessing.'

Slowly, he lowered the canister to the floor.

Jenny said quietly, 'Just… if you're going to hurt me, do it quickly.'

Stunned, Ultan stared at her. 'I was never going to hurt you. Not physically.'

'You have a blade.'

He suddenly looked ashamed as he took the switchblade from his pocket and looked at it. 'I was never going to… it was just for shaving my beard… I'd kept it for that. To get rid of the old me on the day I finally got closure. I planned it that way. I was never going to…' His voice trailed off.

'You scared me.'

'I'm… I'm sorry. I'm just so fucking angry. I always wondered who you were and why you did it. Why, why, why. Always asking and no one there to answer. But still… I would never… Look, I know that men hurt women far more than women hurt men. It's just a truth. But I would never harm you. You're a woman. And you're my mother.'

They held each other's gaze. A moment passed. And another. She heard a faint noise. From the hallway. It was a specific sound: half groan, half squeak. Between the last step of the stairs and the study was a single loose floorboard.

Shane said, 'Do not move.'

Her husband was standing at the door to the hallway, gun pointing directly at Ultan. Jenny recalled her father's motto hung behind his desk in his big company office: *The very moment they think you're finished, your success is assured.* She stared at Shane, taking in his coldness, his concentration, the tension on his trigger finger. Jenny now understood how they had got to this place. The unthinkable had become thinkable and the thinkable had then become doable. Reaching out her hands imploringly towards him, she shouted, 'No, Shane…'

49

SUNDOWN: Shane's arm was outstretched. There was a gun at the end of it. It was a nice weight in his hand. With those bullets in the chamber, all he had to do was squeeze the trigger, as easy as squirting toothpaste. It was aimed at Ultan, who faced him with the switch-blade in his hand. Next to Ultan was Jenny. Her arms outstretched towards him, pleading.

She shouted, 'No, Shane… don't hesitate. Shoot him.'

He pulled the trigger.

The bullet would stop only when it came into contact with its target, and when the target was reached, it would be obliterated. The gun fired. It seemed like the loudest noise he had ever heard. Then there was silence until the silence gave way to a pure, high sound wave – exactly like a test tone.

Shane blinked. There was only Jenny standing before him. Ultan lay on the ground. Or rather, what remained of him. The floor was strewn with bits of his face and skull – it was all there, but would never go back together again. The razor had fallen to the floor a few feet away and spun on the tiles, coming to a halt with the blade pointing back towards him.

Now that Shane knew for certain Ultan was dead, he felt that he had just seen his soul cast away to the atmosphere like a handful of confetti. Had Ultan, just for a moment, experienced silence again?

Sinking to his knees, Shane tried to say Ultan's name, but dry-heaved. His stomach tore at his throat.

Jenny staggered away from the body, saying, 'Blood. So much blood.'

Shane looked up at her and said, 'It's OK. It's all fine now.'

Jenny shook her head, as if suddenly waking up and immediately needing to be alert. Then she walked towards him. Shane was ready to embrace her, but she passed him by, into the hallway and ran up the stairs.

'Jenny,' he called. 'Jenny, are you OK?'

He wanted to follow her. He needed to. But he couldn't move. His eyes wouldn't leave the body. The blood. The mess. *He was going to kill my wife. He was insane. He was armed. I had no choice.*

Jenny was beside him again. How fast was time moving? She was there. She was gone. She was back again. She had something in her hand.

'Your phone,' Jenny said. 'Call the police.'

The sound of sirens carried through the hallway from outside. They were coming already. Otto had done his job. Jenny nudged him. 'Call them anyway… to be sure. Do it.'

He looked at his phone. *What's my code?* Slowly he started keying it in. His fingers would barely move. Jenny was crouching at the body. Was she looking for something? A voice in his ear said, 'Emergency services? What is your type of emergency?'

Footsteps approached the front door. He'd left it ajar when he had snuck in. They were here. He hung up.

Jenny was walking away from the body, crossing the kitchen. She had her own phone out, held up to her face. Who was she phoning? She opened the back door and as she stepped outside, her weeping voice said, 'Mum… something awful has happened.'

50

Six Weeks Later

'See?' Vera said, her pen poised above the deeds. 'I was always going to give you the house. It was just a matter of getting around to it.'

She signed.

It fascinated Jenny, watching Vera's lies immediately gain instant permanence.

Mother and daughter sat across from each other, midway down a conference table, in the boardroom of the family solicitor's office. It was the first time Jenny and Vera had seen each other since the events of six weeks ago. After Ultan's death, Vera had never once directly referred to all that unpleasantness. It was basically as if he'd never existed. Though Vera *had* texted every few days to tell Jenny how good she'd looked in the papers or how well she had come across in an interview. But Jenny wasn't surprised at her mother's behaviour. All of Vera's children had been ego food. They had all been just extensions of her brilliant self.

With everything signed and organised, their solicitor bid them farewell and left the room with the files and deeds. The end line was in sight. Jenny now had Clareville. It was hers and nothing on earth could change that fact. Her mother had also written off the tax liability due on the gift. Signing over the house was the closest Vera had come to admitting responsibility for all that had occurred.

Simultaneously, Jenny and Shane were now fully invested in Otto's property deal. Jenny knew that her husband's eventual acquiescence was because he wanted to spoil her, to be extra kind after the trauma she'd experienced. But there was also something else to it. Perhaps he'd seen something in Otto that he hadn't been aware of. But the bottom line was that within a year their investment would start paying out, and soon she and Shane would have at least a million in cash. The fact was, they'd never have to do anything they didn't want to do again, which is what most people think they want.

The last time Jenny had seen Otto was when he'd tried to kiss her. She knew he was now in therapy with some big shot life coach just up the road in St Catherine's Hill. Jenny was pleased for him, as it seemed that Otto had finally realised that what his life required was a systematic redesign and that it was *him* who would have to make that journey along the Great South Passageway that led to final enlightenment.

Across the table, Vera poured their glasses of the complimentary Chardonnay her solicitor had opened and said, 'Now that you've put all of that nasty business behind you, it's time to move on. I have, too. Unlike the rest of my friends, I refuse to settle for another winter of afternoon television. It's ghastly stuff these days. Daytime TV is now night-time TV. It's been taken over by the obese, unemployed and the incontinent. So … I'm doing an Open University course this winter. I'm going to study botany.'

'Bot—... *why*?'

'Plants thrive in families. Underground, in the soil, they form complex social networks. That's why they're so sturdy and strong. It'll be nice to just have to grow plants to get a qualification. See, Jennifer, I can do college too. I can do anything if I put my mind to it. Joan's lot complained about college all the time. The pressure. The work. La-de-da. I'll show them. I'll show them how it's done.'

'I doubt it'll be a degree, Mum – but impressive nonetheless.'

It was difficult not to admire Vera's dash – the way she seemed to gain energy as she aged; become more adamant about getting her way, shaping the world to her design. Since her mother had once convinced Jenny that she'd loved her deeply and would never measure or judge her, the adult Jenny couldn't help but, even for a brief second, put her on a pedestal.

Vera asked, 'So, what are your plans for the rest of the day? Running off back to work to sort out other people's problems for them?'

Jenny picked up the glass of wine, raised it to sip but changed her mind. 'A day of dealing with other people's problems can smooth out your own.'

The fact was, racing from one new build to another corporate refurbishment didn't allow her much time to think of Ultan and all that had happened. Had it been traumatic? She wasn't sure. The police had arranged for a counsellor in the immediate aftermath, but he hadn't made things easier or clearer or lighter. Perhaps Jenny didn't need them to be.

She remembered seeing Shane pointing the gun at Ultan. She'd had no doubt that her husband would pull the trigger. Jenny knew what Shane was capable of. Anyone who lacked the courage to kill, lacked the courage to live. And Shane lived well. He relished life.

He relished life with her. The immediate thought that went through her head had been – *Shoot him in the face.* Instinctively, Jenny hadn't wanted Ultan lying on the kitchen floor, unshaven aspect up, being stared at, until people – particularly Shane – began to see similarities with Otto.

After the shot was fired, Shane had remained staring at the body, lost in his wish to turn time backwards. She too had wanted to crumple to the ground – with relief, with exhaustion. It was like a Greek tragedy – a long lost son, child of his mother's lover, being killed in front of her by the oblivious husband. Jenny had to summon all her reserves to go upstairs to the bedroom, where she'd hidden her husband's phone. There, she deleted the picture that Ultan had texted.

Back in the kitchen, she handed Shane his phone to call the police. While he was doing so, she crouched by the carnage of her son's remains. Besides the blood, there was a yellow substance leaking from the cavity where the side of his skull had been. But the importance of thieving Ultan's phone from his leather jacket ensured that she didn't vomit.

The final thing she had to do was call her mother. While warning Vera to never tell anyone who Ultan was, Jenny could picture her mother superimposing her own image into the Clareville slaying: bullets, blood and butchering. How could anyone picture such a scene and believe it? A sheet of dread had audibly wrapped itself around Vera. All of this was way out of her league – murder, illegitimate bloodlines, police investigations, perhaps jail? Vera wouldn't have been sure how many, if any, laws she or her youngest child had broken. But the one thing that Vera did know, was that if she wasn't very careful then society's beam would shine onto her life, and it would not be a flattering glow.

Before hanging up, Vera had said, 'Jennifer – I'm so sorry you're experiencing this,' as if she hadn't caused any of it; as if she'd been merely a mother sympathising with her daughter's latest misfortune.

When the police arrived, Jenny had hidden Ultan's pay-as-you-go, over-the-counter mobile behind a shelf in the hall. Later she snuck it out, smashed it and threw it into the bay. The police concluded that Ultan must have done the same when travelling from Otto's to Clareville. In the end, his missing mobile hadn't interested them very much at all.

But the hardest thing Jenny had had to do happened afterwards – the telling of so many lies about Ultan. Jenny told the police that not only was he about to burn the house down, but he'd told her that, 'I'm going to cut your face up so bad that you'll need a decade of surgery just to be able to go outdoors without making kids cry.'

The police quickly found the hostel where Ultan had been staying. It was in a part of the city where middle-class people only went after dark, and only then if they wanted to die. His few belongings had been contained in a small backpack, along with a Canadian passport and Thai visas. After a brief investigation in conjunction with the Thai and Canadian authorities, they'd settled on the convenient conclusion that Ultan had been a loner who left behind a hard life in Canada for the bars of Bangkok.

When the police released Ultan's body, it was shipped back to Canada where his first adoptive parents arranged the burial. Like everyone else (besides Jenny and Vera), his adoptive parents had no idea that Ultan had Irish roots, and supposed that he had only travelled to Ireland to be with Dee – the young woman assumed to be his girlfriend.

A contrite Detective Murray had told Jenny, 'Ultan was just a professional weirdo who went off the rails after his girlfriend's death. Yes, it's strange that he told Shane that it hadn't been about that, and then told you the opposite. But who knows what goes through the heads of these guys? I mean, he kidnapped your accountant Otto, simply because he'd seen him calling into your house. He tortured Otto just to ask questions about you. He'd been going on to Shane about a mysterious picture that doesn't exist. He probably hated women – women who are successful and wealthy and… I suppose, powerful, like you. That's why he blamed you and not Shane, for killing Dee. The resentments these guys harbour can be legion.'

For once, Shane agreed with the police. He believed that Ultan had been a dropout, whose life spiralled out of control before he had a psychotic break after seeing his girlfriend die. Thankfully, Shane wasn't tempted to do his own research into Ultan's story. His aim with all of his books was to create something which told all sides of the story – especially the sides that people had once been too angry, sad or stupid to hear. But he was too close to Ultan's story to write about it without extreme prejudice. Shane had always maintained that the writer should be the court recorder and not the judge.

Over the last few weeks, Jenny had waited for the grief, the remorse, the self-loathing to cascade upon her. But every time she thought, *Oh my God, what have I done*? another reprimanding voice would sound in her head – Vera's. *You don't have to hate a fish to kill it.* Ultan's gate-crashing of her life had been like experiencing pregnancy all over again. She just wanted her son not to exist. To never have existed. To be gone from her body, from her kitchen, from her house, from her life, from the world. Now that he *was* gone, it really was like he'd never existed – as if the events all those years ago in London and Canada were false memories.

It was only recently that Jenny had accepted that it was all over; that things would return to normal; that life would now go on. But there was no feeling of triumph, not even of relief. Instead, she'd thought of her father. Her dad had no doubts whatsoever about right and wrong. Sometimes Jenny wished her own life could be as black and white as that. But, overall, she was glad that she existed in the grey region of morality. She had to make her own way. Every being, every single person, was simply a life built on the ruin of any number of preceding lives.

But while she knew that her father would never have done the things Jenny had done, she knew that her mother would have. Vera would've done it all in the perfectly efficient, self-deluded way in which she managed to turn every unpleasant act she ever performed into a win-win situation for her.

In the boardroom of the solicitor's office, Jenny again lifted her glass of wine and again put it back down without drinking. Vera, who couldn't handle silences very well, was clearly using up all her reserves to say nothing. She inhaled through her nose, exhaled through her mouth, and briefly licked the top of her lip.

Finally, she found something to say. 'Forgot to tell you – Joan got me a present.'

'She always gets you presents.'

'It's something she said that I needed. A cat.'

'A cat? What are you going to do with a cat?'

'I've only had it three days but… I like it. It's a sweet little thing. Curled up and sleeping, eating, and purring. It really likes Joan – Joan has such fun with it.'

Jenny snorted. It wasn't even possible for her to imagine Joan having fun. 'Its name?'

'Lucia. Lucia Cruz – The Light of the Cross.'

Sunlight angled through the window, spraying Vera with a healthy glow. Jenny was reminded of her childhood, where all her memories of her mother seemed to be in bright summer days. In Jenny's mind, Vera had been one of those rare women who were very beautiful and yet unafraid to stand in direct sunlight. She had been so thin and gorgeous; it was why so many people had assumed that she was a good person. Even then, image was everything.

But Jenny's memory of Vera being a proper mother was just an ember now. It was like something from back when there had been no BMWs, SUVs, Hummers. There had been just cars. Red had been red; not claret, damask or vermillion. Blue had been blue; not azure, sapphire or cyan. It was a peculiar sentiment, feeling close to someone she had never in fact properly known.

Vera's mobile chirped the arrival of a message. She looked down on it and smiled before suddenly blurting with relief, 'Oh fab, Joan is ready now. She's so good. Always there for me. Making time. Between the children and… and… it's amazing she even has time to clean the church. But she has such a generous spirit. That's why she does it, I suppose.'

Vera needed to expound upon Joan's inviolability, again and again, over and over, to whoever was listening, because the fact was, she had trained Joan to be absolutely everything for her, and Vera needed to pretend that she wasn't Joan's only reason for living.

Calmly, Jenny said: 'Joan has nothing going on in her life. Her husband left her, and her children have gone abroad to work or down the country to college. Joan never bothered with a third level education, so no interesting job is available to her, and she has too much money to concern herself with a boring job. So, to fill some hours in the week, she volunteers at looking like the holiest of the angels, so your congregation can all see that Vera Donaldson's clan are the tightest, loveliest, most blessed family in the parish. *That* is why Joan cleans the church.'

Vera had actually recoiled back into her seat, as though her body was a violin string; still vibrating but pulled taut. Her eyes were wide – two wells in an arctic sea. 'Shush – don't talk about your sister like that. She'll be here any second.'

'Here? She's coming *here*? To this conference room?'

'Of course. She's collecting me. I told you that she would—'

There was a brief rap of knuckles on the door. Jenny inhaled. The door opened. It was *not* their family solicitor.

Jenny observed her sister as if she were a painting that someone had the remarkable bad taste not only to purchase, but to actually hang on the wall. How she despised Joan's uniform of glamorous international businesswoman, which she wore despite the fact that she had hardly worked a day in her life. She probably thought the in-your-face Ray-Bans were subtle evidence of her great emotional depths. Jenny did not wish her mother dead, but it occurred to her that she *did* relish the many years of misery Joan would eventually have to endure, from her inability to cope, alone, in a life with no meaning or purpose.

Joan asked, 'So, Mom, you're ready?'

'I am.'

'Good. I don't want to spend one more second in that bitch's company than I need to. It makes me sick just to look at her – that self-satisfied, vile—'

Jenny casually interrupted; 'Do get on with it, Joan. Oh, and try not to make too much of an arse out of yourself. You're sober, so you won't have your usual excuse.'

'Don't you dare slander me! I don't know why Mom gave you Clareville. But it's Mom's and she can do whatever she wants with it. However, if you think—'

'What must it be like to be you, Joan? How do you deal with the inescapable familiarity? The same will-sapping predictability? Yours is a life where every day is the exact same and the trick to living is to simply use them up.'

Truly stunned, Joan muttered, 'Excuse me?'

'Joan, haven't you ever asked yourself why your best friend – your *only* friend – is your seventy-five-year-old mother? You're almost fifty and yet when you call in to her – call twice daily to this woman – those are still the highlights of your day.'

Shocked, confused, Joan mangled her attempted riposte. 'Who the hell are you to think you are talking to me like—'

'Haven't you asked yourself why your marriage failed and why you haven't even attempted to find someone else… to even just hang with?'

'How dare you?'

'Don't you know why you're an alcoholic?'

Joan removed her shades, as if allowing her eyes space to bulge.

Jenny, comfortable in her seat, folded her arms on the table. 'Don't you question why you've been such a shit mother? Your kids have been medicated since their teens. Each and every one of them. Every type of anxiety med. That's all down to you. You know that, right? Their angst, their fucked-upness… that's from living with you.'

Joan's breath was coming in quick sudden rushes.

'Don't you ever look in the mirror and wonder where your dreams disappeared to?'

In barely a whisper, Joan said, 'Fuck… you.'

'Newsflash, Joan – it's *her*.' Without looking at her mother, Jenny gestured across the table with her thumb. 'Don't you get it yet? You are her instrument, and you allowed it to happen, you dumb, ignorant, stupid, *fucking* idiot.'

For a moment Joan was still. Then, turning her back to the room, quietly said, 'Mom, I'll be downstairs in the car.' Then she left.

Vera stared across the table. 'Proud of yourself? Talking to your sister like that? If I was you, Jennifer, I'd line up all your saints on a shelf and pray to them one by one.'

'Funny, you never said that to Joan in your house six weeks ago. In fact, you've never said that to Joan *any* of the times she's attacked me over the years.'

'I've told you before – I can't control what either of my daughters says or does.'

Jenny leaned across the table and pointed at Vera. 'Of course you can – you're her mother. You just don't, because you enjoy the show. And even if you didn't, you mustn't upset Joan, the chosen one, the golden child. Jesus Christ! You do know that you've destroyed her? The way you brought her up – it's how people drive hamsters insane in experiments. You give it treats for no reason. Randomly. You don't let it learn how the system of rewards operates.'

Vera squinted. 'What *are* you talking about? I love all my children equally.'

'No, Mum, you don't love all your children equally. You never did. Originally, you loved Hugh-the-golden-child and… well, that was actually it. Joan and I were fine. We did things for you. We did whatever you wanted. Our personal, private dramas were your favourite show, and you could get involved in them and by doing so, we thought it was proof of your love and concern. But it was just proof of your love of game playing. And what's the game? Being the centre of it all.'

Jenny finally took a deep sip of wine. She had waited for so long to point this out to her mother. She had longed to do so for years. Yet, the cleverer part of her knew that it was pointless. Vera would not respond. She would not engage – not meaningfully, anyway. That was not how narcissists worked.

Steadily, Vera returned her daughter's gaze. Her eyes flickered a few times but that was it. It was her usual reaction when blanking everything that she'd just heard and didn't like. The next thing she'd do was to gaslight Jenny – the favourite weapon in her armoury.

Calmly Vera said, 'Are you mad, Jennifer? That wine – is it your first? Have you been drinking too much today? Drink does strange things to us when we're stressed, and you've certainly been stressed recently. I hope you're not on meds *and* drinking. Joan's girls all had such problems when the doctor put them on those anti-anxiety pills. I told Joan it wasn't a good idea. But would she listen?'

Sometimes, Jenny wished that the only thing she'd wanted from her mother was the house; that it was all just a simple matter of demanding something in an arrangement approaching fairness. However, the truth was that she'd always just wanted Vera to treat her like a proper daughter. Even now, after everything her mother had done to her, part of Jenny didn't want Vera to vanish from her world.

But it was time to do what Shane had always wanted her to do. His mantra was, 'The only way to deal with your family is to not deal with them.' In other words, toss them overboard like the toxic waste they were.

'Mum, you and I are done.'

'We are *what*?'

'Finished. I never want to see you again.'

'You can't... What are you saying? After I gave you Clareville? You treat me like this after what I just did for you?'

'You did it for yourself, Mum. You did it because this is the way you want things. Because this is the world you want to live in.'

Jenny could see everything clearly now. Vera didn't allow anyone to be happy unless she was the source of that happiness. If Jenny's world was great, then that would make her mother ratty and envious and Vera would attempt to ruin it, usurp it, or pass it off as inconsequential. For Jenny, the triumphs and delectations of her life had been guilty pleasures. That was because her life was a gift her mother had never intended for her. Vera had birthed Jenny for Vera.

'So, you *tricked* me into giving you Clareville? You've basically admitted it. And all because you want to get me back for... for just being your mother. For just wanting what was best. Always. I thought you loved me, Jennifer. But all this time... you've just been lying.'

Jenny almost applauded. It was a textbook rendition of Vera's *modus operandi* at flash points. She would accuse her adversary of being manipulative (which Vera was). She'd label her enemy as vengeful (which Vera was). She'd call her opponent a liar (which Vera, above all else, was).

'Mum, let me tell you exactly why you gave me the house. You gave it to me so you'll never have to acknowledge how you manipulated Ultan to come to Ireland where he would be killed in my kitchen. So you'll never have to apologise to all the people – me, Shane, Otto, Ultan's friends, even Dee's friends – for everything we all had to go through.'

'You are completely insane. I'm not going to sit here and—'

'I'm not finished. You gave me the house so your life could carry on, uninterrupted. You gave me the house because just a little part of you figured that you owed me something for me ending up as collateral damage in your failed plan. You gave me the house so I could be grateful – because you, more than anyone, know just how corrosive repeated gratitude is to a person's dignity. You loved how Hugh needed you, required you, depended on you. And you love how Joan does so now. You want me to be like that, too. You always have. That's why you kept the house dangling over my head – until a better use for it came along, with Ultan.'

Vera was on her feet, her chair pushed back. Impatiently she began buttoning up her coat. Jenny remained seated, looking up at her mother with calm curiosity as she continued: 'Dad wanted me to have the house. Now I have it. You didn't give me the house. *He* did. And now it's mine. As it should've been for the last twenty-five years.'

'Goodbye, Jennifer.' Vera turned, walked across the room and exited.

Calmly, Jenny stood and gathered her things. So that was that. She was free of her mother. Free of her family. She'd said what had needed to be said and she'd finally received her due, her fair share, justice.

But at what price?

Shutting down that thought, Jenny caressed the serrated edge of the house key inside her jacket pocket, running her finger along its contours. It was the fatted calf.

In no hurry, Jenny left the boardroom and descended the stairs. In the hallway she waved goodbye to the secretary through the glass door to the reception area. Then she was outside on the street, buttoning her coat. Only feet away, Vera was elegantly slipping into the passenger seat of Joan's silver Mercedes. She shut the door and half lowered the window.

'You know, Jennifer, sometimes I think that you're the coldest of them all.'

Her mother said it as though there had been a competition and that, surprisingly, her youngest had won.

As Jenny walked back to Clareville, she couldn't help but be flattered.

51

It was another busy summer evening in Clareville, the pavement bustling with early birds making their way to favourite eateries. Outside Luigi's, Shane had to press himself against the glass to allow a middle-aged woman with two shaggy St Bernard dogs pass him. Shane could only imagine what type of house was required for keeping such large, expensive and impractical animals. Beyond the glass, the clientele were, as usual, all on their best behaviour; not being too loud, not being too famous or too rich; all very aware that perhaps a bigger, more charismatic, more spectacular beast might be about to emerge from the undergrowth.

As Shane walked on, a grey-haired man in a cream suit paused at the entrance and nodded a smile to him. It was one of Shane's neighbours – the judge. They'd seen each other every second day for the last few years and the judge had never acknowledged him. But since the drama of six weeks ago, the judge, like their other neighbours, even greeted him by name.

Do not turn into one of them.

Was it already too late? It was hard to step away from the fun of pursuing the perfect cool, of denying the extraordinary feeling that comes with personally knowing the chef, the front-of-house greeter, or the star.

The fact was, Shane was no longer the person he had been. Whether he liked it or not, money had changed absolutely everything. The deal with Otto was guaranteed to work out and soon they'd have over a million euros, on top of owning their Clareville house. He'd wanted none of this in particular – but now that it had all happened anyway, Shane finally understood the true power of money. It wasn't the mere ability to buy stuff, to travel at will, to skip the queue. Instead, the greatest gift that money could give was the freedom to stop thinking about money.

I'm not one of them. I'm still me. Richer. Freer. But me.

As he approached their house, he recognised the desperate urge – a need – to get to his study and write. It was welcoming. It was familiar. It hadn't changed. It was the only thing he knew, and Shane was aware that part of the reason for this was his ingrained immaturity; he still held intact his adolescent idealism. He remembered when he was sixteen, drinking in the park with his friends before the local disco, and they'd talked about their ambitions which they didn't yet recognise as ridiculous dreams. There were wannabe actors, musicians, football players and even a special ops commando. Shane had wanted to be a writer. Now, when he thought of how none of his friends had become what they'd wanted to be, he was dismayed by their lack of appetite for life. Every one of them had killed the very best part of themselves.

You never killed the best part of yourself... instead, you killed someone else.

When Shane thought of the fact that he was now a killer – that he had slain a man, put him down, shot him in the head, blown his face off – part of him believed that it was not true. That perhaps Ultan had committed suicide. Why else would he *not* have dropped the knife? Why else would he have threatened Jenny and given her time to relay that fact to her armed and adrenalised husband?

Shane knew that Jenny thought Hugh's suicide had been a demonstration of her brother's weakness, his selfishness and his cruelty. She'd wondered how he could've done that to their parents – specifically to Vera. However, Shane had much sympathy for those who chose the time and place of their own extinction. All men seek happiness. Especially those who go and kill themselves. *Maybe that's what Ultan did. Maybe I'm just the equivalent of the guy on the motorway who drives the car that the person purposely walks in front of. Am I just the unwitting instrument?*

Shane walked up the pathway to his front door, opened it and slipped inside. He kept walking towards the kitchen, knowing that Jenny was still out at the solicitor's office. He was then in the backyard, crossing the decking and entering the garage. There was the new Land Rover – silver and shiny, even in the shadows. It didn't interest him much.

Pulling up the rolling metal sectional garage door, he looked up and down the laneway before pushing out the wheelie bin. It felt normal. It felt like the thing a regular neighbourhood dad would do – separate his bottles and tins from the rest of his rubbish before putting it out on a Thursday night. And Jenny would be a typical mother who also recycled, cared about the environment and who worried about the birds in the garden starving in winter. And they would have two, maybe three, children and they would be proud of them, even though their children were extraordinarily ordinary.

And Shane would bring the family to Disneyland every winter and in August they'd go to some beach resort with an excellent kids' club.

Glinting in the setting sun, he saw the last of the glass beads brushed in tight against the far wall of the laneway. He'd never forget Jenny's command – 'Don't hesitate. Shoot him.' It had been the very last thing he expected her to say. If it had been anyone else in the world, he would definitely have hesitated. He would've questioned it. He would've questioned it a second time. And even then, would he have pulled the trigger?

But it hadn't been anyone else. It had been Jenny. And if there was one person that he could trust above all else, it was his wife. Because of that, he needed to protect Jenny, to shield her, to be there for her – always.

At university, twenty-five years ago, Shane had only been a part of Jenny's life – but she had been everything in his. Back then, he'd been young enough to have a powerful sense that what was at stake in their relationship was nothing less than the rest of his life, and that every incident had an unimaginable significance. When they'd got back together in that club seventeen years ago, it still felt like that. And every year after that, it had continued to feel just so.

I'm the guy who got the girl… but at what price?

He looked up to the back of their towering Clareville house. He looked into the garage at their pristine new Land Rover. He thought of his spanking new boat that would be delivered next weekend. He remembered that Luigi's front-of-house had known his name the last few times they'd gone there.

'Where did it all go wrong?' Shane muttered wryly.

You've lost yourself.

This was certainly a moment that his late father would have offered some meaningful advice. His father had taught Shane that he should never feel sorry for himself. 'Have you cancer like David up the road?' 'Are you paralysed from the neck down like Maura's boy in that motorcycle accident?' 'Did you march a hundred miles through a jungle only to watch your family drown in the Red Sea, like those poor people on the news?' His father had a gift for zeroing out the scales. 'Then enjoy your incredible good fortune, Shane.'

Absorbing the low-grade self-loathing, he thought, *enough of this pity party*. Maybe he did deserve the house and the Clareville lifestyle. Over the years, despite his best efforts, they had become part of who Jenny was. And he'd taken possession of all of them. He'd defended them. He'd even killed for them. Therefore, had he not earned them?

Behind him, from the kitchen door of the house, a happy buoyant voice called out to the neighbourhood – 'Shane, I'm back.'

He smiled.

It was time to go home.

Acknowledgements

I would like to thank:

Anne Hughes, first reader and initial editor.

My agent Donald Winchester at Watson, Little Ltd.

Aubrie Artiano, James Faktor and all the team at Lume Books.

My editor Cate Bickmore for her keen expertise and sharp eye.

My parents Carmel and John, and my sisters Pat and Teri.